THANK
ENJOY.

WATCHING

A DIFFERENT TYPE OF TIME TRAVEL

VOLUME 1: THE GARDEN MUSEUM HEIST

JEFFREY JAY LEVIN

J. Levin

Black Rose Writing | Texas

The author grants the final approval for this literary material.

First printing

This is a work of fiction. Names, characters, businesses, places, events, and incidents are either the products of the author's imagination or used in a fictitious manner. Any resemblance to actual persons, living or dead, or actual events is purely coincidental.

ISBN: 978-1-68513-206-4
PUBLISHED BY BLACK ROSE WRITING
www.blackrosewriting.com

Printed in the United States of America
Suggested Retail Price (SRP) $21.95

Watching is printed in Garamond Premier Pro

*As a planet-friendly publisher, Black Rose Writing does its best to eliminate unnecessary waste to reduce paper usage and energy costs, while never compromising the reading experience. As a result, the final word count vs. page count may not meet common expectations.

For Shani, Jessica, Aiden and Liana:

Never Give Up On Your Dreams

To Alexis: For Believing

WATCHING

THAT DAMN SHOW

I used to enjoy watching unsolved crime documentaries. Really, my wife, Adrian, and I enjoyed a variety of documentaries, mostly because of the dearth of actual entertainment being produced nowadays, which I find to be the result of unbelievable egos in a Hollywood ruled, not by the desire to actually create new entertainment, but rather a total fear of taking any chances which may result in the loss of a job, cocaine and hookers. But, I digress. Anyway, Adrian didn't share my enthusiasm for the unsolved crime genre, but put up with it, that is, until we watched a documentary called "It Was a Robbery." As the title may suggest to you, it was about a robbery, in this case the unsolved theft in 1970 of twenty-one old masterpieces, as in the painted/sketched/woodblock variety, dating to the 1400s, none of which had ever been recovered. Not only that, they haven't even been seen since quietly taking their leave of the now defunct museum in which they had resided. My mind immediately went to *"Where the hell can they possibly be?"* Unbeknownst to my conscious mind, it stayed there longer than I had intended.

•   •   •

I always thought of myself as a pretty ordinary guy. I went to school, dabbled in drugs (it was the 60s and 70s, after all), got a job, got married, had kids. You get the drift. I became interested in spirituality but showed no aptitude for extraordinary senses of any kind. I couldn't conjure spirits, tell the future (really, I could hardly recall the past), or use astral projection. I struggled with emotions of any sort, although I have perfected faking it when needed. So, you can imagine my surprise and disbelief when, after binge watching the entire series of *It Was a Robbery*, I found my sleep filled not with dreams, as I've experienced them my entire life, but with something more akin to what I can only describe as "Watching." I know that may not convey my experience, but I'm uncertain how else I can accurately describe it. Rather than taking part in whatever happens in a dream, it was more that I was watching and hearing other people do and say things. Like watching a movie or being the proverbial fly on the wall. And not just any random people. No, these were people with actual names and faces from real life, lifted directly from whatever digital medium was used to record what I have since come to think of as "*That damn show.*" Their names somehow having become etched into my memory as if I had grown up with these hoodlums. I mean, I have relatives whose names I can barely remember, but these guys, I can't will myself to forget them.

•   •   •

Truth be told, I wasn't so much surprised by the "Watching" experience as puzzled by it. My recollection of what I then still thought of as a dream was extraordinary, at least for me. I could vividly see and recall locations, colors, smells, textures, and conversations. It *was* extraordinary!

•   •   •

Jimmy walks into the diner and quickly spots Ralphie and Tiny. Dressed in a black leather jacket over a black silk shirt, with black dress pants and pointy black shoes, Jimmy is certain that he cuts a dashing figure and projects the image he hopes for, a man of taste and class that is not to be fucked with. He casually strolls to the back booth, lighting a cigarette on the way, and joins his compatriots, who are all similarly dressed, almost as if wearing uniforms. The booth is their usual and, for the most part, other customers knew that, if occupied, they needed to leave a wide berth of unoccupied territory. As a result, no other patrons are sitting within earshot of the trio.

"Hey, paisan, nice of you to join us," is the greeting from Ralphie, as he blows smoke in Jimmy's direction.

Tiny, being anything but, takes up most of one side of the booth, so Jimmy slides next to Ralphie, and, making a point of looking at his watch and feigning indignation, says, "What? I'm right on time."

"Only if 20 minutes late is right on time."

"Whatever. What's up?"

Tiny, his mouth opening to reply, quickly shuts his hole as the waitress, offering a menu, approaches and asks Jimmy what she can get him.

Seeing that only Tiny, of course, is enjoying pie, a la mode, he responds, "Coffee, doll. Black."

Nodding, she withdraws, and Tiny once again commences his reply. "That job the other night has the Boss's underwear in a knot."

Looking confused, Jimmy looks back and forth at his companions and asks, "Why? It went off without a hitch. It was a God damn thing of beauty."

Ralphie, agreeing, nevertheless says, "It was. But the amount of heat is something we didn't anticipate. Who knew, eh? Anyway, the Boss says we've gotta stash the stuff for a while, 'till things cool down a bit. Plus..."

• • •

That's when I woke up, if that's what you still call it when returning from a Watching, although, at the time, I didn't know it wasn't an *actual* dream. Immediately, I could smell cherry pie and vanilla ice cream. It smelled wonderful, and I don't even like cherry pie! I could feel the sticky vinyl from the diner's booth and smell the cigarette smoke as if it was clinging to my bare skin. Something, I have no idea what, made me get out of bed, get to my computer, and memorialize everything, which is basically what you've just read. Reading it over immediately after having written it, all I could think was, "*What the fuck?*"

I realize that the clothing and dialogue seem like something right out of an early Scorsese film and is somewhat stereotyped, but, hey, that's how they looked, what they said, and how they sounded. What can I say? And the cigarette smoke! Whoa! It definitely placed it in the right time period.

Anyway, I read and reread what I had written and the first thought that entered my brain was, "*Could these guys have been talking about the art heist?*" They definitely didn't seem like the kind of people you associate with high-end art theft. Plus, "...the amount of heat is something we didn't anticipate. Who knew, eh?" Really? You steal untold millions in high-end art and didn't anticipate the amount of heat that would follow? It would have taken a lot of planning by somebody with brains to have pulled this off. Of that, I was certain. Those guys, if they were real guys at all, could have been talking about anything. A truck heist was probably more in their line of work. That's probably what they were talking about. The payload must have been unexpected; hence the surprise at how much "heat" was coming down. That had to have been it. Convinced, I forced it from my mind and went on with my day.

Ralphie, Jimmy and Tiny, in their almost identical outfits, strut along the street, smoke billowing from their mouths and noses as they suck their unfiltered cigarettes. Turning the corner, the red, green, and white awning of *Mama Nona's Place* comes clearly into view. Loitering outside is a group of four men ranging in age from 25 to 60. All are dressed similarly to the approaching trio, although the eldest of the group is definitely of a higher class and clearly the one deferred to in conversations. His clothes are of a finer material and cut. His cigar smells expensive. There's just a unique aura about him. It's this gentleman that the trio approaches, but not before removing their cigarettes and extinguishing them under the soles of their shiny black shoes.

Jimmy is the first to speak, holding his hand ou
How's things?"

Grasping the proffered hand, Paulie says, "Thi
lot better if you three weren't such screw ups." Rele
Paulie motions towards the door of Mama Nona's and says, "He's
expecting you. Don't keep him waiting."

Glancing at Ralphie and Tiny, Jimmy turns and walks to the
entrance, followed closely by his two trepidatious friends.

The entrance to Mama Nona's opens into a foyer, after which
is the bar. Sitting at the bar are two enormous men. They are
dressed in black pants and tight black t-shirts, over which are
shoulder holsters housing very large 357 Magnum revolvers. As
soon as the trio walks through the door, the men get off their bar
stools and approach the group, one stopping short of the men, with
his hand in position to draw the personal cannon, the other holding
up his hand in the stop gesture of a traffic cop, which all
immediately obey. Nobody says anything as they are quickly and
professionally frisked. Once done, they are unceremoniously waived
through to the restaurant's interior. Gathering themselves
mentally and physically, the three enter the inner sanctum.

The lights are low, the restaurant not being officially opened
for hours. The booths and tables stand mostly empty, without
tablecloths. Mostly empty because the tables and booths which
lined the walkway to the large booth at the back of the room, which
is brightly lit, are occupied by what seem to be clones of the two
guards from the bar. Some are eating, but most are not. All look up
and follow the approaching group with the rapt attention of
trained guard dogs at Stalag 17. The effect is chilling, fulfilling the
intended purpose, as evidenced by the silent gulping of air and
jumping Adam's apples of each of the approaching men.

At the brightly lit table which Jimmy, Ralphie and Tiny
approach sits a man of approximately 62 years of age. His hair is
salt and pepper colored and thick. He is slightly overweight and
jowly, although almost everybody tells him how good he looks. His

skin shone in the bright light, making him appear somewhat sweaty. On the table before him is a black corded telephone, on which he is animatedly speaking, while twirling spaghetti from a large bowl placed slightly to his right. In between rants, the fork makes its way into his mouth, followed by aggressive chewing, forcing the person on the other end of the call to listen and wait until the food had been swallowed and washed down by the deep red wine waiting in the crystal goblet next to the pasta bowl. As the trio slowly approach, they stop in front of the table, leaving about three feet of space, in a show of respect. They stand and silently wait until the telephone has been placed into the cradle and they are silently acknowledged.

"Good afternoon, Don," ventures Jimmy.

The Don holds his hand up, more as a "*Shut the fuck up*" gesture than the traffic cop gesture. Immediately, Jimmy falls silent as the Don continues to eat.

Finally, The Don pushes the bowl away, drinks deeply from his glass of wine, and lookes at the men standing silently before him. "Is it, Jimmy?"

Confused, Jimmy reluctantly asks, "Is it what, sir?"

"Is it a good afternoon? That's what you said when you first appeared. So, I'll ask you again, Jimmy, is it?"

Quickly deciding that this was not a good time to crack wise, he says, "I don't think that it is, sir."

"And why do you think that might be, Jimmy?"

"It seems that you are displeased with us, Don."

Quietly, The Don says, "It does, does it?" Slapping the table, he repeats, loudly, "It *seems* as if I'm displeased, does it? Well, nobody can accuse you of not being perceptive, can they?"

Exercising discretion, Jimmy remains silent.

Looking first at Jimmy, next at Ralphie and finally at Tiny, The Don sits up straighter in his chair and, with his tone of voice definitely registering incredulity, says, "You idiots really have no idea what you've done, do you?"

Jimmy, Ralphie and Tiny look at each other and, finally, at the Don, saying nothing, the looks of confusion on their faces saying it all.

"Well, let me clue you morons in. First..."

•   •   •

And that is where I "woke up." This time the smell of freshly made marinara filled my nostrils such that I could almost taste it. I could feel the high quality fake leather of the booths and chairs. Smell the tannin from the wine. Feel the carpet under my feet. And smell and feel the fear emanating in waves from Jimmy, Ralphie and Tiny. It was enough to make me feel afraid in a way that I've never felt before. Immediately, I jumped from bed and went to my computer, eager to memorialize what I'd just seen, setting down what you've just read.

I must have startled Adrian with how I exited the bed and bedroom, as she soon followed to my office. Concentrating on the keyboard so hard I didn't notice her at the door, I jumped when she called my name, no doubt made worse by the fear still coursing through my being.

"Are you OK? You jumped out of bed so fast I thought you were racing to the bathroom, sick. What are you doing?"

Still clacking away at the keys, I looked up and said, "I'll explain it to you in a few minutes, as soon as I'm done. Just give me a couple of minutes."

Looking at me as if I were part alien, she said, "OK," and went back to the bedroom.

•   •   •

Having completed my written recollection of the night, I returned to the bedroom. In my hand were the pages of recollections from my two "Watching" experiences. I explained, in general terms, what I've been enduring since we watched *It Was a Robbery*. She listened to what I had to say. I explained what I perceived as the difference between dreams and

"Watching". I explained how vivid the images, sounds and smells were. And then I handed her the sheets of paper I had just taken from my printer.

Adrian took the sheets and immediately began reading. I got up and went into the bathroom, both to get ready for the day and to give her some space to read without my staring at her with that *"So, what do you think?"* expression etched upon my face. When I emerged, clean, shaved, and clothed, she was just completing her second pass through my words. I remained silent, but, seeing that she was just about done, sat on the bed and waited.

"Wow. That really is a unique experience," she said.

"Yes, it is. What do you think it is?"

"I have no idea, aside from strange. Is it something you want to check out?"

Thinking before answering, I paused and looked at my surroundings, suddenly noticing the quality of the light and the colors of the fabrics. Finally, I said, "I think I do. I think I have to, if for no other reason than to see if it will stop once I figure it out. And, to be perfectly honest, I'm kind of intrigued as to where this is going."

She looked at me and nodded in agreement. I smiled and said, "So, are you in? I think it's going to take at least two heads to figure this out."

"Are you actually asking for my help?" she asked with an evident quality of incredulity in her voice.

As you might ascertain from that, I'm not one to usually ask for help.

I simply replied, "I am."

"Then I'm definitely in," she said with surprising enthusiasm.

"Awesome!" I leaned over and kissed her before I stood and said, "I've got some work to do, and then we can strategize." With that, I went to my office and left her to prepare for her day.

· · ·

At about 3:00 that afternoon, Adrian and I reconvened at the dining room table. She had the sheets of paper I had provided that morning. I filled a couple of glasses with water and placed one before each of us.

"So," I began, "have you given this any thought today?"

Glancing at the sheets of paper, she responded, "Yes, I have. Let's assume that this was somehow brought up by that show and is somehow tied into it. If that's the case, I think our starting point is 1970 Boston, which is where and when the theft took place. Agreed?"

"My thoughts exactly. And we have 2 locations, the diner and Mama Nona's. I didn't see the name of the diner, but there's no doubt about Mama Nona's Place. We should be able to Google 'Mama Nona's Place Boston 1970' and see what comes up."

"Already done," as she handed me a printout with, not only information on the restaurant, but a picture, circa mid-1970s.

"Holy Crap," was all I could manage as I stared, dumbfounded, at the picture. "It's exactly as I remember seeing it last night." I remained speechless for the next thirty seconds, just staring at the picture. Looking up at Adrian, I said, "You know, until this very moment I thought this could all somehow be explained away, rationally." Glancing momentarily at the picture, I continued, "Any chance of that being the case is now shot to shit." It affected me more than I had thought possible and I took a long drink of water to hide that fact. Placing the glass back on the table, I read aloud the information accompanying the picture. "Mama Nona's Place was an Italian restaurant located in Boston's North End. Owned by the notorious mobster Ricardo Garotini, a/k/a Don 'The Garrote' Ricky, the restaurant served as the Don's headquarters from the late 1960s until 1979, when it closed as a result of Don Ricky's imprisonment. The site of numerous mob meetings and government raids, the food, featuring recipes from The Don's beloved Grandmother, Nona, was purported to be among the best in the North End." Accompanying the article was a picture of the "notorious mobster," as he was being led from the courthouse. I looked at that picture as if I'd never seen such technology, studying it pixel by pixel. Gazing at Adrian, I mumbled, "That is definitely the guy at the table in the back of the restaurant. 'The Garrote?!' No wonder those guys were scared." Sitting back in my chair, I could only ask, "What are we getting into?"

We took a break so that I could make dinner. Yes, I'm the cook, most nights. I had a choice years ago, cook or clean. I quickly chose "cook." This day it was simple: steak on the grill, baked potatoes and roasted broccoli. I was glad that I had chosen a simple menu, as my mind was somewhere in Boston and not centered in my kitchen. That's a good way to cut off a finger, which was not something I wanted to experience. Adrian went back to her office to work on a project while I puttered about the kitchen, trying my hardest not to dwell on The Garrote and all that name implied. As I'm sure you know, the harder you try not to think about something, the harder it becomes not to think about it. This was no exception. I poured myself a little tequila, went to the grill, and lost myself in the sound of the sizzle.

• • •

We were at the dining room table enjoying, if I say so myself, perfectly seasoned and grilled New York strips, in the comfortable silence of a long-married couple, when Adrian, not one for much small talk, suddenly looked at me and said, "The Diner."

My fork was three-quarters of the way to passing my lips when it stopped in mid-air and I looked at her and said, "Huh?"

"The Diner."

"That's what I thought you said. What about it?" as I let my fork complete its trip and waited for the reply, chewing contentedly.

She swallowed the food in her mouth and said, "We need to find out which diner and where it was. The more we know about where these guys hung out, the more we'll be able to figure out."

"There must be 50 diners to choose from back then and I didn't see the name of the one they were in."

Using her fork as a pointer, she began to say something, stopped, bound from her chair, and headed into her office, returning with the sheets of paper I had provided to her just that morning. Could it really only have been that morning? Incredible. Retaking her seat, she skimmed the sheets, found what she'd been looking for and said, "Here it is." Quoting from what I had written, she continued, "*Tiny, his mouth opening to reply, quickly shuts his hole as the waitress, offering a menu, approaches and asks Jimmy what she can get him.*"

She looked at me, waiting.

Staring out the window and thinking, I finally got it, turned and said, "The menu."

Sporting a satisfied grin, she took a bite of steak and said, "The menu." Stopping her chew, she continued, "You saw the menu, so you know the name of the diner."

"But did I see the front or back of the menu? I'm not sure. If I had seen the name, wouldn't I have written it down? I did with Mama Nona's."

"It's all we have to go on. Maybe you didn't think it was important at the time, so didn't take note of it. Now you think it's important, so maybe it will come back to you. Plus, the name Mama Nona's was full in your face from the awning. You couldn't miss it, even if you wanted to. This was much more subtle."

Having finished our meal, she got up to clear the dishes. I usually helped, but this night I stayed rooted in my chair trying to conjure the image of a long gone menu from what is probably a long gone diner. Not really having any idea how to go about the conjuring, I closed my eyes and concentrated, trying to go back to that place and time to see the waitress holding the menu out to Jimmy. Vibrating with the effort, I opened my eyes and took a deep breath. Failure.

•   •   •

The remainder of the evening started out typically uneventfully. We watched some TV, tinkered with our phones, and generally tried not to think or talk about Boston in 1970 and the identity of some long forgotten greasy spoon. You've probably experienced something similar, if not exact. 500 channels and nothing you feel like watching. Adrian was playing a game on her computer pad and I had the remote. Surfing. Happens every night in millions of homes.

Hit the button...an old Seinfeld, with the gang at Monk's Diner.

Hit the button...The Double R Diner in Twin Peaks.

I called to Adrian, not taking my eyes from the television and said, "Adie, you have to see this."

She looked up and I went back to the last two surfing sites and continued on from there.

The Bluebird Café in Nashville.

JJ's Diner in Parks and Recreation.

Lou's Café in Back to the Future.

And finally...

Steve Guttenberg, Mickey Rourke, Kevin Bacon, Daniel Stern and Tim Daly all crammed into a booth in 1959 Baltimore in the movie Diner.

I let the remote drop from my hand and just looked at her. "Really?!? Are you fucking kidding me?!? What is this, every fucking diner that's ever been in a movie or TV show? And then, to drive it home, *DINER*? What the fuck?!?"

Speechless, she could only look from me to the television, with a look on her face that I'd never seen before. A strange mixture of incredulity, humor, confusion, apprehension and, lurking just beneath the surface, a tinge of fear.

· · ·

I had a restless night. Very little sleep and no Watching. My mind was a non-stop jumble of thoughts, concepts, and theories. When the Universe decides to fuck with you, watch out! The next three days and nights were just as bad, if not worse. By the fourth day, I was running on fumes, totally exhausted and irritable. We had dinner plans, it being a Friday night, and there was no way I could beg off, having cancelled for various reasons the last two times we had plans with these same people. Knowing that, with about an hour and a half before we were scheduled to leave, I sat on the couch and closed my eyes, hoping for a few minutes of respite. The next thing I knew, Adrian was shaking my shoulders and telling me it was time to go. I'd dosed off for a little over an hour and felt immeasurably better, if not totally myself. Thankful beyond words, we got into our car and left to pick up our friends.

•   •   •

We arrived at the restaurant without incident. It was one of our favorites and difficult to get into, reservations being required at least two months in advance, so, obviously, we had these plans well prior to whatever had been going on in (or with) my head. All were looking forward to enjoying a wonderful meal with great drinks and good friends. I stayed alert and was enjoying myself immensely, relieved to be out and not thinking about Boston diners at all.

And then the server brought us dessert menus.

She was dressed in a black skirt, white blouse and black vest, as she had been all evening. She reached out to hand me a menu, in what I perceived as slow motion. The white sleeve of her blouse slowly transformed into a yellowish-orange sleeve, leading up to a white collar attached to an old-fashioned yellowish-orange waitress uniform, straight out of the 1970s. She reminded me not so much of the waitress at "*The Diner*" as the waitress on the cover of Supertramp's album, *Breakfast in America*, right down to the little triangular paper hat. I reached out to accept the menu, also in slow motion, and watched as it morphed from a black faux leather cover to an orange and white, plastic covered, stained menu. Depicted on the cover was a stack of pancakes, heaped with butter and dripping syrup, leaning like the Tower of Pisa. Old-fashioned Italian style lettering, in large white letters, spelled out "Bo's Old Fashioned Diner." I knew immediately that "Bo" was short for "Botticelli" and that breakfast was served all day, although I may have gleaned that last bit from the smaller white lettering under the name. Things came back into real time focus with the clattering that resulted when I dropped the menu on my waiting dessert plate. I must have had a strange look on my face, since everybody at the table looked concerned and asked if I was all right. I laughed and said, "Of course. I'm fine. I just remembered something I wanted to tell Adrian and it took me by surprise." Turning to face Adrian, I simply said, "Bo's Old Fashioned Diner."

•   •   •

As soon as we got back home and settled, Adrian simply said, "Tell me."

I related my entire experience, explaining in detail the shift in time perspective, the transformations of the uniform and menu, what the menu looked like, down to the coffee stain under the plastic cover, my reading of the name emblazoned on that cover, and the sudden return to our reality and time perspective.

"That explains why you dropped the menu," she said, smiling. "I think I'd have dropped more than that."

"I've got to tell you, I thought I was losing it for a minute. Once I figured out what I was seeing, I just let it happen. Who knew that the experience of tripping on acid would ever come in so handy? Without it, I think I really would have freaked out."

Shaking her head, she said, "Yeah, who knew?!?", with just a hint of disgust as she punched my arm playfully. Reaching for her computer pad, she continued, "Let's see what we can find about Bo's Old Fashioned Diner."

Computer pad in hand, Adrian typed the name into the waiting square and hit "Enter." Immediately, the Web answered its call, spitting out (metaphorically speaking) the requested information.

Reading aloud, she said, "Bo's Old Fashioned Diner was established in 1962 by Michael Botticelli, an Italian immigrant from Florence, Italy. Mr. Botticelli decorated his diner with paintings by his famous namesake, Sandro Botticelli, to whom he was purportedly related. Bo's Old Fashioned Diner gained a small level of notoriety in the 1970s as a hangout for low-level mobsters and the scene of a shootout that left two people dead in 1970, Sylvia Toscana (47), a waitress, and Edward "Tiny" Lacosta (32), allegedly a low-level employee of "Don" Ricardo Garotini, a/k/a Don "The Garrote" Ricky."

I reached out to touch her arm, causing her to stop reading as I mumbled, "Holy shit."

Looking at me quizzically, she asked simply, "What?"

"That has to be Tiny. The Tiny that I saw with Jimmy and Ralphie. He's really a real person, and he was gunned down in that diner." Standing to pace, I continued, "and that waitress, what's her name?" I asked imploringly.

"Sylvia," came the quick reply.

"Yeah, Sylvia. That could be the waitress I saw handing Jimmy the menu." As I continued to pace, it was apparent to Adrian that I was becoming quite upset, but she wisely said nothing. "Holy shit," I repeated. "These guys aren't fucking around. They killed Tiny because of this fucking heist."

Standing and coming to me, Adrian reached out and stopped my pacing. "Let's not jump to any conclusions, just yet, OK? We don't know why he was killed. He worked for a mobster. He was a mobster. He probably had ambitions to become a more important mobster. Most of the people in his line of work get killed. It could have been for any of a hundred other reasons." She stopped as I visibly began to calm. "And, it all happened a half century ago."

We both retook our seats when it finally came to me, the reason I was so distraught by something that happened so long ago. "That's just the thing, Adie. It did happen a long time ago. But to me, it seems as if it just happened today. I don't understand it, but I feel as if I just got news about something that just happened to somebody I know." I took a deep breath, trying to reset myself. "This is getting to be even weirder than I thought, and I already thought it was pretty fucking weird."

Looking at how seriously affected I was, she said, "Maybe this was a bad idea. We should let this whole thing go and forget about it."

"It's way past that point for me," I replied. "It's like an alien worm eating its way through my brain and the only way to get it out is to figure out what the hell is going on. And I can't figure that out until I know what questions to ask. My biggest question right now is, 'Why is this happening to me?' I need to find out."

"I know you do. I'm sorry you're going through this. Let's take a break for the rest of the night and we'll get back to it tomorrow."

I kissed her and said, "Good idea. Thanks. Sorry I got so upset."

• • •

Now, I'm not an emotional guy, at least I haven't been up to now, but lying in bed that night I couldn't help but feel that something fundamental in that regard seemed to have changed, or, at the very least, was in the process of changing. I didn't much care for it.

• • •

My sleep that night felt forced, if that makes any sense. It was less restful than I would have liked, but better than I expected. At any rate, it was "Watcher - less." I wasn't sure if I was relieved or disappointed about that. Actually, it's a mixture of the two. I was relieved that I got through a night without it and at least get some sleep, while knowing that a night without "Watching" was another night without answers.

The rest of the weekend was filled with a family sleep-over and running around with our 6-year-old grandson. If I wasn't tired before that, I certainly was by the time Sunday night rolled around. Being that preoccupied turned out to be a blessing in disguise. We didn't have time to even think about 1970 Boston, let alone do any research. It didn't even come up in conversation.

It was a welcome break, although short-lived.

• • •

Bo's Diner is strangely quiet when Tiny walks in. He stands at the entry door and looks around, as if waiting for his eyes to adjust to a low light situation, which doesn't really make any sense, seeing as how the Diner is lit up enough to be seen from space. Finally, having had his eyes adjusted or getting his bearings, he turns towards his usual booth and begins walking towards it, in halting fashion. Not seeing either Jimmy or Ralphie in their usual spots, he looks around as he continues his stumbling walk to the booth. Only the cooks and

Sylvia the waitress are visible, and they all ignore Tiny as he continues his slow progress to the booth.

"Sylvia, where is everybody?"

Tiny's speech is not quite slurred, but not crystal clear, either. It seems obvious to Sylvia that he's on the ass end of a bender. Sylvia just shrugs her shoulders and turns away, as if to say, "I don't know, I don't care, and leave me the fuck alone." She has heard rumors about Tiny's drinking over the last week or so and how he tends to shoot off his mouth when he should know better. Nothing ever good comes from that kind of behavior.

Tiny finally reaches the booth, plops down into it, with his back facing the front door, and calls out, without bothering to look at Sylvia, "Coffee." A minute later, a coffee mug is placed in front of Tiny, the steam rising to gently caress his face. He closes his eyes and takes a deep breath through his nose, enjoying the aroma. When he feels someone sit down in the booth opposite him, he opens his eyes to find Joey Animale, the "Animal", has joined him. They stare at each other, wordless, for a full minute before Tiny stammers, "H, hey Joe... Joey. What are you doing here?"

Joey shakes his head and leans forward, making the space feel more intimate and, to those who are familiar with Joey, threatening. "Tiny, you've been drinking quite a bit." He stops and is met with silence and a blind stare. "You've also been talking quite a bit, Tiny. Talking about business and things that you shouldn't be talking about."

Tiny cast his gaze downward, as if searching for an answer in his coffee cup. Finding none, he reengages with Joey, knowing full well that a visit from The Animal is never a good thing. "I don't know where you heard that. I can keep my mouth shut. You know that, Joey. Somebody is trying to set me up."

"I don't think so, Tiny. The Don heard you himself. Are you telling me that the Don is lying?"

Taken aback by this revelation, Tiny is quick to backtrack. "No, Joey, of course not. The Don wouldn't lie. If I talked too much, I'm sorry. I promise, I'll stop drinking and stop talking."

Leaning back, Joey says, "Yes, Tiny, I believe those are promises you can keep."

Visibly relieved, Tiny lets out a breath he didn't know he was holding and leans back, just beginning to open his mouth to thank Joey, when three incredibly loud explosions erupt from under the table. Tiny looks down and sees blood spurting from his chest and stomach area, just before collapsing face down onto the table. Standing, Joey places a five-dollar bill on the table and walks briskly towards the front door. The cooks are nowhere to be seen and Sylvia is just rising from behind the counter when a volley of shots ring out from outside, shattering the large picture window. Joey instantly dives onto the floor, draws his pistol and blindly returns fire as he jumps over the counter and retreats through the kitchen. On the floor behind the counter lies Sylvia, looking just as she had a moment ago, except for the large portion of her skull that now decorates the wall behind where she had just been standing.

•　•　•

I sat up with such force that the bed shook, matched only by the shaking of my body as adrenaline raced through at breakneck speed. Miraculously, Adrian remained asleep as I made my way to the office to record my most recent encounter with the past. As I typed, my ears rang from the sound of the gunshots, muffling all other sounds. The smell of cordite and blood filled my nostrils. I felt sick to my stomach. The violence differed from what we've become used to seeing on television and in the movies. I can't say why. You'd think we've become hardened against the shock of violent death, seeing so much of it on a daily basis. But this was different. Even though I wasn't physically present, it felt as if I were. I could feel the shock wave from the gun blasts, and smell the results, things that don't occur while watching "make believe" violence. My mind was telling me it should be the same as watching a movie, but my body was reacting as if I'd been there when it happened. How does someone like Joey the Animal come to be? So nonchalant about killing that he can leave a $5 bill on the table, holster his weapon and calmly walk away. What had to have happened to him to make him that way, or was he born like that? More questions to which I'll never have an answer. I guess it really does take all kinds to make the world go round.

· · ·

That evening Adrian did her thing with the internet and discovered that my account of the shooting was backed up by what had been reported in the newspapers. It also closely matched a supposition put forth by a detective working the scene, although without the specifics of who was involved. That same detective also opined that Tiny was most likely killed because of his involvement with the still unsolved art heist, and his "lack of discretion in relation thereto." Sounds like a detective with a sense of irony and a love of language. Adrian also discovered that Joey the Animal was indeed a real-life person back in the day. He was named as a suspect in the shooting, but numerous eye witnesses placed him at a party given by the Don at Mama Nona's, so he was never arrested or charged. He was, allegedly, a hit man in the employ of the Don who himself met a violent death in 1973 at the hands of what police suspect was his replacement, although, again, nobody was ever arrested or charged with his killing.

I was beginning to see a pattern, one that didn't lead to a lot of closure.

All of this information was interesting, but it didn't get us any closer to solving anything.

Adrian continued to surf for information when she came across an article that was written on the tenth anniversary of the art theft. It rehashed the information that we had seen in "that damned show," but added the fact that the FBI was still engaged in an attempt at a "successful conclusion to the return of the priceless art." It also mentioned that there was a "no questions asked" reward for either information leading to the return of the art or the return of the art itself. In 1980, the reward was $100,000.00, which was real money back then. The article listed the name of the agent in charge and a 1-800 telephone number.

Our interest became slightly more piqued with this information at hand. Adrian continued her search and discovered that similar articles had been printed on each of the anniversaries ending with a "0." Each of the articles stressed that none of the art had been seen since the theft occurred and that the trail of information, never an easy trail to follow, seems to have been erased over the decades. Her string of articles stopped in the year 2000, at which time the FBI was still "engaged", but there had been no movement for so long that the agent in charge, now a Special Agent Brad Curtis, was only involved on a less than part-time basis while working other unsolved crimes of various genres. Interestingly, by this time the "no questions asked" reward had been increased to $5,000,000.00. That's still real money.

"You know," I said to Adrian, "a $5,000,000 reward could put a totally different spin on this entire experience. I mean, with the going crazy and all."

She looked at me with a wry smile and said, "You know, I believe it could, although I'm not the one going crazy. Plus, we'd be gifting the world long lost priceless masterpieces, so it's a win for everybody."

"It would be a win for everybody! As for going crazy, you don't think I'll drag you down the crazy hole right beside me?" I said, laughing.

"I suppose it would be inevitable," she replied with a sigh.

"Let's give this some serious consideration," I said, in a much more serious tone. "I mean, we've already decided to keep going with this, and we don't know where this is going to lead or the toll it's going to take on us, and by us, I mean me. We have to consider how we're going to get anybody to believe how we came across any information that we might come across.

Can you imagine the reaction from an FBI agent when we tell him or her that I have time traveling visions? Oh yeah, I'm sure they'll take us really seriously," I said sarcastically.

"You're right. Let's take this slowly and see where it leads before we do anything rash, like go to the authorities. This is going to take some planning, and even then we may come across as a couple of nut-bags."

"Agreed," I said. "We have to figure out a way to be believed and at the same time stay out of the spotlight. That will not be an easy feat."

LAW ENFORCEMENT - 1970

On the Monday after the heist, Laurie Polanski, the museum's curator, approached the gothic doors, inserted her key and entered the dark foyer. Approaching the security station, it surprised her to see that it was unmanned, by man or woman. Using her pass key, she unlocked the door, turned the handle and pushed, only to be met with unexpected resistance.

"What the hell," she murmured.

Lowering her shoulder and imitating one of those linemen she so admired from her home town NFL team, the Bears, she grunted with effort as she pushed the door slightly ajar. Redoubling her efforts, she put her leg muscles to good use, as the door slowly pushed something out of the way, finally allowing her to squeeze through and enter the security area. As she did so, her foot hit something solid and unmoving, causing her to look down, revealing a blue uniformed leg.

"Oh, shit."

Stepping over the leg, she entered the room to discover the rest of the body, that of young Michael Ellis. Kneeling, she felt his neck for a pulse. Finding none, she stood, murmured "Shit" to herself once again, and slowly took in her surroundings.

The glassed in area was dark, none of the lights having remained on and the monitors having been switched off. Nothing seemed to be out of place, but perhaps a detailed review by professionals would reveal something different. A sudden realization having come to her, she squeezed back through the door and rushed from the room, being careful not to touch anything, and went into the main gallery. Standing in the center of the room, she surveyed the walls and starred at the 6 empty spaces where masterpieces had hung not 48 hours ago, when she was last at work. As she was about to examine the other rooms, she heard the employee's door open and ran to meet whoever was entering. Seeing Carl Bovetti, a 62-year-old retired Boston police officer and the current head of the museum's security, she suddenly found herself overcome with emotion.

"Oh Carl, we've been robbed!" she said as she struggled to hold back a torrent of tears. "And, Michael is dead."

Carl quickly stepped forward to comfort her and awkwardly embraced Laurie for a moment before he said, "OK, take some deep breaths and calm down. Tell me, where is Michael?" Laurie wordlessly pointed to the security area. Carl turned his head in the direction to which the digit was pointing and said, "The Security Pen?"

Laurie took slow deep breaths in an effort to calm herself, nodded and said, "Please put up a closed sign on the front door."

Carl muttered "Unbelievable" to himself and strode off toward the front door as Laurie moved toward her office in an almost trancelike state.

$$\bullet \quad \bullet \quad \bullet$$

Laurie had been working at the Garden Museum for three months and 21 days when she discovered the break-in and body of Michael Ellis. At a fundraiser held at the facility in her first month on the job, she was introduced to Captain Peter Capprieti, as well as the Superintendent of Police, Edmund diGrazia. Captain Capprieti was charming and seemingly forthright as he handed Laurie his business card, stating, "Please, if the need ever arises, don't hesitate to call me." She reached for her Rolodex, spun the contents until she came to his card, pulled it out and, not waiting for her head of security, dialed the number printed in bold black ink.

Captain Capprieti, together with Laurie, Carl, and Detective Ronald Hillary, toured the museum's galleries, noting each missing piece. Laurie had with her a catalogue of every item in the museum's collection and marked every page which corresponded to a missing item, so that it could be copied and provided to the Captain and Detective. The catalogue contained not only the pertinent information about each piece, such as the name of the creating artist, date on which it had been created, date of acquisition and party from whom acquired, but, more importantly, a picture of each of the stolen artworks.

"Those photographs are going be invaluable in identifying the art, when we find it," said the Detective. "It's a good thing you have them."

"It's standard procedure in the industry," answered Laurie, still somewhat dazed at the scope of the theft and the apparent murder of an employee. "The insurance companies require that we keep pictures of everything, just in case there's a theft." She looked at the empty spaces on the surrounding walls and said wistfully, "I just never thought I'd actually need them."

As they continued the tour of blank spaces, Captain Capprieti and Carl found themselves walking together, the others having fallen behind. The Captain and Carl knew one another from Carl's time on the force, having served in the same precinct together. Unimpeded by the presence of any other ears, Carl said quietly, "Pete, who the hell would have hit this place? Are they stupid or just crazy?"

Captain Capprieti looked over his shoulder to ensure privacy, turned back to Carl and replied, "I have no fucking clue. I do know this, though. There's going to be hell to pay." He opened his mouth to continue, but saw Laurie moving quickly in their direction, so stopped walking and talking. He turned to give Laurie his undivided attention as she said, "Let's turn into this gallery. I think some pieces were taken from here as well."

"Of course," replied the Captain, as he turned into the gallery indicated by Laurie. "Then Carl, Detective Hillary and I need to revisit the scene of the murder."

"Of course," said Laurie. "I believe this is the last room."

· · ·

The government of Massachusetts, including police departments, was so riddled with corruption in the 1960s and 1970s that bribery and fraud became a way of life. Everybody seemed to know it and just rang it up as a cost of doing business. At least things got done, if you knew the right people and had some cash. If you were just an ordinary schmo, then too bad for you.

That everybody seemed to know what was going on included the Federal Bureau of Investigation (FBI), as well as the Massachusetts Bureau of Investigation (MBI). Precisely because of what was going on, the FBI had neither trust in, nor tolerance for, the MBI. It was for that reason that nobody employed by the MBI had been informed of the converted milk truck parked in a parking lot down the street from the home of Don Ricky. Instead of cold dairy products, the truck contained two tepid FBI agents and various state-of-the-art surveillance and wire-tapping equipment, as well as recording devices. Since nobody at the MBI knew, and the FBI had only informed a small, tight-knit group of investigators, there was nobody to pass the information along to anybody in the Boston Police Department. It was this lack of knowledge and lackadaisical attitude concerning their own vulnerability that allowed Captain Capprieti to use his home phone to call The Don at his home. Suddenly, the formerly tepid agents became alert and interested.

"Hello."

"Hello. May I speak with The Don, please?"

"Who's callin'?"

"Captain Capprieti."

"One moment," followed by muffled conversation and rustling sounds.

"This better be important. I told you not to call me at home... ever."

"It is. The museum was hit over the weekend. A lot of art was taken, and a guard was killed. I need to know what's going on, if I'm going to be of any use."

"You don't think I've heard about that? You break protocol to tell me about something that's all over the news?!? The other cops say you're stupid and you're proving them right. What the fuck do you want, Pete?"

"I want any information you might have. Who the hell hit that place and why? Did you know about it?"

"You'll get information if and when I deem it necessary for you to know. Capiche? Whoever did it will have to deal with me. It was not a sanctioned job. As you know, that museum is under my protection. Do you know what this does to my credibility? I'll deal with it. You just go about your business. And don't call me again! Moron."

The call was abruptly ended. The two agents in the truck removed their head-sets, looked at each other and exchanged high fives.

"Finally, some useful information," agent 1 said to agent 2.

"Finally, is right!" agent 2 replied. "For once, our report is going to contain something other than pure bullshit. I'll start typing it right now."

•   •   •

For the first time in over a year, a wire-tap hadn't been blown by a "leak" and had yielded something that might actually be of use. The fact was that, in all likelihood, it was the prior "leaks" that gave the mob guys the confidence to speak, if not freely, then with some level of belief that, since they hadn't been informed of a tap, there probably wasn't one in place.

When referring to the FBI in a major US city, the phrase "Field Office" usually meant something grand and well appointed. The Boston field office at this time consisted of a half-floor rented in a class C office building located in a portion of the city that was definitely not "Downtown." The Agent-in-Charge, David Decker, a 47-year-old, well-respected agent with salt and pepper hair, heavy on the salt, had gathered four other agents into his small and cramped office space, the conference room being unavailable. Containing his desk and desk chair, and two chairs for guests, there was barely enough room to contain all the men, two of whom had to remain standing.

"Eventually, we knew somebody was going to get sloppy," said AIC Decker. Each of the agents present had read the transcripts of the previous night's calls. "Now, how are we going to use it?" His question was addressed to the room at large, not to any particular agent. The AIC looked at each person in the office, waiting for a response. "Come on, this is not the time to be shy," he implored. "What are we thinking?"

"Well," agent Orland said, testing the waters, "at this point we really have nothing specific to go on, other than a phone call from a police captain to a mobster. The Don could just be an informant for this Captain." Orland, a relative newbie at the agency at only 28 years of age, looked around to gauge the reaction of his co-workers and was not pleased with what he saw.

"Not a chance," replied agent Moretti. Moretti was 38 years old, a big, burly guy of 6 feet 2 inches, who had grown up in Boston. "I know these guys. There's no way in hell The Don is an informant. It's more than likely this Capprieti guy is on the payroll, along with 90% of the cops in his precinct. He's probably an informant for The Don, the piece of shit."

This last statement got the attention of agent Hinkle, a slight guy, 30 years old, in good shape who sported a fashionable hair-do, meaning it was just a little longer than most of the others and bordered on insolence. He was also an up-and-comer in the agency. "What did you just say?" he asked.

"I said I know these guys..."

"No, no, at the end, about Capprieti."

"You mean that he's a piece of shit?"

Exasperated, Hinkle said, "We get that Moretti. Before that. About Capprieti and The Don."

"That Capprieti is probably an informant for the Don. That?"

"Yes, that", said Hinkle, as he snapped his fingers. He fixed his gaze on his boss and said, "That could be our entry."

Agent Decker considered where this conversation was going, looked back at Hinkle and said, "Go on."

Having all the attention focused squarely on him, agent Hinkle stood a little taller and gathered himself before he responded, "So, Capprieti has no idea what we do or don't know, as far as his relationship with The Don. What if we play him the tape, just to let him know we've been listening, intimate that we know more than we actually do, and give him the choice of working with us or going to jail? Let's make him *our* informant." He looked around the room for the reactions of his co-workers, hoping that he'd dazzled them.

"Can we trust him?" asked agent Schwartz, a man nearing retirement and playing out the string in an effort to collect his pension.

"Of course we can't," replied Moretti. "No more than we can trust any of the other scumbag informants we use. But that doesn't mean it's not a good idea." That last statement was said with reluctance.

AIC Decker, having taken this in, said, "If we can turn this cop, it'll be our first foothold into the organization. It's worth a try." He turned his attention to Hinkle and continued, "Hinkle, arrange a private meeting with Capprieti. One that will take him by surprise." Now, as he thought and paced in the space behind his desk, as much as the cramped quarters would allow, Decker said, "Someplace outside of his precinct, where fewer people are apt to recognize him, or you, for that matter. Maybe while he's off duty." He continued to pace and think. "Get him alone, show him your credentials and play the tape for him." He paced and thought some more. "And take Moretti with you. It'll be good to show him a face from the neighborhood, someone slightly more imposing than yourself," which drew snickers from everyone in the room. "Oh, and be sure to tape his response, surreptitiously, of course."

"Of course," said Hinkle.

"OK everybody. Let's make this happen."

The team, knowing a dismissal when they heard it, all headed for the office door.

"And one more thing," added Decker, which caused the stampede to come to a halt. "This stays strictly between us."

All the men nodded in agreement as they exited the office.

• • •

Having followed Capprietti for the better part of a week, and now sitting in a car just down the street from the Captain's house, Hinkle and Moretti were pleased to see him exit the house dressed in civilian clothing as he got into his car, parked conveniently right in front of his house.

"He's in civvies. That's promising," noted Moretti as he started the car and pulled out to follow his target at a discrete distance. Instead of driving the standard issue black Ford Sedan, which fooled no one, Moretti was driving his personal ride, a light blue 1968 Chevy Chevelle SS with thick dual black racing stripes across the hood, roof and trunk. It had enough power to use in a chase, if the need arose, but, believe it or not, actually blended in with the other cars on the road, many of which were late 60s, early 70s muscle.

"That it is," responded Hinkle. "Plus, it's his day off. Let's see where this leads."

Where it led was a roundabout and convoluted journey to Newton, Massachusetts, a posh suburb of Boston, about thirty minutes' drive from where Captain Capprietti lived. Instead, the drive took closer to an hour.

"You think he suspects something?" asked Hinkle, knowing full well there's no way to get an answer to the question.

"Who knows?" responded Moretti. "He's been a scumbag for so long, he probably just assumes somebody's tailing his ass, just for the hell of it."

After driving for another few minutes, Moretti said, "I don't think he's made us. I really think it's just his usual precautions."

Having thought about what Moretti said, Hinkle replied, "You're probably right. But, if he's just out running an innocent errand, why the need for any precautions?"

"I think we're about to find out," said Moretti as he pulled over to watch Capprietti's car pull into a driveway leading to the valet parking for the Hyatt hotel. As Capprietti got out of the car, he flashed a badge to the valet, who nodded, got into Capprietti's Cadillac and pulled out to park it in a conspicuous space right out front.

Hinkle quickly grabbed a camera from the back seat and said, "I'm going inside. I have a feeling this could be good for us." He opened the passenger door, got out of the car, turned to lean into the window, and said, "If this is what I think it is, we may have more leverage. I won't be long." He slapped the side of the car as he passed and jogged across the street, where he entered the hotel's lobby.

• • •

The afternoon of the following day, Moretti and Hinkle found themselves in AIC Decker's office. With only the three of them, the space was much more comfortable, which allowed all to sit and utilize the desk. After briefing their boss about the surveillance of the last five days, Hinkle opened a manila folder and placed a series of black and white photographs on the desk. The two agents silently watched Decker as they waited for a response. Decker looked up from the photos, raised one eyebrow, and asked, "What is it I'm looking at?"

"What you are looking at, Boss, is Captain Scumbag with a very well paid lady of the evening, which does not happen to be Mrs. Captain Scumbag," responded Moretti.

Decker gazed back at the series of pictures, which showed the Captain having lunch and being very physically friendly with his companion before holding hands, walking to the elevator, entering the elevator and, as the doors begin to close, embracing the lady while cupping her ass-cheek with one hand. Decker smiled, looked up and said, "Good work, boys."

Hinkle smiled back and said, "We were going to have our chat with him yesterday, but when we saw this, we figured it'd be better to have photos in hand when we had our little tête-à-tête. If he's not worried about the Mob Boss, he's got to be worried about the missus."

Pleasantly amused by his charges, Decker chuckled and said, "Of that I have no doubt. Let's reel this bastard in."

"It'll be our pleasure," said Moretti as he and Hinkle stood and exited the office.

• • •

Not wanting another week to pass before approaching Capprietti at his next rendezvous, assuming the regular nature of such meetings, Moretti and Hinkle found themselves waiting at Capprietti's car as he came out for work two days later. They casually leaned on the car and smoked cigarettes, when the front door of the Capprietti residence opened; Mrs. Capprietti gave her husband a kiss goodbye and closed the door. As the Captain, in full uniform, turned to walk down the steps, he saw the two strangers chatting with each other as they smoked and totally ignored him. One sat on the Cadillac's hood while the other had his foot on the massive bumper.

Capprietti walked down the stairs and approached the car, which was his pride and joy, and called out, "Hey, assholes, get the fuck off the car!"

Upon hearing this, Hinkle and Moretti both looked around, as if trying to determine to whom this statement was directed. Seeing nobody else, they turned back to Capprietti, who by now had come through his gate at a quick pace.

"Are you speaking to us?" Hinkle asked, the picture of innocence, his foot still on the Caddy's bumper.

"Yeah, wiseass," responded the Captain, as he kicked the foot off the bumper.

Remaining calm, Hinkle watched as Moretti, still sitting on the hood of the car, slowly lowered himself to the ground, stubbed his cigarette out on the otherwise pristine paint, and politely said, "That's really no way to behave with fellow officers of the law," as Capprietti stared at the smoldering ashes on his prized possession. Moretti stepped menacingly close to the uniformed officer, their noses only a fraction of an inch apart, before he said, "We came here to have a friendly chat as a professional courtesy," as Hinkle held his FBI credentials directly in front of Capprietti's eyes.

The Captain took a step back, looked at the ashes, and said, "If that's the case, why'd you do that?"

"You were being less than courteous. Sometimes I forget my manners. You know how it is, growing up in this city."

Hinkle moved forward, put his hand on the Captain's arm and said, "Let's have that friendly chat before this gets out of hand, eh? It's really in your best interests, professionally and personally."

Capprietti knew when he'd been threatened, having taken the same tactic on numerous occasions and, anxious to find out what's what, he said, "Sure, let's do that."

Moretti held out his hand and said, "The keys to your ride, please. I'll drive. My partner will follow."

Having no realistic choice, Capprietti complied, got into the passenger side of his car and saw, as they drove away, the curtains of his house slowly dropped back into place.

They drove across town, outside of Capprietti's jurisdiction, to Sam's, a local haunt of FBI agents, which cops never frequented. Ensconced in a back booth, away from prying eyes and ears, they ordered coffee. Hinkle and Moretti sipped their coffee and said nothing as Capprietti fumed. Not being able to contain himself any longer, the police officer, with barely contained rage, said, "OK, what the fuck is this?"

Slowly, Hinkle removed a small tape player from his pocket, placed it on the table, and said, "Pete, may I call you Pete?" and not waiting for an answer, continued, "Pete, we'd like to play a little recording for you. After you've listened to it, we think you'll have an idea about what the fuck this is."

He pressed play and watched as the expression on Capprietti's face slowly resolved from rage to thinly veiled fear as the realization of his predicament sunk in as he heard:

"Hello."

"Hello. May I speak with The Don, please?"

"Who's callin'?"

"Captain Capprieti."

"One moment," followed by muffled conversation and rustling sounds.

"This better be important. I told you not to call me at home...ever."

"It is. The museum was hit over the weekend. A lot of art was taken, and a guard was killed. I need to know what's going on, if I'm going to be of any use."

"You don't think I've heard about that? You break protocol to tell me about something that's all over the news?!? The other cops say you're stupid and you're proving them right. What the fuck do you want, Pete?"

"I want any information you might have. Who the hell hit that place and why? Did you know about it?"

"You'll get information if and when I deem it necessary for you to know. Capiche? Whoever did will have to deal with me. It was not a sanctioned job. As you know, that museum is under my protection. Do you know what this does to my credibility? I'll deal with it. You just go about your business. And don't call me again! Moron."

Hinkle turned the machine off. The FBI agents stared silently as they watched their prey work it out in his head, waiting to see how he was going to play it.

"That means nothing," the policeman finally said, with as much bluster as he could muster.

"Really?" asked Moretti. "Let me quote, *'I need to know what's going on, if I'm going to be of any use.'* Why don't you explain it to us?"

Capprietti thought quickly and said, "I was playing him. I've been letting him think he owns me, all the while using him to put a case together against him."

Hinkle chuckled to himself, took his wallet out of his back pocket and removed a five-dollar bill. He made a show of placing it on the table and flattening it in front of Moretti, before he said, "You were right. That's the direction he went." Hinkle shook his head as Moretti neatly folded and pocketed the money. Hinkle looked at Capprietti and said, "I guess I overestimated you. I thought you were smarter than that. As the Don said, you really are a moron."

As Capprietti began to open his mouth to respond, Moretti held up his hand and said, "Save it," as he placed a manila envelope on the table in front of his guest. When the Captain didn't make a move for it, Moretti said, "Go on, open it. I'm sure you'll find it interesting."

In response, Capprietti said nothing as he opened the envelope and examined the contents as the agents watched him slowly work his way through the photos. He put the pictures on the table and placed his hands palms down on the table in front of him, looked at each of the men seated across from him and simply said, "You bastards."

Hinkle nodded in agreement and said, "You mean you're not going to try and explain that away, too?" He glanced at his partner and said, "Maybe he's not so stupid. He appears to be capable of learning quickly." Refocused on the now deflated cop, Hinkle continued, "So this is what the fuck this is, as you so eloquently put it earlier. We know, and now you know we know, you're in the Don's pocket. We also know that you are a less than faithful husband, a fact which your loving wife might find interesting. You have choices, of course. You can either work with us, in which case things may go easier for you in the long run, or take your chances with the Don and your wife, after we leak to the Don that you've been working for us, and let your wife know of your dalliances. Of course, we don't expect an answer right now. Think it over and get back to us." He looked at Moretti and asked, "What do you think, two days?"

"Yeah, I think two days is fair," responded Moretti, as he looked at Capprietti and asked, "Don't you?"

As Hinkle slid his business card across the table to Capprietti, the cop picked it up, placed it in his pocket as he got up from the table and said, "Fuck you both," before leaving the restaurant in something less than a huff.

To the retreating back, Hinkle mimed a telephone, holding out his thumb and pinky, and said, sweetly, "Call me."

"Well, that was fun," a gleeful Moretti said. "Let's have some breakfast."

"Good idea," responded his partner as he motioned for the waitress.

• • •

Later that day, in what the agents had come to call, euphemistically, "The Palace," the four agents and the AIC gathered in the conference room, sparsely decorated, if one could call it that, but containing an oval table and six chairs. Infinitely more comfortable for the group than the AIC's office. Having been briefed about the meeting with Captain Capprietti, AIC Decker took charge and commended agents Hinkle and Moretti for their work.

Turning his attention to the group at large, he said, "Now for the next phase. The wire-tap on Capprietti's home and office phones is in place. A couple of field agents are currently manning the equipment. Schwartz and Orland, I'd like to keep this as close to the vest as possible, so I want the two of you to relieve them and keep the loop closed to those of us in this room."

"Yes, sir," responded an eager agent Orland.

When neither Schwartz nor Orland made a move to leave the meeting, Decker said, "Now. If the rabbit is going to run or start making contacts, I want one of us there."

Immediately, Schwartz and Orland stood and headed for the door.

"Keep in touch and let me know what's going on," advised Decker.

"Will do," responded Schwartz, as the conference room door closed behind him.

To Hinkle and Moretti, he said, "What's your take on Capprietti? Think he'll cooperate, cut and run, or go to the Don, thinking he can control what happens?"

Moretti and Hinkle glanced at one another, trying to be cooperative partners and not stepping on the other's toes, when Hinkle nodded to Moretti, letting him give his opinion first.

"Well," Moretti began, "my sense is that we freaked the shit out of him. He knows how the Don works, which means, if the Don thinks for a minute that Capprietti's been compromised, Capprietti's a dead man. So, I think he'll help us, reluctantly. Also, I got the impression that the pictures really threw him. He definitely doesn't want his old lady finding out about that."

"I agree," Hinkle chimed in. "The chutzpah these guys have, thinking that they can get away with whatever they want, is amazing. Hopefully, it'll be their undoing."

AIC Decker laughed and said, "Chutzpah, huh? I see you've been hanging out with Schwartz."

"Always looking to broaden my horizons," a smiling Hinkle responded.

Getting back to business, Decker said, "OK. I want you guys following Capprietti's ass for the next couple of days until he gets back to us. Between a tail and the wire-taps we should get a handle on this guy. Keep me up to date."

Hinkle and Moretti rose and simultaneously said, "Will do, Boss," as they headed out the door.

. . .

For the next two days, Schwartz and Orland sat in the converted panel truck, ate sandwiches and smoked. The wire-taps revealed only that Capprietti was trying to keep things as normal as possible. No personal calls were made from either his home or office. After work, Hinkle and Moretti found he went home, where he stayed until leaving for the office the following day. Unlike his usual hands on, some would say, meddlesome, method of being in charge, he delegated tasks to his underlings, not even attempting to micro-manage those tasks. The change did not go unnoticed by those working with and for him, although nobody mentioned it to him directly. At the usual cop bar hangout, however, the talk was rampant, as reported by an FBI agent planted there for that specific purpose. Nobody was sure what brought the change about, but speculation was widespread, ranging from health issues to wife problems to problems with the Don. One intrepid uniformed patrolman offered the possibility of problems with the Feds, but was quickly, and thankfully, shut down. Either nobody thought it was a possibility or nobody wanted to be the one to acknowledge the fact that it was a distinct possibility. The agent made a note of the patrolman's name.

At the end of the second day after the meeting at Sam's, Hinkle had just returned to the office after sitting in his car for three hours, finally leaving Moretti to finish the shift, when his phone rang. Answering after the second ring and having heard the identity of the caller, he glanced at his watch, which read 4:53, and said into the receiver, "Cutting it awfully close, aren't you?"

"I had a lot to think about," replied Capprietti.

"And?" asked Hinkle.

"And what? It's not as if I really have any choice here, is it?" Capprietti asked, rhetorically.

"No, I don't suppose you don't, but before you get all pissy and indignant, don't forget that you have nobody but yourself to blame. Not me, not my partner. It's your actions and your choices that have landed you where you are. Are we clear?"

"Yeah, we're clear. Thanks for the lecture," Capprietti indignantly responded. "What is it you want from me?"

"I want you to remember that you're a sworn police officer and I *expect* you to uphold your oath and do everything in your power to bring down Don Ricky. We're going to need you to contact the Don. Do it in the next couple of days. Find a plausible reason to meet. You need to get back into his good graces. We don't really give a shit about that art heist, but if that's what you have to talk about, so be it. Find some information that you can bring to him. Let him know you don't trust the phone and need to see him in person. Can you handle that?"

"Yeah, I can handle that. How do we make contact?"

"If you need to talk to me," responded Hinkle, "call this number. If I'm not here, somebody will take a message. The message should consist only of a time and place at which we'll meet. If I need to contact you, I have your numbers. My message will also only contain a time and a place. Be there on time if I call. Got that?"

"Got that," said Capprietti before he abruptly disconnected the call.

Hinkle stared at the phone's receiver, muttered "prick," and hung up. He saw that AIC Decker was still in his office and walked over, stuck his head in the door and, after having been acknowledged, said, "He's in."

Decker smiled and said, "Great! Call off the tail after a couple of days, but keep the wire-tap going. Tomorrow, we'll work on strategy."

"Sounds good, Boss. See you tomorrow," responded Hinkle as he headed home for the evening, satisfied with how the plan was going.

• • •

The following day, after reviewing the reports, Capprietti called a meeting of everybody working the art theft case. Since the entire squad knew that this was really the Don's territory, nobody had been working it too hard, fearful of impeding the party that actually had a chance to deal with it. It dismayed the Captain to learn that no real leads had been uncovered and that they were no farther along in the investigation than they were the day after it happened.

"Are you fucking kidding me?!?" an exasperated Captain shouted at his assembled men. He picked up a pile of files that were presumably reports filed by his officers and threw them on the table. "These reports are pure horseshit. There's nothing in there that we can't find out in the newspapers. Maybe I should just hire the reporters." Looking around, he saw the men squirming uncomfortably, and was inwardly pleased.

Finally, his second in command, Lieutenant Morel, being the only other person in the squad to have the standing to stand up to the tirade, said, in what he could only hope was a placating tone of voice, "Cap, you know the score with this. We're concentrating our efforts in other areas where we think we may be of more use."

"Really?" Capprieti mockingly asked. "And what areas are those?"

Taken aback by his Captain's tone, Morel treaded carefully. "There's been a couple of shootings, a jewelry store robbery and a truck hijacking. We've been busy."

"Apparently too busy to investigate a multi-million dollar robbery and murder." The Captain looked around the room and asked, "Does anybody have anything that may not have been in either those reports or the newspapers? Anybody hear anything on the street? You do go out on the street, don't you?" he asked derisively. "Anybody?"

Hesitantly, a uniformed rookie officer raised his hand. The Captain observed the movement and said, "Spit it out, son. What have you heard?"

"Well," the officer began, "I have heard about this guy, Eddie Lacosta. Everybody calls him Tiny, because of course he's a huge guy," he continued with a nervous laugh.

Beginning to lose patience, but noticing how nervous the officer was, the Captain coaxed the young man on. "And what have you heard about this Tiny Lacosta?"

"Um, it seems as if he's been on kind of a bender for the last couple of weeks or so and been shooting off his mouth about some big score he was involved with. He's pissed off because nobody will let him cash in on it. He hasn't actually said what the score was and most people think he's basically full of shit. Oh, sorry sir," he said, embarrassed.

"That's all right, officer," as he strained to read his name tag, "Connelly. We've had more than our share of shit in this room," the Captain responded good-naturedly. As he did so, he could see the tension drain from the room. "Good job." Addressing the room as a whole, he finished the meeting by saying, "OK, everybody. Let's get back out there and do some good today."

Having been dismissed, the men filed out, whispering amongst themselves, many with a look of confusion etched on their faces at the abrupt about-face the Captain's behavior took during the meeting. Most often heard was the word "strange."

Capprieti, having reported to Hinkle, set up a meeting with the Don to take place the following day at Momma Nona's. He correctly ascertained that showing up for this meeting in his uniform would not be met with favor and wisely appeared at the restaurant in civilian clothes. He left enough time to go through the security procedures before being led to the Don's well lighted table at the back of the room, the gauntlet of very large, well-armed men in place and following his every move. As he approached the table, the Don motioned for him to be seated in a chair opposite himself, with his back facing the room. Not comfortable with the situation, which was the whole point, the Captain nevertheless sat where instructed.

By way of introduction, the Don said, "What can I do for you, Peter?"

"First, let me apologize for my error in calling you at your home. It was a stupid thing to do. I'm very sorry."

The Don responded only with an almost imperceptible nod of his head.

Taking this as an acceptance of his apology, Capprietti continued. "Thank you. I'm here because I have some information that I think might interest you."

The Don said, "Continue."

Capprietti relayed the story of Tiny and his bender, repeating, and slightly embellishing, the story told to him by Officer Connelly. As he finished, he closely watched for the Don's reaction, which was, surprisingly, subdued.

"Thank you for the information, Peter. I too have heard tell of similar behavior from Mr. Lacosta. I appreciate your coming forward. Have a nice day." Done with his conversation, the Don picked up the receiver from the ever present telephone and dialed a number.

Having been dismissed, Capprietti decided not to push his luck, rose from his seat and walked the reverse gauntlet to the exit of the restaurant. Once outside, he sighed heavily as he crossed the street to his waiting Cadillac. As he did so, he noticed a black Ford sedan with two occupants parked further down the street. He got into his car, adjusted the mirror and pulled away from the curb, watching to see if the Ford joined him. He was not disappointed.

Having been briefed by Capprietti, Hinkle filled the AIC and his partner in on the meeting at Momma Nona's.

"That was more than we could have realistically hoped for," opined the AIC. "That might be something the Don feels is actionable."

"We can only hope," chimed in Moretti.

"Well, the bugs are in place at Momma Nona's and the phones are tapped. Let's just wait and see."

The briefing over, the FBI men went about their business of the day.

Three days later, Edward "Tiny" Lacosta was dead.

THAT DAMN SHOW...AGAIN

While we were taking it slowly and trying to devise a plan that didn't make us appear to be total lunatics, I thought it would be a good idea to rewatch the documentary. My thought process was that I may have missed some information the first time, since I originally watched strictly for entertainment purposes. I thought it made sense to watch it with a renewed focus on details. While this thought first occurred to me shortly after our discussion regarding a plan, I didn't actually dive right into a rewatch. No, something held me back. A trepidation lurking in the back of my conscious mind. I didn't really think that the cause of my "watching" abilities was the documentary, but I couldn't really be certain, could I? I mean, it did start after my initial viewing, but that could just be coincidence. Couldn't it? That is, if you believe in coincidence, which I didn't. And don't.

So, after giving it a lot of thought and wrestling with numerous scenarios as to why the "watching" began, I decided it was worth the risk to rewatch the documentary. It really didn't seem to be much of a risk, while the reward, namely $5,000,000.00, seemed to far outweigh whatever existential risk might exist. As I thought about it, whatever had brought the "watching" ability to the fore had already occurred, thereby eliminating any further risk. Having convinced myself, I delved into the binge watching experience.

• • •

Adrian was out of town for a few days at an artist's retreat. Her absence coincided with a weekend, so I took the opportunity on Saturday to become one with the couch and spend seven hours or so immersed in the details surrounding an old art heist. I'm not one that watches a lot of daytime television. As a matter of fact, I try to avoid it at all costs. It just seems that there are better ways to spend the daylight hours. So, not only was this totally out of my norm, the fact I was doing it gave me a certain level of uncomfortability, as if I was guilty of something. It was just weird. Nevertheless, I closed the drapes, telling myself it was too sunny to see the screen properly, settled in, and hit "play."

I watched with a heightened level of interest, and stopped only occasionally for food, drink, and bathroom breaks. I wish I could say that I gleaned an enormous amount of new information and insight, but the truth was that my initial recollection of the story was pretty much it. That seemed to be all there was, at least to my bloodshot eyes and tired brain.

Then I went to bed.

• • •

The interior of the warehouse is dimly lit and damp. The dampness comes from its proximity to Boston Harbor, with the brick walls and concrete floors doing nothing to dissipate or absorb the moisture. In the old days, ships could pull up to the dock next to the building and load or unload with relative ease. The dock is long gone, but the harbor remains.

The building is an old three story brick structure. Its exterior has recently been tuck-pointed, indicating that the owner takes pride of ownership and wants to properly maintain his investment. The interior is sparsely decorated, although using the word "decorated" in this context is surely misleading. It is basically an empty structure, except for the stacks of boxes containing various imported goods and the equipment and machinery required to safely and efficiently maneuver those goods. On the second floor is a spacious, well-lit office. One complete wall, the one facing the floor below, is glass. Inside the office, clearly visible from below, but somewhat obstructed by the clouds of cigar and cigarette smoke, are three men. It is clear, somehow, that they are waiting for somebody to join them.

Moments later, headlights become visible, approaching from the street and turning into a parking space just outside the entrance door to the warehouse. The car is a 1969 baby blue Cadillac Calais Coupe. Visible on the driver's side of the long hood is what appears to be a small, round burn mark, as if somebody had extinguished a cigarette. The driver opens the door and confidently approaches the entrance, as if being familiar with his surroundings, not bothering to look around, even though the rest of the street is shrouded in shadow. Upon entering the building, he assuredly climbs the metal stairs to the office, knocks once, and, not waiting for a reply, opens the door and walks through.

Not getting up from behind the antique mahogany desk, Don Ricky looks up, puffs heavily on his cigar and says, "Hello Peter. Thanks for joining us. I hope your wife wasn't too perturbed about your having to work at night." The other two men take a seat on the couch placed along the far wall, out of the way but able to observe all.

Taking a seat, even though not invited to do so, Pete takes a pack of cigarettes from the breast pocket of his expensive monogrammed shirt, removes one of its contents and lights up before saying, "It's not a problem. She's used to the crazy hours of a police officer." Inwardly, he thinks, 'So, they don't know she's out of town. That's a good sign.'

"I'm sure she is. I'm glad we're not doing anything to unduly concern her."

Taking his cue from what the Don had just said, Pete asks, "What exactly are we doing here? It's been quite a while since we've met here," indicating his current surroundings.

"We have some business to discuss, and some of my associates are worried about how safe it is to talk at the restaurant. I believe you hinted about that same concern when you came to see me about Tiny."

Sitting up straighter in his chair, Pete leans forward and says, as if he's somehow forgotten, "Oh, right. Did your boys find anything?"

"Apparently, the FBI is getting both desperate and bold. We found some listening devices. We removed a couple, but left the rest in place so they think we're satisfied with what we found. However, we've found it necessary to move certain conversations to a different location," motioning to their current surroundings.

"Good idea. If you'd like, I can make some inquiries with the FBI to see what they know, or think they know," offers Pete.

"Do you have any contacts in the FBI?" asks the Don.

"There are a couple of guys I could call. You know, law enforcement to law enforcement."

Reaching down and opening a desk drawer, the Don removes a manila envelope and gently places it on the desk in front of Pete.

"What's that?" asks Pete.

"Go ahead and open it," answers the Don.

Pete reaches for the envelope, undoes the string and pulls out a group of pictures. The photos show Pete, FBI Special Agent Hinkle and FBI Special Agent Moretti at lunch, in front of Pete's Cadillac, at a park bench just out of town, and other various places. All told, there are ten photos, taken over a span of three weeks. After having viewed the photos, Pete indignantly says, "You've been following me?!? What the fuck?", as he throws the pictures back on the desk. In his head he's thinking, 'Sometimes the best defense is a good offense.'

Unperturbed, the Don says, "I suppose those are the agents to which you are referring." Picking the photos up, he rifles through them. "Agents Hinkle and Moretti. From what I hear, two very special FBI agents. I'm familiar with Mr. Moretti. Several years ago, his older brother worked for me. He met a terrible end and FBI Special Agent Moretti holds me responsible for his death. It's my understanding that he's vowed to bring me down." Leaning forward with his elbows on the edge of the desk, he continues, "And now it appears that he's recruited you to help him."

"That's crazy! I would never do anything to hurt you or the organization."

Reaching back into the desk drawer, the Don removes a stack of pictures and tosses them to Pete. Pete catches them and immediately sees that they are pictures of him and a female paramour at a physical lunch and even more physical elevator ride.

"Where did you get these?" he asks with barely contained rage.

Ignoring the question, the Don says, "It's my understanding that these were presented to you by your friendly FBI agents as part of an ultimatum to help them get to me. I'm disappointed, Pete, that you choose your wife over me. After all, wives are replaceable."

Finally, coming to grips with his predicament, Pete pleadingly says, "You have to understand, she would've taken everything and ruined me. I can still help you. I could feed misinformation to the FBI..." He stops when the Don holds up his hand.

"I'm truly sorry, Pete, but I can't trust you. Others know of your betrayal. Many of your co-workers have noted the change in your behavior at the precinct. I have no choice but to take action. The big picture takes precedence here."

The two men on the couch, responding to a nod of the head from the Don, approach a totally deflated Pete, take him by the arms and lead him from the room.

The baby blue Cadillac pulls up to the curb in front of a nicely maintained two-story brownstone building built in the 1920s. It is well maintained, with a small front yard behind a wrought-iron fence and gate. The numbers 525 appear on the side of the building next to the front door and mailbox. Immediately after the Caddy parks, a light grey four-door Coupe DeVille drives further down the block and pulls over. Nobody exits the still running car.

The driver's side door of Pete's Cadillac opens and Anthony, a large man, dressed in black from head to toe and sporting a crew cut, emerges, closes the door and goes around to the passenger side door. As he reaches for the door handle, the door is shoved open, hard, in an effort to surprise and dislodge Anthony. Ever the consummate professional, Anthony grabs the side of the door, shakes his head and, murmuring "Really?", takes Pete by the arm and hauls him to his feet. Gently, Anthony implores Pete, "Please, don't make a scene and make me hurt you here on the street. There's nobody around to help you, anyway."

Looking up and down the street while in Anthony's grasp, Pete notices that no other people are anywhere to be seen and the streetlights on the entire block are off, plunging the entire neighborhood into darkness and shadows. As Anthony gently pulls Pete along, he tells him, "As soon as you left for your meeting with the Don, we had this entire block shut down. We've got guys at both ends of the street making sure it stays that way. Let's get moving," as he gently encourages Pete to move toward the house.

"Tony, please don't hurt my wife. She had nothing to do with anything."

"We know. We also know she's out of town, so let's stop the bullshitting and get this over with," now moving Pete forward in a less than gentle manner.

As they climb the steps to the front door, Anthony reaches into his pocket and removes a set of keys attached to the car keys for the car he had just driven. Opening the door, Anthony shoves Pete inside, turns on a light, and shuts the door behind them. Reattaching himself to Pete's arm, he climbs the steps.

"Where are you taking me?" a now panicked Pete asks.

"Your office," is all that Anthony says, continuing to drag Pete along. Finally, at the top of the stairs, he turns to his left, taking his captive with him, enters the office and points to the desk chair. "Sit."

Pete lethargically does as he's told, looking at his office space as if seeing it for the first, and last, time. He takes in the expensive worn brown leather furniture, the bookshelves containing pictures and mementos of his career as a police officer, his diploma from the Police Academy, and other various knick-knacks that once seemed so important. As he continues his survey, he notices Anthony has somehow unlocked the lower right-hand desk drawer, removed a .38 caliber Smith & Wesson revolver, and placed a single bullet in the chamber. Spinning it into the correct firing position, he wordlessly places the gun in Pete's right hand, bends his arm so that the barrel of the weapon is at Pete's mouth, and, in one fluid motion, stomps on Pete's foot, causing Pete to open his mouth in pain, places the barrel into Pete's mouth and, stepping to the side, pulls the trigger. The report is deafening and the results instantaneous, as witnessed by the blood and brain splatter on the wall behind the desk.

Satisfied, Anthony uses a handkerchief to wipe down any surfaces he may have touched, scans the room one last time, and has the strange feeling that he's being watched. Knowing that's not possible, he walks down the stairs, careful to replace the set of keys into the bowl on the table next to the door, and exits, closing the door behind him. Reaching into his pocket for another set of keys, he locks the door, walks down the stairs and through the wrought-iron gate, being careful to close the gate behind him. He then casually strolls to the waiting Coupe Deville and gets into the passenger side of the car. Immediately, the car pulls away from the curb, two other black Cadillacs pull away, one from each end of the street, and the streetlights miraculously return to the land of the working.

•   •   •

HUH...HUH...HUH...HUH. I awoke, gasping for breath, afraid that I was going to hyperventilate. It was dawn and I was freaking out. "What the fuck was that?!?" It was like nothing I'd ever experienced. If I thought my initial "watching" experiences were something, this was a whole new level of intensity...insanity. I forced myself out of bed so that I could record the whole thing while it was still fresh, although, truth-be-told, I felt as if I would never forget a single solitary moment.

I'm not certain I could explain the differences between the initial "watchings" and what I had just experienced. I'll call this new experience "super-watching," because that's what it felt like. Super-sized, super charged, super sensitive, super-freaky. All of those descriptions fit.

Where the initial "watchings" placed me at the location and allowed me to experience certain feelings and sensory perceptions, this "super-watching" placed me at the location so that, not only could I experience feelings, smells, tastes and sounds at a hyper-sensitive level, but also *extrasensory* perceptions. I mean, I could literally hear some of the participants' thoughts. When I wrote "*Inwardly he thought, 'So, they don't know she's out of town. That's a good sign,'*" it wasn't because I was surmising or writing fiction. It was because I actually *heard* this Pete guy think it as it simultaneously manifested in both his brain and mine. When I said that Anthony had the strange feeling he was being watched, it's because I felt what he felt, down to the hairs on the back of his neck rising almost imperceptibly. I felt his relief as he dismissed the idea, knowing that it was just not possible for somebody else to have been there. But I was there, in all but the corporeal sense. I couldn't interact with the environment, at least I don't think I could. The idea to try hadn't even occurred to me until this very moment. That would really be fucked up, wouldn't it? I mean, what if I could have stopped the murder from taking place? Assuming it was an actual historic event, which I'll have to check out. But, assuming it was, and assuming I could have interfered in some way so that it did not take place, how would history have been altered? What ramifications would ripple through time? Would it be better or worse, and by what measure? It seemed I was getting into some pretty esoteric territory. What I took away from this thought process was that I needed to tread very, very carefully.

It was much earlier on a Sunday morning than I usually awoke, but there was no way I could go back to bed with a realistic hope of further sleep. I remained at my computer and decided to find out whether what I had just "watched" was an actual event. I typed in words that I thought might help with an internet search. "Boston Police Officer," "Peter," "1970-1975," "Suicide." Hitting "enter," I sat back, waiting for the results, which arrived almost instantaneously.

An article from the Boston Globe: *"Yesterday, the body of Boston Police Captain Peter Capprietti was found by his wife upon her return from a trip to New York to visit her parents. The police arrived to find a distraught Mrs. Capprietti sitting on the floor outside of Captain Capprietti's home office. The Captain was found seated at his desk, the victim of an apparent suicide. Captain Capprietti, 52 years of age, was a well-respected member of the Boston Police Force for 32 years. Lieutenant John Morel, the second in command at Captain Capprietti's precinct house, said, 'This is a shock to all of us who worked with Pete. There will be an investigation, as in all such cases. I really can't say much more than that at this time. Our thoughts and prayers go out to Mrs. Capprietti and the entire Capprietti family.'"*

Scrolling down, I found a small article from a week later, again in the Boston Globe: *"The death of Captain Peter Capprietti was officially ruled a suicide today, the coroner's office announced. Captain Capprietti was laid to rest yesterday at Holy Mother of God Cemetery in a private ceremony."*

That was the extent of the newspaper coverage of the story. I have no idea if it received more coverage on television news, but, beginning to grasp how things worked in 1970s Boston, I had the feeling that everybody wanted this kept quiet and gone from the public eye as soon as possible. The police, because it reflected poorly on them, especially if serious questions were to have been asked. The FBI, because they didn't want the Captain's cooperation with them, or the way in which it had been obtained, made public. The "Don" because he wanted nothing to be traced back to him or his men. Suicide was readily apparent and an easy way to sweep the matter under the proverbial rug.

Scrolling further down the page, more or less by reflex just to see what I could see, I came across a picture of FBI Agent-in-Charge David Decker. The name David Decker meant nothing to me. However, next to him in the picture, as identified in the caption, was Special Agent Michael Moretti. That name rang the familiarity bell, so I re-scanned what I had written about my most recent "super-watching" experience and found the name, hearing the Don say it in my mind. Utilizing the touch screen on my computer to enlarge the photo, I suddenly felt a surge of energy bolt through my body as I was transported to 1970. I found myself looking at Decker and Moretti at the exact moment the picture had been snapped in front of the building housing the FBI field office. No longer rendered in two dimensional black and white, the walking, talking FBI agents got into the car next to which they had been standing.

"God damn it!" an animated Agent Decker exclaims. "You know what this means, don't you?" as he looks at Agent Moretti, who is maneuvering the car into traffic. "It means we have a mole in our office. Some shithead on the Don's payroll," continues Decker, not waiting for Moretti to respond.

"Not necessarily," replies Moretti. "It could just be another case of cop suicide." Looking at his boss, he says, "It happens all the time."

"Yeah, it does. But I'll bet my pension that this was no suicide," replies Decker, as he whips his head around to look at the back seat.

Noticing the sudden movement by his passenger, Moretti asks, "What?"

"Nothing. I just thought I saw somebody back there. This case is getting me jumpy," answers Decker. "Anyway, my gut tells me this was no suicide. We had the block canvassed, and it appears that very few people were home that night. Those that were said the street lights were out, making it impossible to see anything, even if they had been looking. Then, as if God said 'Let There Be Light', the streetlights came back on. According to forensics, the timing coincides with the approximate time of death. This stinks of the Don. I know it."

Hearing Decker say he thought he saw something in the back seat made me remember my earlier musings. Tentatively, I reached out to flick Decker's ear, not even thinking about the fact that I was able to have a coherent thought while in the middle of a "super watching" experience. Thankfully, I couldn't manifest a hand nor affect my surroundings in any way.

"Well, if that's the case," responds Moretti, "the first thing we need to do is clean house."
"Agreed."

As suddenly as I was thrust into the watching, I found myself back at my desk in the present day, my hand still in contact with the touch-screen. As soon as I realized this, I jerked it away with such force that I thought I would injure myself and looked at it as if a foreign appendage. Adrenaline coursed through my body, bringing about a case of the shakes. Taking slow, deep breaths, I finally got myself under control, at least to the point that I was no longer trembling.

A wake super-watching experience. Well, that certainly brought this to a new level. I know it goes without saying, but I'm going to say it, anyway. Nothing like this had ever happened to me before. *Nothing*. The only part of the experience that I can glean any comfort from was the fact that I could have a coherent thought and make an attempt at physical contact while in the experience. It gave me hope I might be able to exercise some level of control, which, if I was going to maintain any level of sanity, would be a complete necessity.

Still seated at my desk with the search results staring at me from the screen, I hesitated to do anything further. However, against my better judgment, I started a new search, typing FBI Agent David Decker/1970

Garden Museum theft. Hitting "enter" I didn't have long to wait for the determination that that particular combination brought up nothing useful. There were some random mentions of Agent Decker, but none that connected him to the art theft case. Continuing to scroll and read the short blurbs that appeared, I came across an article that outlined the career of the then retiring Agent Decker. Opening the article, I read and determined that Decker's focus was not on the art theft, but rather organized crime in and around Boston. He was named as having been instrumental in the arrest and conviction of Don Ricky, as well as other high and low-level mobsters. It was also mentioned that he was instrumental in ferreting out FBI agents in the Boston field office that were also on the payroll of various mob bosses, including Don Ricky.

That caused me to pause in my internet tracks. Here was more confirmation, if I needed it, and I always needed it, that what I had seen and heard was accurate. Decker and Moretti had talked about cleaning house because they had a mole. Now here, in black and white, was confirmation that Decker was instrumental in doing exactly that.

Sitting there, in the furthest recesses of my mind, I began to formulate a plan, even if I didn't know it at the time. My mind took to wondering if I could enter into a "super watching" experience voluntarily, get the information I was specifically looking for, and then get out, all with my mind in-tact. As I scrolled and ruminated on this, my eyes took in various articles when a name caught my attention. Ralph Scoletti. It was the first name that did it for me. Ralph. Ralphie. There could be a lot of "Ralphs" out there in 1970s Boston, but my mind told me to open the article and my hand responded, revealing a picture of a face that was familiar to me. It was "Ralphie." As I enlarged the picture, being careful not to use the touch screen but rather the cursor, the familiar features became hyper-focused as…

Ralphie walks into a large brick warehouse building located adjacent to Boston Harbor. The concrete floors show tire tracks from the fork lift used to move the pallets of imported goods stored in the building. It was dusk and, as the door closes behind him, he stops to let his eyes adjust to the lack of light. As they do, he sees an unoccupied wooden chair sitting over a floor drain. Knowing as he does that this is not a portent of a good time, he turns to exit the same way he came in when a hand holding a black jack comes down from behind him and strikes him on the back of the head. He crumbles like a marionette whose strings have been cut. Emerging from the shadows behind the door, one of the Don's most trusted muscle men, Anthony, bends, grabs Ralphie under the arms and drags him to the chair. Showing off his dead-lift skills, he hoists the limp body onto the chair and, using the roll of duct tape he pulls from his pocket, affixes the man to the chair. He then steps back into the shadows and waits. A few moments later, the lights in an upstairs office overlooking the main floor come on. A man dressed in a fine Italian black wool suit casually makes his way down the stairs towards Ralphie. Anthony materializes from the shadows, holding a padded chair and places it in front of Ralphie so the Don can sit, which he does. With a slight movement of his head, the Don orders Anthony to wake Ralphie, which he does with a well-placed wicked slap.

Ralphie blinks his eyes, which have a hard time focusing due to his concussed state. He tries to speak, but all that comes out of his mouth is gibberish and drool. Anthony provides one more slap, as incentive, and stands back, behind and to the side of the Don. When finally able to maintain some level of control over his eyes, he sees the Don sitting patiently in front of him, causing him to try to stand, out of reflex. His only thought at that moment is, "What the hell is going on?"

As if in response to this unspoken thought, the Don says, "Ralphie, are you back with us?"

Unable to speak, Ralphie nods his head in answer.

"Good, good. You know, this really pains me to do, but you and your friends have caused me a great deal of trouble. The job at the Garden Museum, that was not a good idea. I'll give you that it was nicely pulled. Nevertheless, not a good idea. I'll take it you and your friends didn't know about my arrangements with the Museum, but

I still can't excuse what you did. You should have come to me first. You know that, right?"

Ralphie gathers himself together and says, "Yesh shir, I know that now." He's having a hard time putting his thoughts into coherent words, and thinks to himself, "Shit, this is not good." At least his thoughts are not slurred.

"I'm glad you know that now. I would have thought that you knew it before, but, OK, you're not the smartest guy around. Which leads to my next question. This job was, obviously, not planned by you and your friends. So, who helped?"

Having trouble keeping his head up, he struggles to right himself and retain what little dignity he has under the circumstances. "It was just us. Me, Tiny and Jimmy. Mostly Jimmy."

"Hmmm. Interesting. Mostly Jimmy, you say? Is Jimmy a smart guy? A planner?"

Starting to reflexively nod, he grimaces in pain as his concussion headache really kicks in. Instead, he steadies himself and says, through gritted teeth, "He is. Really smart. And detailed."

More to himself than to anybody present, the Don mutters, "I wonder why he kept it such a secret?" Out loud, he again addresses Ralphie. "Two more questions and then you can get some rest. First, where is Jimmy now?"

Shrugging as best he could, Ralphie says, "I don't know. I haven't seen him for a couple weeks. I left messages at the usual places, but haven't heard from him."

"What are the usual places, Ralphie?"

"Bo's Diner and his mother's. But since what happened to Tiny, not the Diner so much."

"That's understandable Ralphie. Now, I need you to focus on this next question. Can you do that?"

"Yes, sir."

"Good Ralphie. Now listen carefully. Where did you stash the art?"

Visibly trying to recall the correct answer, he repeats the question to himself in his head. Finally remembering, he says, "I don't know. Jimmy said it would be best if not everybody knew and that he'd take care of it."

"So, just so I understand, Ralphie, Jimmy took all the art, stashed it someplace and didn't tell either you or Tiny where? Is that correct?"

"Yes, it is."

"That Jimmy really is a smart guy," the Don says, and thinks to himself, "And you, Ralphie, are a complete moron." Out loud to Ralphie, he says, "Thank you, Ralphie. That was very helpful. Go with Anthony and he'll take you someplace quiet so you can rest."

Standing, he nods to Anthony, turns and exits the building while Anthony is still cutting Ralphie loose from his bindings. Ralphie, not being quite as out-of-it as he seemed moments ago, thinks to himself, "I'll only have one chance at this," as, finally free of his bondage, with Anthony behind him, he snaps his head back with as much force as he could summon, making bone crushing contact with Anthony's nose. Taken by surprise, Anthony stumbles backwards and brings his hand to his nose, which is now bent and leaking blood profusely.

Muttering "Son of a bitch," to himself, he looks up to see Ralphie stumbling towards the door to the street. Ignoring the blood, Anthony runs after him, catches him just outside the door and slams the blackjack, which had somehow appeared in his hand, into the back of Ralphie's head. It seems to Anthony that the sound of the crushing skull could be heard for blocks. As Ralphie starts to go down to the ground, Anthony grabs him by the coat and drags him back into the warehouse, dropping him onto the floor. Taking a hankie from his pocket, Anthony uses it to catch the blood still streaming from his broken nose. "Son of a bitch." Finding the blackjack still in his hand, he raises it above his head and brings it down with the full force of his years of weight lifting behind it, crushing the rest of the skull and driving bone deep into Ralphie's brain. Thinking to himself, "Shit. Now I have a mess to clean up. Couldn't you just have cooperated, huh? I have a date that I'm going to be late for." He turns to walk back to the door and says to Ralphie's lifeless body, "Don't go anywhere. I'll bring the car in here," as he opens the door, walks through and turns to make certain the door is secure.

Coming out of the experience as suddenly as I entered, I found myself breathing hard once again. "This can't be good for me," I thought. My hand was still on the keyboard, so I quickly raised it and slowly placed it in my lap, for want of a better place. It dawned on me that, although careful not to touch the screen while the picture was being displayed, I still got sucked into whatever that was. I wanted to memorialize this latest incident but was reluctant to touch the keyboard, as if the keyboard were the conduit. Talking to myself out loud in an effort to convince myself that it was safe, I reached for the mouse and quickly closed the web browser. Feeling safer, I opened Word and typed.

•　•　•

Adrian got home late that afternoon. She found me lying prone on the couch, with no television or lights on and my laptop closed. I must have dosed off because I was surprised to find her sitting next to me, just staring. When I opened my eyes, I groggily greeted her and sat up. My hair was disheveled, I hadn't washed or shaved, and my breath must have been atrocious.

"If you don't mind my saying, you look like crap," was how she greeted me.

Rubbing my face, I said, "Thanks. Nice to see you, too."

Bending over to give me a hello kiss, she said, "No, really. You look like you've been through the ringer and spit out. What's up with that?"

"I've had a really rough day," I said. By way of explanation, I handed her my laptop and said, "Here, read it for yourself."

She had a quizzical look on her face as she accepted the proffered computer and opened it. It immediately came to life, displaying the details of the "super-watching" events of the day. As she read, I let myself fall back on the couch, face down. I turned my head slightly, so as not to totally muffle my words, and told her I had rewatched the documentary the day before. I then returned my face to the couch pillow and resumed my prone position while she updated herself on my morning.

She read slowly and methodically, to take in the entire experience. Having finished, she closed the laptop, put her hand on my back and said, in a most sympathetic tone of voice, "Are you okay?"

I turned over on my back, opened my eyes and said, "I didn't get much sleep. I'm afraid to watch anything on television, or read anything on the computer or even look at a book. I have no idea what triggers an experience, so I figured doing nothing would be the safest bet. I don't want to be driving and find myself in another city and time, so I just stayed here all day, trying not to freak out at the loss of control I now have over my sleeping *and* waking moments." Pausing for dramatic effect, I concluded, "So, to answer your question, no, I am most definitely not okay."

"I can understand that," she replied.

I felt a "but" coming and waited. She did not disappoint.

"But," she continued, "trying to hide from this will not help anything."

I forced myself to sit up before I said, "I know, but being home alone and pitiful just felt right. And safe. Now that you're here, I don't feel so concerned about getting into one of those 'watchings' and not being able to get out."

She put her arm around me and said, "Ah. I hadn't really thought about that as a possibility. I get it more now that you said that." After a pause, she asked, "What are we going to do about this?"

Not answering right away, I finally said, "I don't really know. It would probably help to know what's causing this so we could make at least a half-assed half-educated attempt at control." I paused to think before I continued. "It seems that both of the waking experiences were triggered by photographs. Touching or not touching doesn't seem to matter. And, while I'm sure there were other photos that I scrolled over, they didn't suck me in.

Only the ones with at least some connection to the theft, even if I don't know what that connection is." Getting a sense that I might be onto something, I straightened up and speculated. "So, that tells me that my mind, whether consciously or sub-consciously, is still maintaining some level of control." I looked at Adrian for a sign.

"Go on," is all she said.

"So, if my mind is still in control of what I see, there's got to be a way to train my mind to respond to my conscious thoughts, don't you think?"

"It makes sense to me."

"So now, the question becomes, how to do that?"

We both remained silent as we mulled the question over in our minds. Finally, Adrian said, "Earlier you said that it would probably be helpful to know what's causing this. The brain is full of electrical and chemical reactions. Maybe we should have some kind of scan done."

"That actually makes sense," I said, not meaning it as though I was surprised that she came up with it, but as a truly good idea. "Although, that would mean going to a doctor and coming up with a plausible reason for having the scan."

Adrian had the answer to this dilemma ready. "There's always Jennifer."

"Jennifer" was Dr. Jennifer Silver, who has been a friend of ours for the last 35 years or so. She also happened to be a well-regarded neurologist with a practice not more than an hour from where we live.

Smiling, I said, "There's always Jennifer. And," I continued, "we can tell her the truth."

• • •

One week later, Adrian and I found ourselves at Jennifer's house. Located in an upscale area of Scottsdale, it was a large, modern desert dwelling, except for the patch of grass she insisted on keeping, despite our efforts to get her to rid herself of the mowing and watering it required. It reminded her of her upbringing in the Midwest and she was having none of our argument. She wanted it, and that was that, as they say. Plus, her ex-husband really wanted to get rid of it during the period in which he lived there. Keeping it was her way of extending her middle finger to him.

We were seated around her kitchen table, where so many conversations take place among good friends. We were munching on cheese and nuts and drinking cold, filtered water. Adrian and I had spent a good portion of the morning trying to explain what I had been experiencing. As an additional aid, I had brought my laptop so she could read my recollections of the "watching" and "super-watching" experiences. Jen had just finishing reading the last of the writings when she closed the laptop and stared at me, as if attempting to see into my brain without the aid of any technology.

"What?" I asked.

"What do you mean, what?" she asked, incredulous. "This is extraordinary."

"I know. I mean, why are you staring at me like that? There's nothing you can see that lends itself to a clue as to why this is happening, is there?" I asked, hopefully.

"Unfortunately, no. I didn't realize that I'd been staring. I was just thinking about possibilities."

"And?" prompted Adrian.

"And...I'm uncertain. There has been a case study of someone that claimed to be able to astrally project herself from her body, which differs from what you're describing. She claimed to be able to leave her body and float above it, while maintaining an awareness of her physical self. She underwent brain scans while claiming to do so. The researchers found that something dramatic was happening in her brain. The fMRI showed a deactivation of the visual cortex with a corresponding activation of the left side of several areas associated with kinesthetic imagery, which includes mental imagery of bodily movement. But what you are experiencing is different."

"I wish I could pretend to understand most of what you just said. I got she showed signs of different brain activity. There should be a chance I would show something, too, don't you think?" I asked.

Deep in thought, she nodded to herself and said, "There's a chance." Refocusing on me, she asked, "Do you think you could initiate one of these experiences while in the scanner?"

I looked at Adrian, shrugged my shoulders, and said, "I have no idea. But in the interests of science, and sanity, I'm willing to try."

"OK, so am I." She smiled and said, "What the hell, after all these years of knowing you, maybe you'll finally serve a useful purpose and give me a topic for a paper." She stood and headed for the front door, while Adrian and I remained seated, not knowing what Jen was up to. Turning back to us, she said, "Well, come on. There's no time like the present. It's Saturday, nobody is at the office and I can have free reign over the scanner."

With her show of eagerness, we quickly got up, gathered our belongings and headed out with Dr. Jennifer.

•　　•　　•

In Jennifer's office, she directed me to sit in a chair and roll up my sleeves, which I did. She approached with a blood pressure cuff, wrapped it around my left arm, and pumped it up. Looking at the little dial and counting to herself, she unclasped the cuff and said, mostly to herself and Adrian, who was also seated in the room, but out of the way, "130 over 85. Not bad."

I looked at Adrian and she gave me the thumbs up, as Jennifer walked to another part of the office, rummaged in some drawers and returned to my chair, her hands suspiciously behind her. She leaned over to swab my right arm with a gauze pad, prompting me to jump out of my seat and say, "Whoa, whoa, whoa. I thought we were here to play with my brain. What are you doing?"

She sighed and said, "I need to get a blood sample. If we're going to do this right, I want to be able to review the results of your blood analysis while viewing the results of your scans. I was trying not to alarm you, knowing your aversion to needles. That's why I took your blood pressure first."

"My 'aversion' is right! You know I hate those things! Fiddle with my brain all you like, just leave needles out of it." It was clear I was agitated.

Adrian finally walked over to me and said, "If you want to get this thing under control, sit down, close your eyes, and let Jen do what she needs to do," leading me back to the chair I hadn't realized I had vacated.

Returning to my chair, I sat, glared at Jen, and held my arm out.

"Now that's a big boy," she said, not even attempting to keep the mockery from her voice.

I stuck my tongue out and said, "You're buying ice cream after this," just as she stabbed the needle into my arm and removed what must have been a gallon of blood.

"See, that wasn't so bad," the Doctor said while trying not to laugh.

"That's because it wasn't your arm, Dr. Mengele," was my response as she walked away with my blood to do whatever it is they do with blood. "Can we get to my brain, please?"

She returned without my blood or any other dangerous looking device, and said, "Yes, we can get to that thing you call your brain. Follow me," as she led us out of this treatment room, down a hallway and into another larger room. As she turned on the lights, she said, "I think you're going to like this."

With the lights in the room on, we could see a large circular machine with what appeared to be a bed protruding from one end. The opening to the machine didn't look large enough for a full sized human to get through it, but, not seeing any stray body parts lying around or hanging from the opening, I surmised that I'd actually fit.

"How am I going to get my computer in there with me?" I inquired. "There doesn't seem like there's even room for me."

Jennifer finally saw what we were looking at and laughed to herself. "Oh, you're not going in that. You're using this." She pointed to a table on the other side of the room which held a plastic head on which sat a rubbery plastic face-mask/bald cap contraption out of which protruded what seemed like a hundred different wires. A cross between Michael Myers and Daddy Warbucks.

I walked over to inspect the thing and said, "It looks like a prop that someone stole from an old sci-fi horror movie."

She lifted it while still on the stand, and said, the awe apparent in her voice, "It does, doesn't it? It's the latest thing in fMRI technology. It's so much better than having to lie in that banging coffin." She turned to look at Adrian and me and said, "and I've made some modifications of my own."

She motioned to a nearby comfortable looking, nicely upholstered wing chair, and said, "Shall we get started?"

•   •   •

After sitting in the chair and, dare I say, actually getting comfortable, Jennifer gently removed the portable fMRI, which was what she called it, from its stand and began to place it on my head. She was careful to move my rather long hair out of the way in an effort to get as tight a fit as possible. She had said that it was important that the various feeds attached to the helmet made as close contact with the skull as possible. They were sensitive enough not to require shaving of the head, thank goodness, but a tight fit was essential. That was her reason, so she said, for getting it so tight that my eyes were almost creased closed and the skin on my cheeks looked as if I were then currently sky-diving. I suspected she was making it that tight just so she could make me look as ridiculous as possible. After all, what are good friends for?

Having completed her fitting torture, she stepped back and, with Adrian at her side, said, "He looks as if he's had terrible plastic surgery, doesn't he?"

Adrian assessed me and heartily agreed, not quite stifling a girlish giggle.

"If the two of you are done with your critique of how I look, can we get on with this, please?"

"I had no idea that tight skin would turn him into such a grouch," was Jennifer's comment to Adrian, who could only laugh in response. Turning back to me, Jennifer was again Dr. Silver in her domain. "OK, I'm going to go behind the glass, over there," as she pointed to a small control room behind her. "We'll begin with some base line readings while you just sit and look at the walls around you. After that, I'll have you read a book, watch a little of a movie and then listen to some music. This will allow me to see the reactions in your brain to each of these separate stimuli. Once I'm comfortable with how the scans are working and your ability to focus on the various stimuli, Adrian is going to hand you the computer. She will have already done a search, so the results will immediately be available. I want you to scan those results and, when you find an appropriate article, attempt to begin a 'watching' experience. Got that?"

Not in the mood for any witty repartee, I simply said, "Got it."

"OK." She turned on her heels and headed into the control room. Over a loudspeaker in the room in which I was seated, I heard Jennifer's voice. "When I turn the power on, you'll feel a slight tingling sensation. It's normal and nothing to be concerned about. I'm going to begin the scan in 3...2...1...now."

At that moment, I felt a slight surge of electricity and, as warned, a slight tingling sensation on my skull and a little throughout the rest of my body. It wasn't painful. More like the electrical feeling from a tenser machine turned to 11. In any event, I was glad to have received the warning. I could relax and sink into the comfy chair, still alert and not freaking out. Over the speaker, Jen said, "Now, look around the room. Really take in your surroundings. It's OK to move your head. When you're done, bring your focus back to the wall right in front of you and keep it there until I tell you otherwise. Ready?"

"Ready."

"Go."

As instructed, I slowly moved my head, deciding on a clockwise direction to begin. I took in the color of the walls (cream), the color of the ceiling (white), and the posters on the walls (all medical). Changing direction, I saw Adrian sitting at a table working with my computer, the color of the carpet (a tan pattern), the old style banging coffin MRI machine, and, finally, back to the bland cream color wall directly in front of me. I tried to empty my mind of thoughts and just mindlessly stare.

"Good, you're doing great. Now, please read the book to yourself until I tell you to stop." About to ask, "What book?", I saw Adrian materialize in front of me and hand me a copy of a book titled *Timeshots*. Apparently, she thought a book which I had never heard of would be best for this test. I opened to the first page and read silently. After 11 pages I heard Jennifer say, "Good. You can stop reading now."

"I was just getting into it."

"You can take it home with you. Please hand it to Adrian." Once again, I hadn't noticed my wife approach. I handed her the book, and she handed me a laptop on which was showing *The Princess Bride*, one of my favorite movies. Jennifer must be looking at differences between familiarity and non-familiarity. I smiled, sat back and watched as Miracle Max worked his magic and the boys went off to storm the castle. Again, I was interrupted by Jennifer. "That's good. Please hand Adrian the computer and put on the earphones she's going to hand you." Rather than complain, I did as I was told. Putting on the headphones, from my chin instead of over my head, because of the fMRI machine, I was subjected to a series of different styles of music ranging from rap and opera to classical, modern adult alternative and classic rock. Over the loudspeaker came Jennifer's voice yet again. "Good. You're doing great. Please take the headphones off and give them to Adrian while I make some final adjustments. This may take a few minutes, so just relax." This time I turned my head in time to see Adrian walk to me and hold her hands out. I handed the headphones to her as she silently mouthed, "You're doing great," before she went back to her seat at the table across the room.

After three or four minutes, Jennifer came back on the speaker. "OK, are you ready to try this?"

I gulped, not noticing until then how dry my mouth was. "I suppose so. It's the reason we're here. Before we start, can I get a glass of water?"

"Sure." I heard some rustling, water flowing from a tap, and a door opening. Adrian handed me the glass, from which I thirstily drank.

"Thanks," I said, as I handed the glass back to Adrian, who quickly returned to her table and placed it gently down.

Once again, Jennifer asked, "Are you ready to do this?"

"I am."

As soon as the words were out of my mouth, Adrian handed me my laptop. On the screen were the results of a search she had started. The search parameters were "Jimmy/Garden Museum theft/1970/Boston Mob." I thought, "clever" as I scanned the search results. My eyes landed on a newspaper article entitled "FBI Questions James Russo in connection with the Garden Art Heist." The name James Russo was unfamiliar to me, but I had a gut feeling that it might be Jimmy. I clicked on the article and...

Jimmy is seated in a sparsely decorated, or rather, undecorated, room. He is in a stiff wooden chair. In front of him is a metal table, which holds Jimmy's pack of cigarettes, and two FBI agents seated in their very own stiff wooden chairs. One wall is covered by what I easily identify as a two-way mirror. Opposite that wall is a window that looks at a section of Boston which could only be described as seedy. In the corner junction where two walls meet, mounted just under the ceiling behind the agents, is a large camera. Jimmy is not cuffed. He is smoking a cigarette, as is one of the agents. One agent is Moretti. The other is an agent named Hinkle. Jimmy appears to be very relaxed, although he finds he has to squint because of the harsh fluorescent lighting.

"Jimmy, we have it on good authority that you were involved in the Garden Museum theft," says Agent Hinkle.

Jimmy is amused, which is evident by his chuckle and the fact that he thinks to himself, "Ha. These guys got nothin'. This should be fun." To the agents he says, "On good authority? That's really rich boys." Leaning forward with his hands on the table, he continues, "You know, if you look up 'On good authority' in the dictionary, it says 'Don't got shit.'" Satisfied with himself, he leans back, takes a long drag from his cigarette, and blows the smoke towards his interrogators.

"Don't be such a smart little prick, Jimmy," says a pissed-off Agent Moretti as he leans forward and threateningly begins to rise from his chair.

Reaching out to stop his partner, Agent Hinkle says, "Don't. This little prick isn't worth it," as he turns to look at the camera. As Agent Moretti sits back down, Agent Hinkle thinks to himself, "This little prick is right. We don't got shit." To Jimmy, he says,

"Jimmy, you have no idea what we do or don't know. I can tell you this, though. We know enough of what went down to arrest you right now."

Jimmy aggressively stands up, leans forward, and holding his arms straight out in front of him, palms up, exposing his wrists, says, "Then do it! Go ahead!" Waiting, he stares at the Agents, neither of which moves. Sitting down, Jimmy resumes his relaxed position, crosses his legs and looks straight ahead. "If you had anything at all. Even the tiniest little shred of a piece of evidence, you'd do one of two things. You'd either try to turn me against the Don, or you'd threaten me with a long and hard prison term. The fact that you've done neither tells me you ain't got shit," he lectures. "So, either charge me with something or let me go." Watching the reaction of the agents, he thinks, "These guys really took me for an idiot. Same as the Don."

Not moving from his position in his chair, Agent Hinkle says through gritted teeth, "Get out." Turning to look at the two-way mirror, he thinks, "I knew it was a mistake to bring this guy in."

Not needing to be told twice, Jimmy stands, pockets his pack of smokes and swaggers out of the room.

I came out of it in a much more controlled, less hypertensive manner. It must have been because getting pulled into it did not come as a total surprise. That, and the fact that nobody had been shot or bludgeoned to death. At least that's my non-scientific theory. Immediately, I opened my "watching" folder and transcribed what you've just read. Jennifer and Adrian were both patient and quietly waited until I had finished, saved the file and closed the laptop. Once that was done, both cautiously approached. Seeing their hesitancy, I laughed and said, "It's OK. I'm not going to go postal on either of you. And, you may have noticed, I'm not even close to hyperventilating."

Adrian gave me an enormous hug and, since we were in physical contact, I could feel the tension drain from her body. Jennifer was still in business mode as she began to extricate me from my wired helmet, being careful not to pull any of the wires or tear any portion of the contraption. Still, I thought the look on her face was odd. A combination of worry, awe and calculation. Noting that, I said, "So, was there anything you could see?"

Continuing to untangle me from the machine, she avoided eye contact and said, "There was definitely something going on. Until I have some time to really analyze it I don't want to say anything." Completing the headdress removal process, she said, "There we go," as she moved to replace the piece on the waiting plastic head. To lighten the mood, she said, "Feel free to move about the cabin."

Adrian was more outwardly curious about what, if anything, I'd experienced. In response to her inquiry, I opened the laptop and handed it to her. Jennifer appeared at her side and they both moved to the table at which Adrian had been sitting and read what I had written.

"At least nobody was murdered," commented Adrian. "That's a vast improvement over some of those other 'watchings.'"

"I couldn't agree more," I said as I advised them both of my theory as to why I wasn't hyperventilating and freaking out.

Jennifer was strangely quiet, and I commented on that fact. She replied, "I'm just trying to process everything I've learned today. It's been quite a lot and totally different from anything I've ever come across." Walking to the control room, she turned the equipment off, shut the lights and said, "Let's blow this pop-stand, shall we?"

Adrian and I gathered our things and joined Jennifer in closing up shop. On the way to the front door, I said, "I believe that somebody is buying ice cream."

In reply, Jennifer said, "I believe that somebody is. I know just the place."

• • •

For the rest of the week, I spent my time concentrating on avoiding visual stimuli that could in any way be connected to the Garden Museum theft. I avoided television shows or movies that even had art in them. To my surprise, it was harder than I'd imagined. I noticed that art appeared everywhere. I went to books. Fiction. That was much safer, especially with the lack of pictures. I worked some, trying to avoid using my computer to search the web for anything, lest I stumble upon something that would transport me before we heard from Jennifer. Finally, Jennifer called and asked us to come see her the following Saturday, once again when nobody else was around. Neither of us could discern anything based on her tone of voice or inflections. Our curiosity would just have to wait.

• • •

Saturday arrived, and we found ourselves at Jennifer's office rather than her home. She had told us it would be easier to explain if she could use some of the machinery to show some things to us. Our curiosity was aroused.

She greeted us warmly and led us into her office. It was spacious and well-appointed. In addition to her large mahogany desk, there were professional looking leather chairs, a couch, a coffee table and a decent sized conference table. On the conference table she had arranged a coffee service, soda and, knowing my preferences, chocolate milk. She had also set up a computer. On the wall near to the conference table was a lighted viewing square. You know, the kind the TV doctors snap x-rays into so they can explain to the patient how bad the break is. I cracked open an individual container of chocolate milk and took a gulp as Adrian and Jen helped themselves to coffee. Small talk ensued as we got comfortable, that is, until I couldn't take it anymore.

"OK, Jen, what's going on? Based on all this," I said as I motioned to our surroundings, "I'd say that you were trying to find a really nice way to tell your patent that's he's got 2 weeks to live."

She sighed, as if concluding that she couldn't put off the conversation any longer, and having realized how much her preparations had freaked us out, she became very conciliatory as she said, "Oh no," coming to hug us both. "I'm sorry, I didn't mean to let you think that." Motioning to the chairs and taking a seat herself, she continued, as we sat down, "I wanted you to be as comfortable as possible, but not because you're dying. I'll show you what I found, but first I'll just give you a general overview. When we did the scans and you went into the experience, what I was watching was something that I don't think anybody has ever seen before. First, do you guys know what a fMRI scan usually shows?"

Looking at both of us in turn as we shook our heads in the negative, she continued, "It's used to monitor blood flow to the brain under varying conditions. It lets us see which sections of the brain are being activated by increased blood flow. Your blood flow levels were slightly increased, but nothing to indicate any concern." She stopped to drink some of her coffee and asked, "Do you remember me telling you I had made some modifications to the head-piece?"

We both said, "Yes."

"OK. Those modifications allow me to monitor not only blood flow but levels of other chemicals present in the brain and the functioning of electrical impulses." Stopping to ensure that we were still following her, she continued after we both nodded. "Your hippocampus was literally glowing from activity." She was trying to control herself, but her excitement was obvious. "I've never seen anything like it. I showed it to some colleagues and none of them had ever seen anything close to it either. And these are some of the best in the business."

"So," I interjected, "is my head going to explode, or what?" Involuntarily, my hands went to the top of my head, as if I could somehow feel what was going on in there.

"I don't think so," she answered.

"That's not very comforting. I'd really prefer a definite NO."

"There's no sign that, outside of your 'watching' experiences, anything out of the norm is going on in that section of the brain. All the baseline readings I took before your experiences were well within the norm for someone of your age and gender."

Adrian said, with definite relief in her voice, "Well, that's comforting."

"So," I asked, "what about during the 'watching'?"

"That's when you really began to light up. I was concerned, of course, but, because of your normal base readings, and the fact that you exhibited no signs of anything abnormal, besides your normal behavior," she interjected, "I became less concerned."

"So, Jen," a slightly exasperated Adrian cut in, "what were the other chemicals you observed in the hippocampus, and what do they mean?"

She turned to the computer on the table and powered it up and said, as we waited for the screen to show whatever it was Jen had planned, "First I really want to show you the scan." The screen came to life and the inner workings of my brain were laid bare for all to see.

I had to admit that what we saw was fascinating. I also have to admit that it may as well have been a cartoon depiction shown to a high school biology class. It meant absolutely nothing to either Adrian or me. Nevertheless, we watched it with Jennifer. I couldn't help but sneak peeks at her. Her reactions were as interesting, and more meaningful, to me. When the show was over, she looked at us expectantly. We just stared at her in confused silence.

Excitedly she asked, "Did you see that?!?"

I looked at Adrian and back at Jen. "We did. But Jen, as you may remember, we are not neuroscientists. We don't even play them on TV."

Somewhat dejected, she responded. "OK. Sometimes I forget that not everybody is as into this as I am."

Adrian attempted to cheer Jen up and said, "It's not that we're not interested, Jen. God knows that's why we're here. We just don't understand it like you do."

Mollified, at least a little, Jen said, "You're right. OK, what you just watched was not only an explosive blood flow to the hippocampus but also an amazing amount of electrical activity accompanied by a flood of an enzyme called hexosaminidase A." She watched us for any sign of recognition, and seeing none, she continued. "When you got married, did you have a screening for Tay-Sachs disease?"

Adrian and I looked at each other and remembered. "We did," I responded. "The test was negative."

"That's because you had the enzyme. The absence of the hexosaminidase A enzyme causes Tay-Sachs. What they don't measure in those tests is how much of the enzyme is present. As long as it shows up, that's all the test is concerned with."

"OK. So, what does this have to do with me?" I asked.

"That, my friend, is an excellent question. And I don't have the answer."

"You seem very chipper for somebody that doesn't have an answer to a very important question," I noted.

"It's not a question that's ever been asked before." Her excitement was once again becoming apparent. "You remember I took blood, right?"

"As if I could forget."

"An analysis of your precious fluid showed that your hexosaminidase A levels were off the charts. Nothing like it has ever been reported," she advised.

"Maybe it's because nobody ever thought to look at quantity before," chimed in Adrian.

"I don't think that's the case," said Jen. "They know what the norm is. I looked it up. It came up in the Tay-Sachs research." Pointing to me, she said, "and your boy here has an exponentially higher level present than is normal."

"What exponent?" I asked.

"Fifty," was the reply.

"I wish I could say that explains everything," Adrian said.

"Me, too," answered Jen.

After a silence fell over the table, I asked, "So, where does this leave us in our quest to understand my time traveling non-corporeal experiences?"

"It takes us closer to an understanding," replied Jen.

"How so?"

"Do you know what the hippocampus is?" Jen asked.

"Where hippos go for higher education?" It was out of my mouth before I even knew it.

After the requisite eye rolls and groaning from both women, Jen entered lecture mode. "The hippocampus is thought to be principally involved in storing long-term memories and in making those memories resistant to forgetting, though this is still a matter of debate. It's also thought to play an important role in spatial processing and navigation." Ignoring the blank stares with which she was being met, she plowed ahead. "The subregions of the hippocampus are connected by two principal neural circuits: the trisynaptic circuit and the monosynaptic circuit. The trisynaptic circuit forwards information from the entorhinal cortex to the dentate gyrus via the perforant path, which perforates through the subiculum. Information flows along bundles of axons known as Schaffer collaterals. The circuit is completed by outbound projections to the subiculum and the entorhinal cortex." Satisfied with her "simplified" explanation, she waited for a response.

Pointing to Adrian and myself, I said, "Not neuroscientists. Can you put that in baby talk, please?"

She gently shook her head, as if dealing with children, and said, "The Hippocampus controls our perception of space and time."

Now Adrian and I both sported expressions of understanding and amazement.

Not waiting for our response, Jen summed up by saying, "It's my theory that the combination of blood and the high levels of the hexosaminidase A enzyme, which is somehow bonding to the blood cells and causing increased electrical activity, is causing your 'watching' experiences."

After considering in silence for a moment, I said, "The good news is that there is an actual, possible, physical explanation and I'm not merely going crazy."

"And the bad news?" asked Adrian.

"We still have no idea why it started and we're no closer to being able to control it than we were before we had that information."

• • •

The next day I couldn't help but look up Tay-Sachs disease. I remembered I had been tested those many years ago, but did not recollect the specifics. It turned out that it's a rare disorder passed from parent to child. The absence of that enzyme which I have in so much abundance causes fatty substances, called gangliosides, to build up to toxic levels in a child's brain and affects the function of the nerve cells. As the disease progresses, the child loses muscle control. Eventually, this leads to blindness, paralysis and death. Wonderful...not. The high-risk groups for Tay-Sachs disease included having ancestors from certain French Canadian communities in Quebec, Old Order Amish communities in Pennsylvania, Cajun communities of

Louisiana, and last, but not least, Eastern and Central European Jewish communities, known as Ashkenazi Jews. That last group explained why I had to be tested before we got married. This knowledge wasn't helpful in any way, other than to satisfy my curiosity.

During the remainder of the week, Adrian and I discussed various ways of approaching future 'watching' experiences. We concluded that the best I could do at this point was to make sure that, when reviewing information, or even thinking about the case, I was mentally prepared to be pulled into a scenario long ago and far away. Control my breathing and try not to put myself in a position where entering an experience could be potentially dangerous. I hadn't forgotten about that waitress experience and the menu. While not a "watching" experience, it was something unexpected and totally different, and I didn't want to be caught unaware. So, we determined to limit my driving and motorcycle riding to those instances of sheer necessity, only. Also, no sky-diving, cave diving, or other insane activities, none of which I had any plans to begin, anyway. We also talked about the best way to contact the FBI. Our goal in doing so would be two-fold: first, maintain anonymity, and second, have credibility. On our own, because of a total lack of experience in dealing with the FBI, or any law enforcement agency, we just couldn't come up with a plan that seemed viable in reaching our goals. We decided it would make sense to talk to somebody that had the requisite experience. It just so happened that we had another long-time friend that would come in handy.

•   •   •

One night, about a week and a half after our last meeting with Jennifer, Adrian and I were at home watching a movie. I can't tell you which one because it didn't make much of an impression on me, at least not as a movie. What made an impression was a scene, leading up to a climactic plot point, which contained a lot of explosions and flashing lights. Something clicked in my mind and, with no warning to Adrian, I stopped it mid-explosion and hit "rewind," to use an old-fashioned term.

"What are you doing?" a very annoyed wife asked.

"Just bear with me a moment," I said, as I went to the beginning of the show. Finding what I was looking for, I muttered, "There it is." I hit play and almost immediately hit pause, looking at Adrian expectantly.

"There what is?" Still annoyed.

I pointed to the screen, which displayed the following in the upper left-hand corner of the screen:

WARNING, THIS VIDEO HAS BEEN IDENTIFIED
TO POTENTIALLY TRIGGER SEIZURES FOR
PEOPLE WITH PHOTOSENSITIVE EPILEPSY.

"So? Neither of us has epilepsy."

"No, neither of us does, and I've seen that same warning a hundred times before," I said, as I cut her off from cutting me off, "and it never meant anything to me. But, the 'watching' experiences only started after watching something on television. And they got more intense after watching it again. What if there was something, an underlying photo sensitive issue, that was the trigger?" I looked at her expectantly.

Considering, she didn't answer immediately, although I could see some of the annoyance drain from her face. She looked back at the warning and then at me. "I suppose it's a possibility," she reluctantly admitted.

"That's what I think."

I grabbed my phone and typed a text message: *Hey Jen. Could my "watching" experiences be considered a seizure of any type?* I showed it to Adrian, who nodded. I hit send.

I stared at my phone for a couple of minutes, expecting an instant response. When it didn't arrive, I looked at Adrian, who said, "You know, she has a life. She might not be available at your beck and call."

Reaching for the remote, I acknowledged that fact by saying, "Well, she has some nerve." I fast-forwarded to the climactic scene where I had so suddenly stopped and hit play. To me, the scene was anti-climactic, but that's just me.

Finally, after an excruciating two hours, my phone sounded its text message alert chime: *From a technical standpoint, I suppose it could be classified as a seizure. Seizure is defined as a sudden, uncontrolled electrical disturbance in the brain. Aside from altering behavior and movements, it can alter levels of consciousness. So, the short answer is, yes.*

I handed my phone to Adrian, who read and reread the message. "Interesting," was all she had to say. Since she had had a few glasses of wine and I had indulged in some of my favorite tequila, I really couldn't have expected much more. We trudged off to bed.

·   ·   ·

The next morning, all bleary-eyed and bushy tailed, I knew I had to research whether "It Was a Robbery" contained the seizure warning. Loathe to even start the video, for reasons I would think are obvious, I instead started with a simple internet search. "Did the documentary 'It Was a Robbery' contain an epilepsy trigger warning?" Nothing like being direct, or so I thought, until the search results gave me all kinds of information about various robberies and the history and causes of epilepsy, but failed to answer my question. Plan B. "At how many frames per second are most movies shot?" Enter. Amazingly, the answer actually appeared, that answer being 24. Seemed simple enough, until I dug just below the surface. It turned out that 24 frames per second was used for most movies. Television didn't seem to have a standard. Europe generally used 25 frames per second, while Japan went to 30 frames per second. And then there was this: *Most videos you play on Netflix should be 23.976 frames per second. However, Netflix also offers tests for 59.940 fps. (Unfortunately, there's no way to tell if a show or movie plays at 23.976 or 59.940 frames per second.)* Well, great. We happened to have watched the thing on Netflix. New search. "At what speed was the documentary 'It Was a Robbery' filmed'?" Enter. Seemed simple enough, right? An article appeared detailing the fact that while It Was a Robbery was supposed to have been filmed at 24 frames per second, there was a problem during shooting that resulted in a portion of the film actually being filmed at an incredible 80 frames per second. A large portion. Due to time and budgetary constraints, the producers decided to just leave it as it was, it being cheaper to go with what they had already shot, even though using more film at a higher speed, than to reshoot at the lower speed. I also learned that while showing a film, the projector shutter breaks the light beam once as a new image was slid into place and once while it was held in place, meaning that each frame was actually projected on the screen twice. The higher the frames per second, the more flashing. The result was that a good portion of the film contained a high rate of flashing which, while not noticeable to the naked eye, could be transmitted to the brain subliminally, which, I'm pretty sure, was what happened to my brain. Just because I couldn't help myself, I did a little more research on seizures and the effects of flashing lights. It turned out that certain patterns of light, such as flashing bright lights at particular frequencies, can synchronize cells within the visual cortex. If the neurons then fire through their networks at too high a level, they could recruit other neurons into a hyper-synchronous discharge. While I'm uncertain what that actually meant, in the scientific sense, I'm pretty sure that it meant a seizure was happening. In my case, the seizure was not a typical epileptic one affecting my motor controls, but instead, due to the strange combination of that enzyme and the bonding action with my blood, and the resultant electrical brain storm, which could be the result of a hyper-synchronous discharge of neurons, my hippocampus altered my level of consciousness by sending me through time and space. At least that's the theory I was going with. I'll post it to Jennifer just to get her take on it, but it's what I'm sticking to until something better comes along.

LAW ENFORCEMENT – PRESENT DAY

The Boston FBI field office currently resided in a modern glass and steel structure in Chelsea, Massachusetts. A nice, new, clean structure in a nice, new, clean neighborhood. A far cry from its humble beginnings. They also had ten satellite offices throughout Massachusetts, New Hampshire, Maine and Rhode Island which handled a vast array of crimes, none of which were art thefts. The reason that art thefts were beyond their jurisdiction was, in 2004, the FBI created the Art Crime Team, which consisted of twenty special agents dedicated to the investigation and recovery of stolen art, headquartered in the FBI's main building in Washington, D.C. Unfortunately, even though the name conjures the image, they did not wear special decorative spandex suits or capes. Twenty agents may sound like a large team, until one realized that this team was responsible for the investigation of stolen art throughout the United States, as well as assisting worldwide in cooperation with foreign law enforcement officials and FBI legal attaché offices. That was for both new and old unsolved cases, including one particular art theft which occurred in 1970 Boston. As one might imagine, the special art crime agents were spread thinner than old runny grape jelly on crunchy toast.

The head of the Art Crime Team, or ACT for short, was Maurice Bonet, a short, balding gentleman of fifty-seven, with the beginnings of a slight paunch becoming evident under his unbuttoned sport coat. Agent Bonet was well respected within the art world, having obtained both his Master's and PhD in Art History from New York University and assisting in the authentication of numerous stolen works of art, many of which he was instrumental in helping to recover.

While Agent Bonet may have been well respected within the art world, within the hallowed halls of the J. Edgar Hoover Building, the ACT was thought of as a lazy stepchild filled with "namby-pamby artists and not real agents," as one upper echelon FBI bureaucrat so succinctly put it at a private meeting of other upper echelon FBI bureaucrats. This status was belied by the placement of the ACT offices on the first floor next to the library. Not quite the basement, but not too far removed, either. Their offices were comprised of a reception area with a desk for a receptionist, Agent Bonet's less than spacious office, and two smaller offices, each containing an antiquated metal desk, office chair and one chair for a visitor. The total of three ACT agents in the building was due to the fact that the remaining seventeen agents were spread throughout the other fifty-six field offices located in the country's major metropolitan cities. Thin.

The receptionist's desk was occupied by Marcia Wilson, a fifty-six-year-old black woman and native of Washington, D.C. A product of the local public school system, she began working at the FBI after two years of junior college. After all her years at the Bureau, she was an expert at maneuvering the ins and outs, ups and downs, and twists and turns of Bureau politics. Which was a good thing for Agent Bonet. At this point in his career, he was basically an academic with an administrative job. He loathed office politics and paid such matters no attention at all. He was last in the field about eight years ago, at which time he determined that he'd rather be at home with Martha, his wife of thirty years, and their two teenagers, William and Sarah. Being in charge of a division that nobody else cared about or paid much attention, he had the ability to assign other agents to handle the bulk of matters without drawing too much attention to the fact, stepping in only when needed, usually at the end of a tedious and time-consuming investigation.

On this day, Agent Bonet was in his office reading an article about watercolors in Artforum Magazine. A leading publication in the art historian world, such reading not only fulfilled a personal desire, it also fell into the "continuing education" category. When his office phone rang, he was so deeply concentrating on the written words that eight rings had sounded before it registered in his consciousness. On the ninth ring, he found his hand involuntarily reaching for the receiver, picking it up and bringing it to his ear.

"Yes?"

"I was about to come in there to make sure you weren't slumped over your desk gasping your last breath," an exasperated Ms. Wilson said.

"Well, that is a little overdramatic, isn't is Marcia?"

"Oh, who are you kidding, Maury? You love the drama," she replied good-naturedly. "Plus, you took so long to pick up that I thought it might be a distinct possibility this time."

Chuckling, Maury said, "Sorry about that. I'm reviewing an article and got really into it. What can I do for you?"

"There's a lawyer on the phone, a Josh Lowenstein."

Agent Bonet thought for a moment and said, "The name means nothing to me. Should it?"

"Not that I can recall."

"What does he want?"

"He says he represents a client that may have some information regarding an old case. And by old, I mean from 1970," a skeptical Ms. Wilson replied.

"Wow, that is an old case." He paused to consider and finally said, "Give him to Agent Hebert. It could be an interesting exercise for her."

"Will do."

•   •   •

Special Agent Starling Hebert was twenty-six years old and in her second year at the Bureau. She had graduated from the University of Kentucky with a Master's in Art History and, immediately upon graduation, applied to the FBI, with an eye on the Art Crime Team. She was grateful that no spandex costumes would be required. Her first name came from the fact that her mother was an avid birder, the Starling being her favorite, and her father was a huge fan of both *Silence of the Lambs* and the FBI. He often told her she was destined to be an agent, which, it turned out, was true.

When Agent Hebert returned to the office, she greeted Ms. Wilson, grabbed her mail, and headed into her personal domain. Seated at her desk, adorned only with a picture of her parents on one corner and her late dog, Jake, a large white boxer, on the other, she noticed the flashing red light on her phone, indicating that at least one message awaited. She settled in to view her mail and tried to ignore the strobe like effect of the message waiting light, but, as hard as she might try, it could not be avoided.

"OK, OK," she said to nobody as she reached for the message center's play button and, unable to avoid it any longer, felt her finger push down.

"Beep. Friday, 1:43 p.m. Hello Agent Hebert. My name is Joshua Lowenstein. I am an attorney representing a client who has information which may be of importance in the recovery of stolen art from the Boston Garden Museum theft of 1970. I'd like to discuss the situation and attempt to come to an agreement regarding the reward. My number is 928-555-0114. Thank you."

She glanced at her watch and noted that the time was 4:47 p.m. She decided to brush up on the referenced theft before calling Mr. Lowenstein back on Monday. She completed her mail review, most of which then found its way to the circular file cabinet on the side of her desk, and searched the computer records for any available information on the Garden Museum heist. To her chagrin, but not her surprise, no detailed information had been entered into the system for an event that occurred so long ago.

Again, speaking to nobody in particular, she said, "Looks like I'll have to do this the old-fashioned way." On the computer, she retrieved an Archive Requisition Form, completed it, and sent it through the proper channels. "With any luck, I should have something back by the middle of next week." She shut the equipment down for the weekend, walked to her door, turned the lights off, and went home for the weekend.

Due to the fact that her caseload was already on the full side, it was late Wednesday morning before Agent Hebert, aided by a calendar reminder, noticed that her Archive Requisition Form request had fallen on deaf ears. Once the reminder had been received, she also realized that she had yet to return that lawyer's telephone call. Perturbed by the lack of response, she called the Archive Section, only to be told that they were running about two weeks behind for document requests, but they would try to get them to her by the end of the following week. No sooner had she hung up from that call than Ms. Wilson rang to tell her that Joshua Lowenstein was on line two. Resigned to talking to him without the benefit of having reviewed any files, she picked up the phone and punched the button for line two.

"This is Agent Starling Hebert. How can I help you?"

"Agent Hebert, my name is Joshua Lowenstein. I am an attorney and represent a client who may have some information that could lead to the recovery of items taken from the Garden Museum in 1970."

"Yes, Mr. Lowenstein. I was waiting to return your call until I had the opportunity to review our file in that matter. Unfortunately, I won't be able to do so until the end of next week at the earliest."

Taken aback by the lack of excitement and urgency, Mr. Lowenstein said, "Well, that is too bad. I had hoped for and expected a higher level of interest when the possibility of closing out a fifty-year-old open file presents itself."

"Mr. Lowenstein, please don't take the timeline as an indication of lack of interest. I'm sure you can appreciate that, the case being as old as it is, the file is not contained in our computers and that is just how long it's going to take to retrieve them," she replied, annoyed at his implication. "Do you have reason to believe that the items are in imminent danger of being moved or destroyed?"

Chastised, and not wanting to alienate his only contact at the FBI, Lowenstein quickly backtracked his attitude and tone of voice, becoming much friendlier. "I'm sorry Agent Hebert. I didn't mean to offend. I was caught-up in my client's excitement. And, no, I have no reason to believe that the items are in imminent danger of being moved or destroyed."

Having accomplished her goal of putting the lawyer in his place, Agent Hebert also took on a friendlier tone. "Well, that's good to know. What's the nature of your client's information?"

Hesitating before answering, Lowenstein chuckled to himself and said, "There is a very complicated answer to your very simple question. However, I'm not yet at liberty to disclose that. My client would first like to nail down the terms of an agreement relating to the reward."

"Reward?" is all that Agent Hebert said.

"Yes, agent Hebert. There is a five million dollar, no questions asked reward for information leading to the return of the stolen objects. It is my understanding that the Garden Museum closed down several years ago, but their insurance company paid a very sizable claim prior to that. I believe the insurance company is still offering the reward."

Intrigued, she said, "That is a sizeable reward, but since it's not being offered by the FBI or any other government agency, I'm afraid that you're going to have to deal directly with the insurance company."

"Agent, my client has instructed me to deal only with the FBI, which remains in charge of the still unsolved case. The reason being that, if the information comes forward and the items are recovered, they don't want to become the target of an FBI investigation, which, you'll have to admit, would be inevitable. They have no connection to anybody that may have been involved in the theft and were still in high school when the theft occurred, in a city far from Boston. All of which can be easily verified. They want to get out in front of that. However, they are also very aware that, in this age of social media and the internet, if their identity gets revealed and the circumstances of the information coming to them become public, their lives will be turned upside down, and not in a good way. They'd rather just forget the whole thing. The FBI maintains jurisdiction of the investigation. If we can come to an agreement as to anonymity and verification of the information and, if it leads to recovery of any of the missing items, once the FBI makes the recovery and verifies to the insurance company that my clients provided the relevant information, the insurance company won't be in a position to withhold payment."

Having taken in this information and digested it, Agent Hebert asked, "Your client is willing to forgo five million dollars unless we agree on this?"

"They are. They know that, aside from all the unwanted attention and on-line trolling, if there were a separate FBI investigation, they'd have to hire counsel to protect themselves, which would cost a fortune. They're just not willing to go through all of that."

"And you can't disclose the nature of the information?"

Using his most conciliatory voice, Lowenstein said, "I'm really sorry, but I can't. It's quite complicated and, once I can disclose it to you, I'm certain you'll understand."

As she thought to herself that she's got nothing to lose and, career wise, everything to gain, she said, "Send me a draft agreement and I'll run it up the flagpole while I review the file."

Satisfied, Lowenstein replied, "Thank you. I'll get that to you in the next day or so."

Having disconnected the call, she leaned back in her chair and closed her eyes, trying to recall anything she could about the Garden Museum theft. Not being from Boston and having been born decades after the furor surrounding the theft had died down, she could not summon any information from the depths of her mind. She opened her eyes and straightened up in her chair, as she muttered, "What the hell? Maybe this will prove interesting," as she got back to work.

. . .

I disconnected from the call and turned to Adrian, who was sitting next to me and listening, as I had the call on speaker. "What do you think?"

Considering, Adrian said, "It's hard to tell, Josh. She had no knowledge about the theft, which could be both good and bad. At least she seems willing to consider your proposal."

"Yeah, that's a good sign. She probably figures she's got nothing to lose at this point. Howard was pretty good at letting me know what we could get away with when dealing with the FBI." Howard was Howard David, a longtime friend and fellow attorney with whom I had attended law school. He dealt with criminal matters as a major portion of his practice, unlike me. He gave me an excellent introduction as to what tact I should take. I just hope that this turns out to be an exception to the old adage about a lawyer representing himself having a fool for a client. "I'll prepare a draft of the agreement and send it to her. She'll have to send it to the FBI's legal department, I'm sure, so it could take a month or so to get it nailed down. At least it's a start."

Adrian stood and said, "That it is. I've got errands to run." She kissed me, headed for the door, grabbed her car keys, and was gone.

•   •   •

As with most things, when dealing with a vast bureaucracy, the archived files did not arrive until many days after they were scheduled to have made an appearance. Agent Hebert had never been to the archive section, but in her mind she envisioned a large cavernous space containing box filled shelves from floor to ceiling as far as the eye can see, reminiscent of the final scene in *Raiders of the Lost Ark*. In reality, her vision was not far from the truth. When they did finally arrive at about 3:00 in the afternoon, Agent Hebert was on the telephone with a soft-spoken person in Paris, France, who was not pleased to be working at 9:00 p.m. her local time. The delivery man, without bothering to knock, threw her office door open, which caused it to bang into the wall and scared the hell out of her. Paying her no heed, the man wheeled in a cart loaded with eight banker's boxes, which he proceeded to noisily stack in the far corner of her office, two stacks of four boxes each. Unable to address the deliverer, she could only glower while she strained to hear her phone conversation and understand the person on the other end of the line, watching as he rolled his cart out and slammed the door shut.

Her call finally completed, she returned the receiver to its cradle, leaned back in her chair, and blew through closed lips, creating a sound much like a horse. Staring at the stacks of boxes, she said, "So, you're the famous Garden Museum files. Quite an entrance," as she rose from her seat and approached the two monoliths. Perusing the writing on the exterior of each box, she was pleasantly surprised to note that they had been stacked in chronological order, oldest to newest, top to bottom. "Maybe that guy actually knew what he was doing," she mused. She grabbed the top box in the first stack, as she continued to herself, "May as well start at the beginning," as she carried it back to her desk. She placed the box on the floor next to her chair, removed a stack of manila files from the front and placed them on her desk. She placed the top file it in front of her and began the tedious process of familiarizing herself with the fifty-year-old case.

After nearly an hour and a half of reading and note taking, it became abundantly clear to her that the boxes actually contained very little information regarding the Garden Museum theft. The FBI, in the late 1960s and 1970s, had been deeply involved in investigating organized crime in the Boston area, and these files contained the fruits of the agent's labors in relation to that investigation. Most of the files concerned someone by the name of Ricardo Garotini, a/k/a Don "The Garrote" Ricky. The files that didn't relate directly to Ricardo Garotini related to his known associates. There were detailed notes from agents involved in following Garotini and those in his employ, as well as reams of paper containing transcribed conversations from wire taps. Nothing that tied him to the theft in which she was interested. Realizing this, Agent Hebert skipped to the box which contained files nearest to the date of the theft. As she rummaged her way through the files, she came upon one labeled "Garden Museum." "About fucking time," an exasperated Agent mumbled to herself as she removed the file and placed it on her desk, noting to herself that the file was amazingly thin. Opening the file, she found a copy of a rather skimpy Boston Police Department file. In it she found a typed note written by Special Agent David Decker. She knew from her file review that Agent Decker was the Agent-in-Charge, so she was excited to see what he had to say. Removing the note she read, *Boston PD doesn't seem too interested in doing an investigation. Seems that The Don, having most of the PD on his payroll, has instructed BPD to let him handle his own investigation. Let's check out Capprieti and see if we can find something to use to squeeze him.* Looking up from the note, Agent Hebert took a few moments to consider what she'd just read. "Hmm. Interesting." She picked up her pen and made a note to find out who Capprietti was. About to delve back into the file, the sound of her cell phone, which had been sitting silently on the corner of her desk, startled her. As she reached for it, she noted the time, muttered to herself, "Shit," and answered the call without even saying hello. "Sorry. I just got involved in something and lost track of time." After listening for a few moments, she responded, "I know. I'm leaving now. I'll be there in twenty minutes." Disconnecting, she took one last glance at the papers on her desk, rose, and exited her office.

• • •

Arriving in her office early the next morning after a restless night of sleep, she dove right back into the boxes of files. While tossing and turning in bed last night, she found that her thoughts continuously returned to the mysterious Capprietti mentioned by Agent Decker. She had a feeling that, somehow, he had a pivotal role to play, although she had no idea how. Determinedly, she approached the boxes and rifled through contents while searching file headings, until she finally came across a file labeled "Captain Peter Capprietti." "Yes!" she exclaimed as she pulled the file from the box. In doing so, she noticed it contained more material than the entire Garden Museum file had. Primed for some serious note taking, she picked up her pen and began to read. She learned that he was in charge of the precinct in which the Garden Museum had been located and became hopeful she would actually be able to garner some useful information. As she continued to work her way through his file, those hopes were dashed against the rocks and smashed. "Jeez. First, he's in the mob's pocket, while he's also an unfaithful husband. What a total sleaze," is what went through Agent Hebert's mind. Out loud, she said, "No wonder he shot himself, the coward." About to close the file and return it to the box, she spotted a small piece of paper, apparently torn from the corner of an envelope, on which somebody had scrawled,

"Suicide??? Bullshit!"

The underlining had been done so hard that the paper was torn. She held the note in her hand, turned it over and searched for a clue as to who had written it. Finding none, she replaced it and made a note, remarking that it had to have come from Agent Decker, as he was in charge at the time and it was obviously written with a lot of emotion by somebody with a stake in the investigation. Returning the file to the box, she took a moment to contemplate and realized that she was in dire need of a pick-me-up, so she left her office and headed for the coffee machine.

• • •

At her desk once again, cup of coffee in hand, she contemplated the many boxes and files and came to a realization. "There's nothing in the file that even tells me what the theft was." As she sipped her coffee and stared at nothing in particular, she closed her eyes and retreated into her mind and tossed around what little information she had relating to the theft. Suddenly, her eyes sprung open and she said, "They weren't even investigating the theft. They didn't give a shit unless it led directly to this Don Ricky guy." This realization led her to scoot her chair closer to her computer, knowing that, for information regarding the theft, she was going to have to do an internet search. As she began her search, she thought, "I work for one of the largest intelligence agencies in the world and I have to go to Google for information about a theft. Unbelievable."

Ninety minutes later, she had filled up pages of her notebook, printed copies of many of the missing works of art, and had a much better understanding of what actually happened, to the extent that anybody can have such an understanding. Among her notes were the names of numerous articles and a documentary which had been produced entitled *It Was A Robbery*. Satisfied that she had enough information to at least speak intelligently with Josh Lowenstein, she sent him an email:

Mr. Lowenstein:

I just wanted to let you know that I have forwarded your draft agreement to our legal department for review. Once I receive any comments from them, I will forward same to you.

I was able to familiarize myself with the Garden Museum theft and am very interested to hear your client's evidence, especially how they came by such evidence. Please contact me to arrange a convenient time to discuss this further.

Thank you.

Special Agent Starling Hebert

FBI Art Crime Team

After having proof read the missive, and being content with how it read and what it said, she hit "Send."

Exhausted, she sat back in her chair and took a deep breath. She reached back to her computer, signed out, shut down, and headed home.

• • •

I was at my desk working when I heard the familiar tone indicating a new email. Opening my email browser, I saw it was from Agent Hebert and quickly opened and read it. Hitting "Reply" I wrote a response:

Agent Hebert:

Thank you for getting back to me. Once the agreement is in place, I will advise as to a convenient date and time for further discussion. My preference is to meet in person, if that would be acceptable to you.

I look forward to working with you.

Sincerely,

Joshua Lowenstein, Esq.

I hit "Send" and mused to myself about what we had put into motion. There'd be no turning back now.

• • •

During the time between when we met with Jen and now, I'd been extremely careful not to put myself in a position where a "watching" experience could catch me by surprise. But, it seemed to me, and Adrian agreed, that, with what we'd set in motion, I needed to get more information. After all, the goal was to recover the art, and we were no closer to doing that than we were before we watched that damn show.

After much discussion, we focused our attention on Jimmy. He seemed to have been involved in almost all the "watchings," if not in actuality, then at least peripherally. Of the three main characters that seem to have been involved in the theft, he was the only one that had survived the Don. In addition, based on the Don's musings and my ability to hear thoughts, Jimmy may have been something other than he would have everybody believe. So now the question became, how did I go about creating a "watching" experience that got me the information I needed?

I thought back to the "watching" in which Jimmy was being questioned by the FBI. The trigger in that instance was a newspaper article. I figured that if I went back to that same article and concentrated on the FBI interrogation, I just might wind up somewhere in the same time frame with the same people. Adrian agreed it seemed like a reasonable conclusion, so we picked a time, right after dinner, when I could concentrate, uninterrupted, and she could monitor, also uninterrupted. That meant phones off.

We brought my laptop to the couch, muted the lighting, and got comfortable. A glass of ice water awaited on the coffee table. I found the article, took a few deep breaths, visualized Jimmy in the interrogation room of the FBI and let myself be carried away in the image, until...

Jimmy swaggers out of the FBI offices, not looking back and exuding confidence. Exiting the office building, he hails a cab and drives away. After ten blocks of instructing the cab driver to make various and numerous sudden turns and changes of direction, all while Jimmy looks out the back window, the cab drops him off at a busy subway station. Jimmy heads down the stairs, shedding his black leather jacket and mussing his hair as he goes. Paying his fare, he waits in a corner with his back to the wall as he watches the people coming into the station. Confident that he hasn't been followed, but still taking no chances, he darts onto a train just as the doors close, again keeping a keen eye for anybody else that makes the same move. As the train rumbles through the old tunnel and the lights in the train car flicker, he unbuttons his black shirt, takes it off, turns it inside out, and returns it to its proper place, revealing a clean green shirt. Not taking a seat, he stands by an exit door, waiting and watching. As the train approaches the next station, he prepares to exit, noticing a man sitting next to the door wearing a Red Sox baseball cap. As the door opens and he steps through, he reaches back, grabs the hat and places it on his head, just as the doors close. Not looking back to see the bewildered face of the now hatless passenger, he scampers up the stairs and out into the busy Boston street. Walking a block and crossing the street, he enters the Boston Hilton Hotel, nodding to the doorman. Bypassing the reception desk, he heads straight to the elevators, exiting on the tenth floor. Surreptitiously looking around as he walks towards room number 1032, he fishes the key from his pocket as he quickly approaches the door. In one swift move, he strides to the door, inserts the key and enters, silently closing the door behind him.

In the room, he puts the key on the dresser and removes a crisp, newly laundered white shirt from a drawer. Placing it on the bed, he goes into the bathroom, where he quickly showers. Towel drying his hair, he brushes it in a style completely different from that usually worn. After putting the shirt on, he removes a light gray pinstriped suit from the closet, together with a dark blue tie. Once dressed, including clean, polished black wing-tip shoes and a gray Burberry overcoat, he grabs his room key and heads for the door. Stopping suddenly, as if just remembering something, he detours to the bedside table. Opening a drawer, he removes a Smith & Wesson snub nose .38 caliber revolver, checks to make sure it's loaded, and places it in the waistband of his slacks at the small of his back. Satisfied, he leaves the room, closing the door behind him, casually checking the hallway for occupants as he strolls to the elevator.

Outside, the doorman hails a cab, and Jimmy gets in, giving the driver an address. Driving straight to the tendered address, Jimmy exits in front of a medical office building. It appears that most of the offices are closed, it being dark and after normal business hours, but luck was with Jimmy as the main door opens, emitting two people that had the misfortune of having to work late. Jimmy grabs the door just before it clicks shut, mutters a muffled "Thanks," as he bends his head and turns his face away from the possible witnesses, and heads into the building, letting the door shut behind him. With no hesitation, he heads to a stairwell, enters and climbs to the third floor, taking the stairs two at a time. Opening the door on the third floor, he turns left, with no hesitancy, approaches a door on which stenciled lettering proclaims it to be the offices of Frederick Shainen, D.D.S., and, removing a key from his pocket, opens the door, enters the empty, dark waiting room and gently closes the door behind him. Quickly moving to the inner sanctum of the record keeping room, he removes a small tool kit from his overcoat pocket, and puts on a pair of gloves that had been keeping the tool kit company. With practiced efficiency, he easily picks a file cabinet lock, rifles through the files and, having found his target, removes the contents. Documents in hand, he moves to another file cabinet and repeats the exercise. Finding a particular file, he removes its contents and replaces them with the contents from the first file. Quietly, he closes and locks that file cabinet, returns to the first, and refills the now empty folder with the contents just removed from the other cabinet. Carefully, he closes and locks the file cabinet. After leaving the office and locking the door, he removes his gloves and retraces his steps to exit the building.

Once out of the building, he turns to his right, walks three blocks to a public covered parking garage, enters on foot and, moments later, drives out in a black 1965 Ford Fairlane.

Twenty minutes later, having parked the car on a dark side street, he walks to a building in a slightly questionable part of town.

The sign above the door reads "1270 Club." Entering, his gait changes slightly, something between a prance and a glide, as he looks around the dimly lit room, apparently searching for a particular occupant among the all-male clientele. Finding the individual for whom he is searching, he prance-glides to the table, sits and drinks from the waiting cocktail. Removing the overcoat and placing it on the empty chair next to him, he says, in a voice unlike his own, "Hi sweetie. I hope you haven't been waiting too long, but I had some last-minute business to attend to."

Reaching for his hand, his companion says, "It's not a problem, Richard. I've been waiting for this date for a month. What's another thirty minutes?"

Patting his hand, Jimmy/Richard says, "I've been waiting, too. I'm so glad the time is finally right."

Jimmy/Richard's cohort, Thomas Duarte, is of very similar height, age and build. Facially, they could be brothers. As the night progresses, it becomes clear that this is the first date between the two. After about two hours, during which Jimmy/Richard appears to have been drinking heavily, but in reality, not being nearly as drunk as he appears, the two leave the bar and walk/stagger to Jimmy/Richard's car. At the car, Jimmy/Richard asks Thomas if he would mind driving.

"Not at all. I think it's probably a good idea," although he is actually drunker than Jimmy/Richard.

"It's a great idea," thinks Jimmy/Richard, laughing to himself in his head. Out loud, he says, "Great, I know just where we can go. I'll give you directions as we drive."

As they drive, Jimmy/Richard pretends to get lost, both of them laughing and having a great time, not a worry in the world. Finally, Jimmy/Richard says, "Over there. Just pull over there," pointing to a place under the elevated train tracks running along the Charles River.

Obediently, Thomas follows the instructions and pulls the car under the tracks. He parks, looks at Jimmy/Richard, and says, "Oh, you are a naughty boy, aren't you?"

Opening his door and getting out of the car, Jimmy/Richard wickedly replies, "Oh, you have no idea."

Following suit, Thomas gets out of the car and walks around to the passenger side, approaching his "date" for an amorous embrace. Instead, he finds Jimmy/Richard waiting for him, a gun pointed at his chest.

"What the hell?"

Winking, Jimmy/Richard says playfully, "It's just part of a game. It helps me with...you know." Opening the car door and reaching into the back seat, Jimmy/Richard removes a gym bag and throws it to Thomas, instructing him to change into the clothing in the bag.

Now more relaxed, Thomas opens the bag to find a black leather jacket, black silk shirt, black dress pants and pointy black shoes. Looking at Jimmy/Richard, he says, "This is weird, but OK, I'm game," and proceeds to change clothes. Having completed the transformation, he takes a step back and does a modeling pirouette. "So, what do you think?"

Studying the trasnformation, Jimmy/Richard thinks, "If I didn't know better, I'd think he was me." Out loud he says, "Perfect." Smiling, he reaches down and unzips his pants, motioning with his head for Thomas to step forward and pleasure him, the gun nowhere in sight. Eagerly, Thomas steps forward and kneels down, reaching to unbutton the pants before him. As he does, Jimmy/Richard's hand, suddenly holding the gun by its barrel, smashes the gun stock down hard on the back of Thomas's head, knocking him out cold. Replacing the gun in the small of his back, Jimmy/Richard says to the prone body, "Sorry, buddy. Nothing personal." Dragging the unconscious Thomas to the driver's door, Jimmy gets him seated behind the wheel in an upright position, head leaning back against the top of the seat. Closing the door, he walks to the passenger side, opens the door and, after removing his overcoat and suit jacket, which he places on the hood of the car, leans into the open door, gun in hand. Waiting and listening as if he were prey attempting to avoid a predator, he finally hears a train approaching overhead and, at the height of the train's clamor, pulls the trigger twice, obliterating Thomas' skull, careful not to get blood or other material on his clothing. Closing the door, he retrieves his suit jacket and coat, opens the trunk of the car, and removes a container of gasoline. Remembering, he retrieves the gym bag and tosses it into the car. Thoroughly dousing the body, interior and exterior of the car, he calmly dresses himself, and lights a cigarette. Tossing the empty container away, he stands back, smoking. Satisfied, he opens the driver's door and tosses the cigarette into the car, igniting an inferno. Mesmerized by the flames, he watches as the car and its contents become engulfed. Pulling himself from his reverie, he backs away from the now oppressive heat and eradicates the marks left by his dragging of the prone body. Taking one final glance at the pyre, he nods to himself, satisfied, and calmly walks away.

I returned from my journey through space-time with a start, my eyes shooting open and my breath coming in fits and starts. Thankfully, Adrian was sitting there and took my hand, which instantly calmed me. I drank deeply from the waiting glass of water and then quickly went back to my computer to record what I had just "watched." Adrian remained silent as I typed, just monitoring my actions. Finished, I handed her the laptop so she could read about my experience while I silently watched for any facial reactions. It became clear when she reached the section regarding shooting and burning Thomas Duarte, so I reached for her hand and squeezed it. She squeezed back as she completed her review and looked at me.

"Holy shit. This guy is really something else."

"In more ways than one, it would seem," I replied.

I handed her the glass, and she drained it of whatever remained.

Having finished the water and regained her composure, she said, "This guy really had everybody fooled. The Don, the FBI, probably even his mother."

"Definitely his mother," I said. "Otherwise, she would have drowned him at birth."

"Wow," was the only response.

"We should search for any article about his death," I said.

Instantly, her fingers worked the keyboard. Moments later she read aloud:

"Last night, the fire department was called to a vacant lot under the elevated train tracks, where they found a burning car. By the time they arrived, the car had been totally consumed. Witnesses reported that there appeared to be a body in the car, but those reports have not yet been confirmed."

Scrolling down for any updates, she found an article from two days later and again read aloud:

"The Boston Police Department has confirmed that a body had been found in the burning car under the tracks on Leigh Street. Due to the intensity of the fire, a positive identification has not yet been possible. However, the car was registered to James Russo. Mr. Russo was recently the subject of questioning by the FBI, which refuses to comment. The Boston PD has advised that dental records are being checked to confirm the identity of the victim."

Continuing to search for updates, Adrian came upon another article:

"The Boston Police Department has confirmed that, based on a review of dental records, the body found in the burning car registered to James Russo was indeed Mr. Russo. Confidential sources at the Boston PD have also confirmed that Mr. Russo died as a result of two gunshots to the head. Mr. Russo was purportedly in the employ of alleged mob boss Ricardo Garotini, a/k/a Don 'The Garrot' Ricky. Mr. Garotini, when asked whether he knew Mr. Russo, replied, 'I did not know him personally and he was not in my employ. However, if he was in fact a criminal, it's not surprising that he met such an end.' The FBI still refuses to comment, citing an ongoing investigation."

When Adrian finished reading the articles, we just looked at one another in amazement.

"The son of a bitch got away with it," I said, the awe in my voice apparent. "It seems that he *was* smarter than everybody gave him credit for."

"It sure seems that way," Adrian replied. "This whole thing took a lot of planning and cold-blooded ruthlessness. Who is this guy?"

"And where the hell did he stash the art?"

Contemplating, we each came to the same conclusion at the same time. "We need to keep following this guy. He's the key," I said, stating the obvious.

"Yep." After a momentary pause, "Hey, let's not lose sight of the fact that you had a controlled 'watching' experience!" she pointed out. "That's huge!"

I chuckled to myself and said, "You're right, it is. If I did it this time, there's no reason I shouldn't be able to do it again. Believe it or not, though, it really tires me out. I don't think I should go back in tonight."

"Yeah, I can see that."

"By the way," I asked, "how long was I out, gone, under, whatever?"

Looking at her watch, she said, "I think it was about forty-five minutes or so."

Thinking back on the experience and the time frames noted in my written recollection, I noted the vast discrepancy. "The entire experience, in the time frame of where I was, took place over the course of hours." Pausing, I looked at her and checked the time on my phone, confirming, more or less, the time that had elapsed since I first went under. "How the hell is that possible?"

"You're wondering how time can be different?! How the hell is any of this possible?!"

Shaking my head in wonder, all I could say was, "Good point."

•   •   •

The next day, I awoke with a tremendous headache. Not quite a migraine, but not too far off that path, either. I'm not prone to such headaches, although I have had them in the past. In my experience, they are usually stress related. I hadn't thought about the "watchings" in terms of stress, but, now that I have, I suppose it wouldn't be unreasonable to attribute the headache to what's going on in my brain. After all, if it is some kind of seizure, and it lasted for forty-five minutes, that would be very stressful. In any event, I took three ibuprofen and went to back to bed, keeping the bedroom as dark as possible. There would be no forays through space-time today for this boy.

When I finally got my act together enough to get out of bed, somewhere around noon, I headed straight to my office and fired up my computer. Checking my email, I found one from Agent Hebert. I eagerly opened and read it.

"Mr. Lowenstein:

Attached please find a copy of your draft Agreement that has been sent to me by our legal department. As you can see, our lawyers had some changes. Please review and get back to us so that we can proceed with the recovery of the missing art.

Sincerely,

Special Agent Starling Hebert

FBI Art Crime Team

"Of course they had comments," I thought to myself. Most lawyers reject the first draft of a proffered document as a matter of course. If nothing else, they have to make it seem as if they are doing their job, especially in a giant bureaucracy.

Opening the attachment, it pleasantly surprised me to find that the comments were not at all unreasonable. However, there were a couple of points that needed tweaking. I made my requested revisions and attached the document to an email.

"Agent Hebert:

Thank you for sending the revised document. I have reviewed the revisions requested by your legal department and have a couple of revisions that I require. Kindly send this to your attorney and have them reviewed. Please ask him/her to contact me directly with any questions.

Sincerely,

Joshua Lowenstein"

Sending that off, I decided I better do some actual legal work for actual clients, which is how I spent what little remained of the day.

• • •

Adrian had been gone all day. When she got home, she found me lying in bed with a damp, cold cloth over my eyes. As she gently approached my prostrate form, I lifted one corner of the cloth, opened the now exposed eye, and grunted a greeting. Addressing the perplexed look on her face, I explained the situation, moving my head as little as possible. Replacing the cloth, she turned to leave the room when I remembered she didn't know about the comments to the agreement with the FBI. Without removing the cloth again, I said, "Hey, I heard from the FBI lawyer. They had some comments, but nothing too bad, which was surprising. I sent some comments back. We should probably have something in place in a few weeks."

"That's great. Hopefully, that should be enough time to get some more information together."

She returned to the bed and sat gently on the edge. I removed the cloth and was immediately struck by the look of deep concern etched on her face. "If what you're doing keeps taking this kind of toll on you, I'm not sure we should continue."

"I'll be fine by tomorrow. We have to continue or the FBI is going to come after us for trying to pull a hoax over on them. I imagine they frown upon that."

"We could explain it to them."

"They're not the type of people that like to listen to explanations from people they think are nuts. We started this and we'll see it through. I'll be fine."

She bent down to kiss me, gently, and said, "OK, but you need to be honest with me about how you feel after your excursions. If this keeps up, maybe Jen can help."

"I will. Besides, I think if I'm having problems, it will be fairly obvious."

Agreeing to nothing, she said, "We'll see. I'm going to make some dinner."

I returned the cloth to my face and made some kind of noise in response.

. . .

Agent Hebert, her curiosity piqued more by what she hadn't found in the files than what she had, spent what little extra available time remained in her day trying to gather information about the investigation into Boston's organized crime in the 1970s. She thought, not incorrectly, that if she were going to search for the art with Lowenstein, she should have as much information in her mind as she could store. Papers spread over her desk in seemingly random fashion, they had, to her, an almost elegant logic. Early on, she noted that the investigation centered on Don Ricky, even though there were other crime bosses in the area. She wondered why they had focused on this particular mobster and continued to search the files for an answer. In doing so, she reviewed the personnel files for the team and, reading through Agent Moretti's file, noted that his brother had at one time allegedly worked for the Don and was killed in an operation gone bad. Apparently, his personal vendetta was enough to persuade his boss and friend, Special Agent Decker, into focusing his hunt on Ricardo Garotini.

Remembering the hand written note regarding the supposed suicide of Captain Peter Capprieti, she searched for more insight into why somebody, presumably Decker, felt that his death was something other than what it seemed. Unable to find anything to support Decker's theory, she continued reading. She learned that the Garden Museum theft, while not being investigated by the agency, was what was being used to get Capprieti to approach the Don. Following that tenuous thread, she noted that the names of three men, Edward "Tiny" Lacosta, Ralph Scoletti and James Russo, continuously cropped up in relation to the theft. Unfortunately, each had met a violent death, leaving no clues as to the whereabouts of the art, which was all that really concerned her. After what appeared to be a cursory investigation at the time of the murders, none of the deaths had ever been solved and, although they remained open on the books of the FBI, no cold case investigation had begun.

Sitting back and reflecting on what she had found, or not found, in the files regarding the theft, she became more intrigued by what the lawyer, or more correctly, his clients, could possibly know. No actual evidence was in the file, nobody was ever charged, and there wasn't even a hint of what happened or where the art went. Her best guess was that it had been sold off, piece by piece, on the black market. Even so, when that's been the case in the past, in almost all instances, at some point a stray piece turned up somewhere. Usually by mistake, but, nevertheless, something usually showed up. For there not to be a hint, not even a rumor, of any single piece for *fifty* years, caused her to consider shifting her thought process, although she hadn't quite gotten to that point, yet. Her training, and experience of other agents, was just too ingrained and overwhelming. She'd just have to wait and see what Lowenstein and his clients had, although she really couldn't believe that they had anything of significance. Already becoming disheartened at the prospect of failure, she thought to herself, "Damn! I'd really love to bring this one home!"

. . .

I don't know if I underestimated the severity of my headache or over-estimated my ability to recover, or a combination of the two, but it took much longer than I expected. I waited through the following day, fully expecting to be able to delve into another episode on the next day. When I realized that I still had the lingering effects of the headache, I began to get antsy. I knew that if I couldn't come up with the location of the art by the time I met with Agent Hebert, I'd need to have something to show her. Something solid.

Adrian really wanted me to take a break from leaping through space-time. I really wanted to do something constructive. We discussed it and soon came to the realization that there were at least three unsolved murders and one assumed suicide that we could shed light on. I may not have mentioned it before, but Adrian is a really talented artist. She can work in various mediums. So, we came up with the idea that I would describe the person who committed the murders and she would sketch him, just like they do on television.

Our first attempt focused on Peter Capprieti. It seemed to be a more compelling case than the other two, from the standpoint of interest to the FBI, although the same could be said for Jimmy's staged death. We flipped a coin and the policeman won.

I went over my notes of that particular "watching" experience to make sure that I remembered the details. Instantly, I could recall everything about it, almost as if I were reliving it, but without the seizure. I closed my eyes and focused my mind on what Anthony looked like. Without watching what Adrian was doing, I slowly described the man responsible for the deaths of Capprieti and Ralphie, and who knows how many countless others. I didn't rush, waiting for Adrian's cues as to when to start and stop. Finally, she said, "OK, open your eyes."

The face that stared at me from the page of her sketchbook totally amazed me. I carefully studied the drawing, and we made minor corrections here and there. An eyebrow was thicker. There was a small scar under his left eye. His hair was just a little less poofy. Those types of things. When we had finished, I looked from the page to her and said, "That's him. Without a doubt."

I looked at my wife in amazement. "Damn, you're good," I said as I reached out to embrace her.

Gratified, she returned the embrace and simply said, "Thank you."

Both of us sat staring at the drawing, mesmerized, as if we expected it to speak to us. Hopefully, it would speak volumes to Agent Hebert. Finally, Adrian broke the spell and said, "There are at least two more people that we should do this for, don't you think?"

Thinking, I saw where she was going. "Joey Animale, the 'Animal', and Thomas Duarte," I replied.

"Exactly." After a brief pause, she asked, "Are you up for it?"

Smiling, I said, "I appreciate your concern, but doing this really doesn't have any adverse effect on me. It's probably more tiring for you. Are you up for it?" I asked.

Making a derisive sound, she answered, "I could do this all day. Let's get going."

I went back to my notes and we repeated the process for each of the remaining subjects. It was time-consuming and tedious, but the end results were spectacular. In each instance, Adrian had fully captured the image I had, until then, really only seen with my mind's eye. Again, it was difficult to avoid just sitting and gazing at the sketches, which we did for longer than was practical. With an almost physical exertion, I pulled my attention away and concentrated on Adrian.

"I think I'll prepare packages for each of these to give to Agent Hebert."

"What type of packages?" she asked.

"I'll put together the written recollections for each and include the appropriate picture. I have no doubt that, when she hears where the recollections came from, and how we came about having these sketches, she's going to be incredibly skeptical. Hopefully, the packages will form a basis for her to investigate further, so she can either prove us to be frauds or authentic."

Adrian couldn't control the laugh that she suddenly emitted. "Skeptical is putting it mildly," she said. "Her reaction is going to be really interesting."

Nodding my head in agreement, I could only respond, "Interesting. It will be that."

MEETING AGENT HEBERT

I had fully intended to go back into my time warp, mind melding, seizure inducing experience before meeting with Agent Hebert, but, as it so often does, life had other ideas. Between work, family and other commitments, when the email from Agent Hebert appeared in my inbox stating that the agreement had been accepted and signed, the time for such an endeavor had passed. I contacted the Agent and arranged to meet her in Washington, D.C. in three days. She was anxious to hear what I had to say and didn't want to waste any more time. I, too, was anxious to hear what I was going to say and how it would be received. Even if I didn't have the ultimate prize, yet, it was worth it to get the ball rolling. After all, absent showing up with a trailer full of stolen art, the hard part of getting her to believe our fantastic tale would be germane to our ultimate success.

Adrian was unable to join me on the trip, so I booked a room at the Hotel Harrington rather than at a more modern, luxurious hotel. It's an older hotel, still very nice, but not what I would have chosen had I been planning a romantic weekend getaway. Its proximity to the J. Edgar Hoover Building was the deciding factor.

I had arranged to meet Agent Hebert in a conference room at the hotel. I had an uneasy feeling about being at FBI headquarters when I unloaded the background of our information. Had I been locked in a room surrounded by FBI agents, I felt I may not have gotten out unscathed. Agent Hebert was reluctant to give up home field advantage, but, at my insistence, meaning it's the only way that I'd meet, she agreed.

The hotel was kind enough to have beverages and snacks waiting for us in the conference room. Precisely at 10:00 a.m., which was the appointed time, Agent Hebert stuck her head in the open doorway and gently knocked on the door frame. I looked up to see a young woman, approximately five feet six inches tall, dark auburn hair, light complected and dressed in what I have been told was business casual attire. I was wearing a clean pair of jeans and an actual shirt with a collar, which, in my mind, also qualified as business casual. Standing, I went to the door and greeted my guest.

Holding my hand out, she took it in a firm grip and said, "Good morning. Mr. Lowenstein, I presume?"

Smiling, I replied, "Yes, and I'm very thankful to be here to welcome you," thinking that there's no way she'd recognize the quote.

To my surprise and delight, she smiled and said, "While we're not going to be exploring the wilds surrounding Lake Tanganyika, based on what little my research has been able to uncover, if your information is legitimate, it could prove to be an interesting journey on its own."

Laughing, I motioned to a seat and said, "And that's *before* you've heard what I have to say."

Ignoring the snacks, we each grabbed a bottle of water and took seats across from one another at the table. Agent Hebert, apparently an avid note taker, placed a well-worn notepad in front of her, held a pen in hand and said, "OK Mr. Lowenstein, why don't you tell me the nature of your client's information?"

"First off, please call me Josh."

Nodding her assent, she said, "Josh it is."

I noted she did not offer to have me call her Starling.

Instead of answering her question, I asked, "Were you able to find any information or evidence regarding the theft in your files?"

She hesitated before trying to regain control. "Josh," she pointedly said, "we're not here to discuss what evidence or information I may have. I believe you contacted us to discuss the information your client may have."

"True," I said, stating the obvious, "but I'm just trying to determine if you'll be able to verify what I'm going to tell you." Watching her facial expression, I knew I had to clarify. "Not so I know what we can get away with, if that's what you were thinking. Rather, the opposite. In my view, it's paramount that you be able to verify as much of our information as possible. I need you to believe what I'm going to say, and the only way for that to happen is for you to come to that conclusion on your own."

I waited and watched for her reaction, staying silent. At last, she said, "Fair enough. In that case, you should know that the information in our files regarding the theft is minimal, at best."

Sitting back in my chair and taking a drink from my water bottle, I said, "I thought as much." Leaning forward, I continued, "It seems to me that the Bureau's focus was on bringing down Don Ricky, not on recovering the stolen art." I waited for her response.

Instead of a direct response, she merely said, "Go on."

Nodding, I continued by asking, "Have the names Captain Peter Capprieti, Ralph Scoletti, Edward Lacosta, known as "Tiny," and James Russo come up in your files?"

Even though she tried to hide her reaction, and did a fairly decent job of it, I could immediately tell that I had struck a chord of recognition. Recovering, she said, "Let's just say that those names are familiar to me. The question is, how are they known to you in relation to the theft?"

Not immediately answering, I thought about how best to proceed. After a few moments of silence, I delved right into the story, thinking, "I've got to go there eventually, anyway."

"My client first heard those names as he watched a documentary called 'It Was a Robbery.' Are you familiar with it?"

"Only to the extent that I saw it mentioned in an internet search."

"Check it out for yourself. There's probably more information in that documentary than in your files."

Wearily, she said, "I'll keep it in mind." Leaning forward, with a definite edge to her voice, she continued, "So, we're sitting here because your client watched a documentary about the theft and he or she thinks it will net them five million dollars?" Sitting back in her chair, she said, "You've got to be joking," as she closed her notepad and began to gather her belongings.

Trying not to show panic, I said, "No, of course not," a little too loudly. It did, however, get her attention. I took a deep breath and continued. "After watching the documentary, my client began to have, for lack of a better description for you, 'visions' of the past involving each of those people, and more."

I was about to continue when the look on Agent Hebert's face stopped me cold. It was a look of total disgust and hatred. She slammed her hand down on the table, stood halfway out of her chair, leaned forward threateningly, and shouted, "Who put you up to this, you asshole!?! Who?!?"

Reflexively, I jumped back, even though still seated, causing my chair to roll on its casters.

"Nobody put me up to this. What are you so upset about?"

Hastily gathering her things, while continuing to fume, she spit out, "Fuck you! I hope you and your pals had a great laugh!" Turning to face me full on, she said, the venom in her voice apparent, "Just remember, I'm still in the FBI and I'll be looking for you." Turning, she headed for the conference room door, muttering, "Asshole."

Not knowing what else to do, I acted instinctively and ran to cut off her exit, blocking the door before she could pull it off its hinges and escape. Admittedly, not a wise move when faced with an angry, armed FBI agent.

"Stop," I pleaded. "Honestly, I have no idea what you're talking about. I knew that when I told you about the 'visions' it would be hard to believe, but I had no idea it would piss you off like this."

We both just stood facing each other and breathing hard, each trying to control our emotions.

Seeing that she was getting more under control, I ventured on. "Listen, I can prove to you that these 'visions', or rather, 'watchings,' as we've come to call them, are real." I waited. Not having been pushed aside or shot, I continued. "Just come back to the table and I'll show you."

As she thought about what I said, I could see her calming down. "Please." I tried not to sound as if I were pleading. I don't think I was successful.

Once again under control, we returned to the table and took our places. Neither of us said anything, instead opting to drink from our water bottles in an effort to let the situation normalize. After a few moments, I reached over and opened my laptop carrier, withdrawing the packets which I had prepared. Each was labeled in accordance with the person to whom they applied. I slid them over to her and said, "Just look at these."

The top packet was labeled "Caprietti." She looked at it and tentatively reached out and touched it, seemingly afraid that it would somehow harm her. At last, she picked up the top packet, opened it and withdrew its contents. Rifling through to see what it was, she saw the printed recollections of each "watching" experience involving Captain Caprietti. The final page was a sketch of a stranger's face. She looked at me questioningly and I quietly said, "Please, just keep an open mind and read through the material. I won't bother you." As she began to read, I busied myself on my phone, attempting to surreptitiously watch her now and then. Each time I looked, she was deep into the reading, which I greatly appreciated. After twenty minutes or so, I felt her look up at me. I stopped what I was doing and our eyes met, just as a single tear escaped from her eye and rolled down her cheek. Instinctively, I reached out with my hand and covered hers, asking, as gently as I could, "Hey, are you OK? I didn't mean to upset you in any way."

Regaining her composure, she took a deep breath and drained the remaining contents of her water bottle. Once again under control, she said, "You didn't upset me. As a matter of fact, if this is truly genuine, and you trust the person who wrote this, it's a greater comfort to me than you can ever know."

Assessing the situation and taking stock of the person in front of me, and taking into consideration her initial reaction and her new attitude, I had a quick decision to make. The decision made, I said, "If you can assure me I can trust your confidentiality, and you'll trust me with whatever caused you to react the way you did, I'll tell you about my client." As she started to say something, I held up my hand to stop her. "But," I continued, "I need your word that you won't reveal the identity of my client to anybody."

She considered before she replied, "I'll promise not to reveal the identity, unless I'm forced to by the agency or a court. I'm not going to jail to protect the identity."

"Fair enough," I responded. "That means you'll tell me about the reasons behind your reaction and your change of heart?"

She nodded her assent, but I said, "I need to hear you say it."

"Yes, I'll tell you about the reasons behind my reactions, and I'll trust in your discretion not to reveal it."

"Deal," I said, as I held my hand out to her. She took my hand and, looking directly into my eyes, shook it and said, "Deal."

• • •

I retrieved an unopened bottle of water and tore open a package of cashews, munching, while I gathered my thoughts. Agent Hebert also opened a fresh bottle of water and a package of cheese crackers. It seems that we both needed some sort of nourishment to continue. Finally, I was ready to begin.

Making direct eye contact with Agent Hebert, I said, "I can tell you I have complete confidence in what was written, and the experiences it recounts, because," I paused and took a breath before continuing, never breaking eye contact, "the experiences and recollections are mine."

I sat back, unexpectantly relieved not to have to hide the truth, still waiting for her reaction. Instead of saying anything, she peered deeply into my eyes, making me slightly uncomfortable. I did not break eye contact, feeling that this was some kind of unspoken test.

She sat back and said, "Thank you for sharing that and trusting me." Pausing, she continued, "I know better than most what's at stake." Leaning forward, she asked, "Can you tell me when these 'watchings' started?"

Feeling that we were now on a different level of relationship, I chuckled and said, "Oh yeah. I can tell you precisely when it started. Do you remember the documentary I mentioned, '*It Was a Robbery?*'"

She responded by nodding her head and said, "Uh huh."

"Well, they started the night I watched that damn show," I said. I recounted my second viewing of the documentary, the increase in intensity of the experiences and our visit to Dr. Silver. I told her about the scan Jen ran on my brain while I was having a "watching" experience and what her results showed. I told her about Tay-Sachs and the chemicals involved and what seemed to be going on in my brain. I also told her what I discovered about the rate of frames per second at which the documentary had been filmed and my theory as to why whatever was happening in my brain started. I explained how we did a controlled "watching" and the effect it had on me. Finally, I told her about how the sketches were created.

Sitting back in my seat and relaxing a bit, I looked at her and said, "So? Does any of that make sense to you?"

She smiled, again surprising me. "You'll probably be surprised to hear that, yes, some of it makes sense to me."

"I am definitely surprised," I replied, not even attempting to hide my amazement. "Now I have some questions. Why did you react as if somebody was playing a cruel trick on you? How can any of this make sense to you?" I watched her as she gathered her thoughts, but did not begin her tale. I prompted her and said, "Your turn."

"OK, here I go. I was adopted as an infant by a couple in Kentucky, where I spent much of my childhood. When I was seven or eight, my father, my adoptive father that is, took me to the movies. We went to see a Disney movie, *Tuck Everlasting*. It meant little to me at the time, but having heard what you said about the frames per second, I remembered that there was some issue with the theater's projector, causing some strange flickering. I remember people shouting for the manager to get the thing fixed. Anyway, shortly after that, my father started having what he called visions. He let people know about it and, as you can imagine in a small, close-minded religious community, people started talking. They weren't religious visions or anything like that. He claimed to see things that happened in the past. Well, he started to get a reputation around town, and even into surrounding communities, as being a 'little off,' is how people put it. Then he claimed to have 'seen' our Sheriff, Sheriff Joe Johnson, rape and murder a little girl, Missy Williams. She was six years old when she disappeared and was never seen again. This was five years before my father claimed to have 'seen' this. As you can imagine, the Sheriff, who was still Sheriff and very popular and powerful, did not take kindly to this accusation." She stopped to take a drink of water and gather herself, as she was becoming emotional. I kept quiet and let her go at her own pace. After a few moments, she continued. "Anyway, Sheriff Joe, as he was known, started a quiet campaign to have my father declared legally incompetent. He went so far as to tell my mother that, if she didn't cooperate, he'd be sure to have me removed from our house and sent to foster care. That was just too much for my mother to deal with and, having some doubts of her own about my father's sanity, agreed to cooperate. My father was declared incompetent. Basically, they found him to be insane, and committed him to a state institution. He died after being locked up and subjected to all sorts of insane treatments, including shock therapy. Through it all, he never recanted his story about what he had seen Sheriff Joe do."

Having completed her saga, she sat back, fighting tears. She looked at me and said, "So, I totally understand why you want to maintain your anonymity."

"Wow. I'm so sorry that you had to go through that."

"Thanks, so am I."

"You said that you grew up in Kentucky, but I don't hear any kind of accent."

Smiling, she said, "Shortly after my father died, we moved up North, to Chicago, where my mother had a cousin. They drilled the accent out of me."

"Really," I said. "I grew up in Chicago, too."

We played Chicago geography for a couple of minutes when I had a thought. "Hey, you said you were adopted. You pronounce your name 'Aye-Bear' instead of 'Her-Bert.' Your father wasn't Louisiana Cajun, by any chance, was he?"

She looked at me as if I had just sprouted wings. "How did you know that?"

"I didn't know, but the last name 'Hebert,' as you pronounce it, is a clue. Remember I mentioned Tay-Sachs and the tests our neurosurgeon friend performed?"

"Yes?"

"Well, in my research I discovered that, besides Ashkenazi Jews, which explains my predilection, one of the groups most prone to Tay-Sachs is Louisiana Cajun." I let that sink in for a moment. "We may have just figured out what was going on with your father. He wasn't insane at all. He *was* having 'visions,' as he put it."

"Oh my God," she said as she covered her mouth with her hand and started to shake. I came around the table and put my arm around her in a comforting gesture. After all, I have girls not much older than she was, and it hurt to have her suffer like that.

After a few moments, she once again regained her composure, after which I returned to my chair.

"Thank you," she said with as much sincerity as I have ever heard coming from anybody. I just nodded. "You know, this could mean that that bastard Sheriff Joe is guilty."

I had thought that, but didn't want to bring it up and open another wound. I simply said, "It could."

In the ensuing silence, I heard both of our stomachs make growling sounds. We both laughed, each a little embarrassed. "Let's go grab some food. I have this room for the entire day. After lunch, we can come back and get into what's in those packets I prepared."

Agreeing, she said, "Good idea. Lunch is on the FBI," as we headed out the door.

•   •   •

We had a very pleasant lunch at one of the few remaining Jewish delicatessens in the area, where I had the pleasure of introducing her to a chocolate phosphate. Turns out she's almost as much of a chocoholic as I was. We each made a point to avoid discussing "watchings" or visions, 1970s Boston mobsters or the Garden Museum theft.

Returning to the conference room refreshed and trusting each other much more than we had when the day began, we dove into the packets I had provided. The first one, dealing with Peter Caprietti, was of particular interest to Agent Hebert, or Starling, as I was now permitted to call her. She told me not only about the official file and the finding of a suicide, but also about the handwritten note that she assumed had been written by Special Agent Decker.

Recalling something I had "watched" and written about, I said, "Hold on" and got my laptop. I pulled up my recollection of the conversation between Moretti and Decker that took place in the car after Caprietti's death. Handing her the computer, she read while I waited. It was a short writing, so the wait was not a long one.

"So, it was Decker who wrote that note," she said as she looked at me.

"It seems like it to me."

"And he thought the Don was behind it. He even mentioned the lights going out, just like you did." She stopped to quickly go through the writing once again. "Do you think he felt your presence in the car?" she asked, her voice steeped with incredulity.

"It sure seemed like it to me, but I suppose it could have been a coincidence, if you believe in that sort of thing," I replied.

"In coincidences?" she asked.

I just nodded.

"You don't? Believe in coincidences, that is?"

I looked at her and said, "I don't." Watching for a reaction, I saw her contemplating the issue. "Do you think that, with all the agents working for the FBI, and with my having originally called your boss, it's a coincidence that I wound up sitting in this room with you?" I asked.

"I guess I would have, if you hadn't brought it up."

"Really?" I asked. "It just so happens that I'm sitting here with probably the only agent in the entire Bureau who has any chance of understanding what I've experienced and actually believes what I've said and seen. To me, that's no coincidence. It's what supposed to happen if we're to get to the bottom of our mystery."

"Well, when you put it that way, I can see what you mean," she said, not quite convinced.

"Think about it," I advised.

She looked at her watch and discovered that it was much later than she thought. I said, "It's OK if you have to get going. Frankly, we've been at it a lot longer than I thought would have been possible, especially since I half expected you to kick my ass out the door hours ago."

She laughed and said, "Thanks for understanding. It's been enlightening, in more ways than one," as she gathered her belongings.

I said, "Can you run those sketches through facial recognition or some other magic program?"

"I can," she said. "I'll let you know what I come up with. Just don't think any answers will show up in an hour. This isn't television."

"Well, damn. I've been programmed to expect instant gratification."

"Ha! The FBI will cure you of that expectation."

Ready to leave, I held out my hand. She ignored the hand and came in for a hug, which I gladly returned. Standing back, she said, "Thank you. For everything. I'll be in touch."

"Thank you for not having me committed," I said with a smile. "My flight leaves at noon tomorrow. If you have a miraculous discovery in the morning, I'll be here. Otherwise, I'll wait to hear from you. Hopefully, I'll have some more information relevant to the location of the art."

"Be careful," she said as she headed out the door.

I watched her leave, shaking my head in amazement as to how the day had turned out. "That was un-fucking believable!" I said to the empty room as I grabbed my stuff and headed upstairs. "Adrian will never believe it!"

• • •

The day after the meeting, Agent Hebert found herself in her office, unable to concentrate on anything other than the fact that "watching" experiences were real, and, by extension, so were her father's "visions." The enormity of that fact hadn't struck her until the middle of the night when, in full REM sleep, she sat up, opened her eyes, and said, "Holy shit!" She knew that her case load wouldn't lend itself to freelancing, but she desperately wanted to dive into her father's case. If she could clear his name, and put that bastard Sheriff behind bars at the same time, she would feel that her career choice had paid off in full.

Before she even knew what she had done, her cell phone was in her hand and her mother's phone was ringing.

"Hi Honey. Is everything all right?" Her mother was one of those that assumed, if you're calling, it's bad news.

"Hi Mom. Yes, everything is all right. How are you?"

"I'm fine, dear. Just getting ready to go to Aunt Jeanine's and play cards with the girls."

"That's nice. OK, have a good time and say hi to everybody for me."

"Star? What's going on? You know I can always tell when there's something on your mind. You didn't just call to say hello. What is it?"

Exasperated, Star replied, "Yes, Mom. You can always tell. It's like a strange sixth sense with you."

Satisfied, her mother said, "So, what is it?"

"It's about Dad."

Star could hear her mother take a deep breath and steady herself. Her mother had never quite gotten over having to choose between her husband and daughter and was still guilt-ridden over it. Not waiting for her mother to inquire, she continued. "I just wanted to let you know that I'm working on a case and," she hesitated and gathered her nerves before she said, "I can't tell you how, but I'm convinced that, because of what I've learned in this case, Dad was actually having visions of the past."

After a sharp intake of breath, her mother said, "Star, we've been through this before, right? There's no way he could have seen what he said he did. You'd be best to just let it lie and let him rest in peace."

"That's just it, Mom. We *have* been through this before. But that was before I knew what I know now."

"And what is that, dear?" she said in her placating Mom tone of voice.

With an edge to her voice, Agent Hebert said, "I know the cause of those visions, and, as a matter of fact, I'm dealing with somebody else having the same visions."

"Somebody else is having visions of Sheriff Joe raping and murdering a little girl?" her mother asked, the disbelief apparent in her voice.

Rolling her eyes and shaking her head in her own display of disbelief, she said, "No, Mom. Not the same visions, but different ones, visions that I can prove." She hadn't actually discovered that she could prove them yet, but she needed to make a point.

"And how did you find this person?"

"I'm working on a case with him, and he's very credible."

"OK, let's say you're correct and your father was actually having these 'visions.' So what? It's ancient history and your father is dead and buried. Leave it be, please!"

"Why, Mom? Why are you so desperate to just let it be? Don't you want to clear his name?"

"If he were alive, yes. Now? Now it's just like shaking a hornet's nest. There's no good to be had from it. It's best to just run for cover."

"You know I can't do that."

Sighing, her mother said, "Yes, I know. Just be careful not to get stung."

Resigned to give up this particular fight at this particular time, Star said, "OK, Mom. I do have a question, though."

"Yes?"

"Did Dad ever do any writings or talk about his 'visions' with you? Is there anything around that might give me some insight?"

A strange sound came from her mother before she said, "Sometimes he'd start to talk about them, but I shut that down quickly. I didn't want people to think he'd gone crazy. *I* didn't want to think he'd gone crazy. I don't know, maybe things would've turned out differently if I'd talked to him and gotten him help." Star could hear a quick hitch in her mother's breathing, as if she were trying to hold back tears. Staying silent, she waited for her mother to continue. "As for writing, nothing that he ever showed to me."

Disappointed, Star said, "Oh. That's too bad. I was hoping he may have written some thoughts or, I don't know, something."

"I'm sorry I couldn't be more help, Star. I really have to run now. Love you."

"Love you, too, Mom," as she disconnected from the call.

Gathering her thoughts, Agent Hebert was about to get back to work on her case when she realized something about what her mother had just said. She didn't say he wrote nothing, just that he didn't show her anything. If her mother had been unwilling to talk to her father about what he was going through, what were the chances that he would vent his thoughts into writing, but not share them? After all, it was probably clear to him that his wife wanted more to protect his reputation, and by extension, hers, than to believe something that, to the both of them, was probably fantastical. She hoped the chances were high and quickly sent a text message.

"Mom, I know there are some boxes of Dad's stuff around that you kept. Please look and see if there are any notebooks or anything like that. Thanks. Love you."

Having done all she could on that front, she turned her attention back to the Garden Museum theft and the packets provided by Josh. She had already reviewed the "Caprietti" packet, so she turned her attention to the next one in the pile, which was labeled "Ralphie." She removed the documents and placed them on her desk. She couldn't help but notice the last page, which was another sketch by Josh's wife. "She is talented." Having already reviewed the Caprietti packet, she thought that the sketches for both were the same. Just to make certain, she pulled out the sketch from the previous file and laid them side by side. "Hmm. They are the same." Eager to discover why, she began reading.

"So, this guy was a paid killer for the Don," she said to nobody. She found that talking, even to herself, helped the discovery process. She turned the sketches over, because she hadn't before and wanted to make sure that there was no information written that she had missed. Not having a last name, she was unable to run any kind of check. Had she started a search for "Anthony, 1970, Boston" the computer would probably have laughed at her before spitting out pages and pages of results. Satisfied that facial recognition software was her best chance of identification, she scanned the sketch and, when completed, set the software to work. It would continue to run in the background until it either came up with a match or determined that no match existed.

Next, she picked up the packet labeled "Tiny" and performed the same type of review she had performed on the Caprietti and Ralphie packets. With her notepad at the ready, she read about the various "watchings" in which Tiny had been involved. The description of the murder at Bo's Diner fascinated her, spurring her to make notes of the names of the individuals involved. "Finally, a full name," she said as she scribbled the name Joey Animale. While believing what Josh had told her and written, at heart she was still an FBI agent and needed as much verification as possible. As a result, she dug through the boxes of files that still called her office home for any information regarding the Bo's Diner shootout. One box held separate files for each of the Don's various "associates," so she carried it over to her desk and was able to find one for each of Tiny, Ralphie, Jimmy, and Joey the Animal, all of which she placed on her desk. Strangely, there was no file for the mysterious Anthony with no last name.

"Hmmm, that's odd." To be certain, she rifled through the contents of the box again, still finding no Anthony file. Picking up her pen, she moved to her ever present note pad and jotted *"Where's the file on Anthony?"* Considering, she took to her notepad again. *"Was there a file on Anthony? Was it removed and forgotten? Was it removed and hidden/destroyed? By whom?"*

Her questions jogged something in her memory and she went back to the packets of material that Josh had provided. Going through each, she was unable to find what she needed in order to justify her thought process. Sliding her chair closer to her computer, she wrote a quick email.

"Hi Josh. I have a recollection of something I read in one of your writings about a mole in the FBI's office. I can't find it in what I have. Can you confirm?

Thanks.

Starling"

She hit "Send" and stared at the screen in anticipation of a quick response. When one wasn't immediately forthcoming, she resigned herself to waiting and, giving up the staring contest with an inanimate object, went back to her review of the files.

The files on Tiny, Ralphie and Jimmy were each similar in that not a lot of information was available. Based on the notes placed into the file, she was able glean the fact that the agents didn't feel that any of them were worthy of their own investigations. They were of note only because they were low-level associates of their primary target. It was noted that each may have been involved in the Garden Museum theft, but no evidence had been gathered or saved that tied any of them to the theft. There was only conjecture based upon hearsay and what they had heard from Caprietti and no further time or energy had been expended on them or the theft. Each of their files had been marked "Deceased/Closed." As for Joey the Animal, there was a surveillance picture taken as he was leaving a restaurant called Mama Nona's. It was a grainy black-and-white photo taken from inside a car parked at least a block away from the entrance to the restaurant. "Jeez, my phone takes better pictures," she said, noting the obvious difference in technology from back in the day. Comparing the picture with the sketch that Mrs. Lowenstein had drawn, it was evident that they were the same person, a fact which she found extremely gratifying. "Great!" Any corroboration of Josh's story was good news in her mind, both for the immediate case and her father's. Going back to his file, she read that Joey had been a suspect in the killing of Tiny at Bo's Diner, but, with eye witnesses swearing that he was in attendance at a party at Mama Nona's at the time of the shooting, the agents were unable to pursue it further. She also found a newspaper article that mentioned an unnamed Boston PD detective who speculated that Tiny's killing was related to the Garden Museum theft, although the file contained no corroboration of that musing. The file was also marked "Deceased/Closed," noting that Joey had been shot in the head by an unknown assailant, a fact affirmed by the coroner's slab photo, which she also found in the file.

Having completed her review of all but the packet labeled "Jimmy," she was getting ready to open and review that information when an email alert sound caught her attention. Sliding back to her computer, she found a return message from Josh.

"Hi Starling. I can confirm. I've attached a copy of the relevant pages. Find something?"

Josh"

Quickly responding to let him know she hadn't found anything concrete, she opened the attachment and read through it, confirming her recollection of the conversation between Decker and Moretti. "Hmm. Any connection between that and the missing Anthony file?" She quickly jotted a note to that effect and was about to jump back into the "Jimmy" information when her office phone rang. She reached for the phone without bothering to check caller ID and was greeted by Ms. Wilson.

"Agent Hebert, I just wanted to remind you of your meeting in five minutes with Agent Bonet."

"Oh shit," she said, not meaning to have said it aloud. "Sorry. Thank you, Ms. Wilson. I'll be there in a minute."

Having disconnected from the call, she hurriedly gathered information about another case, grabbed her notepad, and jogged out the door.

. . .

The man is standing at the reception desk of the hotel, his two large suitcases waiting patiently off to the side of the desk, having been brought down by the bellman. He's dressed in freshly cleaned and pressed blue jeans, with a dark green Nehru jacket over a white Beatles T-shirt, and blue and white Adidas Campus sneakers on his feet. His brownish blond hair is stylishly long and he wears round horned rimmed glasses with yellow tinted lenses. Approaching the receptionist, he flashes a friendly smile and says, "Good morning, Liz. I'd like to check out."

"Certainly, Mr. Martin." Holding her hand out, she says, "Your room key, please."

Complying, Mr. Martin hands her his key, the tag clearly showing room number 1032.

"Thank you." Turning her attention to her task, she says, without looking up, "I hope your stay with us was pleasant."

"Oh, most definitely," as Mr. Martin hands her a credit card.

"Thank you." Running the credit card and it having been accepted, she hands it back to Mr. Martin, saying, "I hope we see you again soon, Mr. Martin. Would you like the bellman to help you with your luggage?"

"Yes, please."

Liz motions for the waiting bellman, who takes the luggage through the revolving door, where the doorman hails a waiting cab and the bellman places the luggage into the trunk of the car. Tipping the bellman and doorman, careful not to tip either too much or too little, he says, "Thank you" and gets into the waiting back seat of the Yellow Cab. Before the door closes, and within earshot of the still loitering doorman, he instructs the cab driver to take him to the airport, checking to make certain that the doorman, making every appearance not to be listening, clearly heard the direction. Smiling to himself, Mr. Martin closes the door and the cab pulls away from the curb.

Having traveled out of sight of the hotel, Mr. Martin says, "You know what? I've changed my mind. Instead of the airport, please take me to the Regent Hotel in Cambridge."

Looking at his passenger in the rear-view mirror, the cabbie asks, "Are you sure? That's really out of the way."

Returning his gaze through the mirror, the passenger responds, "I'm sure. I'll also be sure to make it worth your while, especially if you can maintain a certain level of discretion."

The cab driver, taking his attention from the road, again uses the mirror, seeing his fare tilt his head and nod. In response, the cabbie says, "Whatever you say, boss," as he puts his turn signal on and changes course.

Once on the new route, Mr. Martin closes his eyes and is seemingly asleep when, after about twenty minutes, his eyes suddenly pop open and he begins to silently wretch. The cabbie, unable to ignore this display, looks into the mirror and, seeing his rider in distress, immediately pulls off the road and stops the car, turning around to ask through the clear bullet-proof plastic divider if there was anything he could do. Mr. Martin, looking outside and seeing what appears to be a deserted shipping container storage area, nods his head and points, saying through clenched teeth, "Go behind one of those. I don't want to throw up where somebody might see me." Obediently, the driver turns and drives to the indicated spot behind a stacked row of rusty looking containers. Once the car has come to a complete stop, out of view of any potential witnesses, Mr. Martin throws the door open and runs further behind a container, where he bends over and dry heaves. Concerned, the cabbie opens his door and exits the vehicle, approaching his passenger.

"Hey, is there anything I can do for ya?"

Nodding his head and motioning for the driver to come closer, Mr. Martin croaks out, "Yes."

The driver, now close enough to touch his fare, puts his hand on Mr. Martin's shoulder and asks, "What do you need, buddy?"

In response, Mr. Martin quickly stands straight and, with a short upward thrust, hits the cabbie full on the chin with a blackjack, catching him completely by surprise as the sound of breaking bone reverberates against the sides of the various metal containers. Before the cabbie can react in self-defense, Mr. Martin is standing over him, raining blows from the weapon on and about his victim's head, knocking him down to the ground and rendering him unconscious. Seeing the prone body in the dirt, he stops to catch his breath, breathing hard and noting the blood spatter on his Nehru jacket. Sufficiently recovered, he drags the still breathing body to the car, placing it face down on the back seat. Closing the passenger door, he gets into the driver's seat, starts the car and wends his way through the maze of containers until he finds the one he's been looking for. Stopping outside and to the side of the chosen container, he gets out of the car, finds a key in his pocket and unlocks the heavy padlock keeping the container secure from prying eyes. With the door open wide, he enters and strips off his shirt and jacket, sunglasses, fake eyebrows and wig, revealing the face of Jimmy Russo. Walking back to the cab, he removes his luggage from the trunk, stopping to make sure the cabbie was still unconscious. Opening the suitcase, he changes his shirt and shoes and puts on aviator style sunglasses. Placing his luggage into the vehicle which waits inside the container, he gathers his disguise, takes it to a nearby trashcan and sets it on fire, waiting until the blaze is burning sufficiently to incinerate the contents before reentering the container and driving out in a 1964 blue Ford Falcon panel van. Stopping the van outside of the container, he returns to the cab, starts the engine, and drives it into the now empty container. Exiting the car, he opens the passenger door and sees the still unmoving body of the severely injured, but still breathing, driver. Reaching into his pants pocket, he removes a four-inch stiletto style switch blade knife, grabs the cabbie by the hair and pulls back, revealing the throat, and calmly slices through the flesh deep into the carotid artery. Dropping the head into the quickly forming pool of blood, he briskly wipes his fingerprints from any surface he may have touched, closes the car door, and exits the container, replacing the padlock and locking the car and body inside. Looking around to be certain that nobody was lurking, he calmly walks to the van, gets in, starts the engine, and drives away.

"God Damn It!" were the first words out of my mouth when I returned from my latest foray into time/space. Adrian was waiting with a large glass of cold water and four extra strength ibuprofen, which I quickly accepted and put to use. She looked at me with a mixture of concern and curiosity. I held up my finger in a "give me a minute" gesture and typed. When finished, I handed her the computer and she read. When she had finished, she looked at me with a look of complete incredulity.

"Who the fuck is this guy?"

"Jimmy Russo the gangster, Richard the gay man, Mr. Martin the who knows what. He's the man of a thousand faces," I said, not quite able to hide the fact that I was slightly impressed. No. More than slightly. Not with the cold-blooded killing, of course, but with the planning and execution (no pun intended) of that plan. "I mean, he could have been an actor or novelist, and been successful at either, or both." Stopping to reflect, I continued, "Although, it was probably easier to do what he did than to get into either acting or publishing," I said, the cynic in me coming out.

"Well, whoever he is, or was, and in whatever disguise, he always seems to be a psychopath," noted Adrian.

Agreeing, I said, "So, here's the five million dollar question. Was the art in that van?"

"Yeah, that is the question, isn't it?" she responded. "Why couldn't he have at least opened the back doors to make sure everything that was supposed to be in there was actually still there?"

"Because that would've just been too easy. For us, I mean. Really, he just seems to be so supremely confident that nobody could possibly have found it." Thinking for a moment, I said, "And, you know, I can see his point. The container was still locked with his lock. And the van was still inside and unmoved. If somebody had gotten in there, they would probably have just stolen the van and driven the hoard away."

"Good points, but still, I wish there was a way to confirm that that's where he stashed the art. Otherwise, we're still in the middle of a wild goose chase with no proof that he's even got it," she said, the frustration evident in her voice.

"I don't disagree," I said, "but I think we have to proceed under the assumption that he has it and that's where it was. Another question is, where is he taking it?"

"The more we discover, the less we seem to actually know," she pointed out.

"Seems to be the story of life itself," I said in my most philosophical tone of voice. Putting my hand to my head, I winced and said, "Even with the ibuprofen, I'm getting a headache." Looking at Adrian, I asked, "Can we do a sketch of the cab driver and what the storage area looked like? Maybe Agent Hebert could find where it is...or was."

"OK, but let's do it quickly so you can lie down and minimize that headache."

We did, and I did.

•   •   •

Back in her office the following day and eager to get back into her review of the information packets, Agent Hebert hurriedly completed a report on another case for her boss and placed it in her outbox. The packet labeled "Jimmy" had been calling to her from the side of her desk and did not quiet until she pulled it to her, opened it and removed the contents, placing them in front of her. Quickly sorting through the pages, she immediately noted that there was more information to read in this one packet than, seemingly, in all the others combined. Curious, she started at the top and, over the next forty minutes, read through the material, just to become familiar with the information. Next, she opened her notepad to a fresh page and read through the material a second, slower time, mulling things over in her mind, jotting notes, and getting the feel for Jimmy. Much like Josh and Adrian, she found herself both fascinated and repulsed by his actions saying, "Who is this guy?" more than once. Just to make certain that she hadn't missed something in the FBI files, she revisited the thin James Russo file from the boxes and confirmed that the agents running the initial investigation hadn't been focused on Jimmy at all. "Holy shit. If this guy really faked his own death, he definitely had everybody at the agency fooled." Focusing her attention on the sketches which had been provided by Josh and his wife, she was able to compare a photo of Jimmy, apparently taken on his way out of Mama Nona's, with the sketch, and determined that it was definitely the same person. As for the other sketch, the one of Thomas Duarte, she had no other frame of reference. Before focusing on Duarte, she scanned Jimmy's sketch and began the facial recognition software on the off chance that some or all of his aliases might be revealed. Having a full name for the other sketch, she bypassed facial recognition and instead ran a missing person's inquiry. Since missing persons cases were more frequently updated in the computer system, even from that long ago, she remained hopeful that something would come up.

Having done all that she could to this point with the information available, she took some time to review her notes and turn the information over in her mind. Something was bothering her, but the more she chased it, the more it eluded her. After not thinking about it for a few minutes, she was finally able to trace the problem back to Jimmy's faked death. She reread Josh's account and then retrieved the FBI's file from the ever present boxes. She reviewed the agency's file and compared what she found against Josh's account, confirming that the official version completely dismissed any possibility that it was anybody other than James Russo that had died in the burned-out car. Forensics, such as it was, did a thorough examination of what they had, which was not much at all. The body no longer contained fingerprints and what remained of the clothing was examined and processed in the lab, the determination being that they matched the clothing known to have usually been worn by Jimmy. The only method left to determine the identity was dental records, which were used to confirm that it was, in fact, Jimmy. Still, something nagged at her. She reread Josh's account yet again, and then it hit her. Back in the official file, she scoured the report and finally found what she's been looking for...the gas can. Josh had said that Jimmy had tossed it aside and the FBI file clearly stated that it had been found, tagged and bagged. Laboratory examination determined that the only fingerprints on the can were that of James Russo. Conjecture, as stated in the field notes, was that the killer either forced Jimmy to soak the car and himself, before being shot, or the can was conveniently already in the car and the killer, wearing gloves, didn't leave any of his own fingerprints. In either event, nothing further was ever done, it having been determined that James Russo was the victim, so it mattered not if his fingerprints were on the container of the evidence destroying gasoline. "More corroboration," she muttered. Maybe she was prejudiced by the information she had that the original investigating agents didn't, but she thought the fingerprints should have triggered some sort of alarm. However, after putting herself in their shoes, she came to understand their conclusion. The fact was that James Russo was three steps ahead of everybody else involved in the investigation, including the FBI. He understood how the investigation worked, knew the limitations of the forensics of the day, and had absolutely no compunction about killing to enhance his chances of success. A deadly and successful combination. Yet, the question remained, was he involved in the art theft or was he up to something else entirely? There was still nothing concrete to tie him to the heist, even with Josh's ability to go back in time. She was about to email Josh when she received a notification that a new email had arrived. Seeing that it was from Josh, she thought, "Coincidence?" and laughed nervously. Opening it, she read.

"Good morning/afternoon Starling. I've attached to this email an account of my most recent 'watching' experience. I've also attached some sketches that Adrian was able to do based on my descriptions. One is of a cab driver, one is of a location somewhere outside of Boston, and one is of a Mr. Martin, yet another alias of James Russo, if that is even his real name. Once you've read the account,

you'll understand why each of the sketches has been provided. Before you get your hopes up too much, please know that I have still not yet determined the location of the art, although I feel we are getting closer. I think we should put our heads together and discuss what we've got so far, what you've been able to corroborate, and where we go from here.

I look forward to speaking with you soon.

Josh."

She shot off a quick reply, letting him know that she'd get back to him and opened the attachments. As they were appearing on her computer, she received an email notification labeled "Thomas Duarte Inquiry." "Thomas Duarte?" she murmured. Suddenly, it came to her. "Oh!" Quickly transferring her attention, she retrieved the message, which consisted of a copy of a file and a picture of the missing person.

The file was from the Boston PD, since there was nothing to indicate, back then, that FBI involvement was required. Nobody suspected that the subject had traveled across state lines or been involved, even peripherally, in a federal crime. So, it was left to the Boston PD to track down clues and find the missing individual. Since the missing individual, Thomas Duarte, was an adult, no investigation was started until he had been missing for seventy-two hours. When it was finally reported to Boston PD by a friend at work, where he failed to show up, the investigating officers, following a lead from that same friend, tracked his movements to the 1270 Club, which was enough to doom the investigation. The 1270 Club was a notorious "gay" club and, in the world of the 1970s Boston Police Department, anybody frequenting such an establishment did so at their own risk and deserved whatever they got. Nevertheless, the investigating officers did follow-up enough to determine that Mr. Duarte left with a "date." Nobody knew the name of the date or had ever seen him before. No description of the man was in the file, and no additional or further sightings were uncovered. No further clues or evidence revealed themselves and, as a result, the investigation was closed and the information entered into a missing persons database where Thomas Duarte was still listed as "Missing."

"As if a gay man in 1970 could ever get a fair shake from any police department, let alone Boston," Agent Hebert lamented.

Opening the remaining attachment, which was an actual photograph of Thomas Duarte, she retrieved the sketch sent by Josh and held it up next to the computer monitor.

"These could be one and the same," she remarked. "Amazing."

And, she thought, yet more corroboration. The more confirmation she could gather about Josh and his "watchings," the stronger she felt about the chances of recovering the art, which was still her main concern, although not far behind was her belief that the key to clearing her father's name and justice for Sheriff Joe and his victim lay in what Josh was able to do.

• • •

After a working lunch and several meetings, Agent Hebert was again sitting in front of her computer and able to focus on the latest email from Josh. Opening the attachments, she forced herself to read the account of the "watching" before viewing the sketches, which was a feat in itself, her eye wanting again and again to return to the drawings. After all, she had a Master's degree in Art History. She wanted to have a frame of reference when viewing the illustrations rather than just marveling at their detail and the skill required to create them.

Following her usual pattern, she read through the account once, just to get the gist of it. Then she reread it more slowly, taking notes as she went. Finished with that portion of her task, she leaned back, rubbing her tired and bloodshot eyes.

"Holy shit. This guy is a fucking psychopath!"

Now ready for the show portion of this tell and show, she focused on the art. Each of the pieces was labeled, so it was easy to discern which picture was of what subject.

First, she looked at Mr. Martin. Retrieving the drawing of James Russo, she held it next to the monitor and closely examined the two. She could clearly see the similarities in bone structure, but the subtle differences, the eyebrows and hair, together with the tinted glasses, were enough to change the appearance so that one would have to know Jimmy to ascertain that Mr. Martin might be one and the same.

Next she reviewed the drawing of the storage container ghost town. Not being familiar with Boston or its environs, it meant nothing to her, so she quickly set it aside.

Finally, she brought up the drawing of the cab driver. Knowing his fate caused her to lose the perspective of the cold FBI observer and made her view the picture with a sympathy that she otherwise reserved for non-work-related matters. She could imagine his feelings of empathy toward his ill passenger, feel his desire to help. The fact that he was so ignominiously butchered caused a rage to arise for which she was unprepared. Forcing herself to look away, she felt herself shaking as a tear escaped. Wiping it away, it dawned on her that this victim, intending nothing but helpfulness, was akin to her father, both having been condemned to death for their troubles. Until this instant she hadn't realized how this case, or, more accurately, what Josh was doing in relation to this case, had brought thoughts and feelings about her father to the fore which she hadn't realized were so deeply buried. She knew she was balancing on the precipice of unprofessionalism and fought to bring herself under control, a battle that she won, for now.

After leaving her office and taking a short stroll in what passes for fresh air in D.C., she returned re-energized, the remains of the Grande Mocha Latte in her hand having had something to do with that. Sliding to her computer, she typed an email.

"Josh, we need to talk. Are you available sometime tomorrow? Let me know a time and I'll send you a Zoom invite."
Thanks
Star"

• • •

After I received the email from Star, I arranged for a video conference so that Adrian could participate and meet Agent Hebert. It was set for 3:00 p.m., so I had plenty of time during the day to fixate on what it was she wanted to discuss. I had heard nothing about what she had discovered and was more than a little curious about her findings. Instead of thinking about it, I tried focusing on work, but it proved difficult to ignore the continuous taunting of the ever present clock in the corner of my computer monitor. Finally, we approached the appointed time, so I gathered myself and Adrian and we huddled around my laptop after having placed it on the dining room table.

After logging on, introducing Adrian to Agent Hebert and vice versa, and generally exchanging pleasantries, we got down to the business at hand.

"Josh and Adrian, I've read through all the material that you provided, including that last account of Jimmy and the cab driver. If I may be unprofessional for just a moment…Holy Crap!"

"Holy crap is right!" I responded. "And there's nothing unprofessional about it, as far as we're concerned," I said as I looked to Adrian for confirmation, which she readily provided by nodding her head. "This guy, Jimmy, or Richard or Mr. Martin, or whoever he is, is a real piece of work."

"A true psychopath," said Adrian.

"He is that," said Agent Hebert.

Before she could continue, I asked, "Out of all the information we gave you, were you able to corroborate any of it?"

In response, she told us about the information in the FBI's files, or rather, the lack of information. She told us about what in my 'watchings' she could corroborate based on those files. She confirmed that Thomas Duarte was listed in the Missing Persons database, but that no way existed of identifying the remains, as they'd been buried or disposed of fifty years prior.

"He really did get away with murder," I noted.

"More than once, it would seem," commented the Agent.

"What about the death of Captain Caprietti?" I asked.

"Besides the note in the file, which we talked about, nothing. Which leads me to the fact that, while I can corroborate almost everything you've said or seen, to some degree, there's absolutely nothing I can do with any of it."

"I was afraid of that," I said, despondent.

"These guys all seem to have covered their tracks on anything having to do with anything you've seen."

Adrian asked, "What about the location of that storage container facility? Is there any way you can figure out where that was?"

"We have a modified version of facial recognition software that we use for locations. I have the program running your sketch, but so far, nothing." After a pause she said, "By the way, Adrian, your sketches are excellent, and I'm saying that as an art historian, not just as a viewer."

"Thank you. I appreciate it."

"So," I interjected, "where do we go from here?"

"I hate to state the obvious, but we're no closer to finding the art now than we were before you called me," said Agent Hebert, stating the obvious.

"You noticed that, too, huh? There's no putting anything past the FBI," I said, maybe just a bit too snarkily. "Sorry, I didn't mean it to come out like that, but yeah, we noticed the same thing."

"Josh, I know these 'watchings' take a toll on you, but I don't see any way around it. First, we need to know if the art was in that van and where it was going. Is there any way you can revisit that and get the state and number of the license plate? We might be able to track something with that information."

"I don't think I have any choice," I said, resignedly. "While I'm back there, I should also find out the cab driver's name and maybe the cab number. Maybe there's something you can do for his family, with the right information."

"I'm running his sketch through Missing Persons, but so far, nothing. If you get a name there might be nothing we can do, officially, because, if it's like everything else so far, there won't be any actual evidence left, but I'll see what we can do."

"OK. The location of that storage container facility might be helpful, too. I wonder if there's a possibility that it still exists."

"I wouldn't count on it, but who knows? Stranger things have happened." Looking at Josh, she laughed to herself. "As if I have to tell that to you."

Adrian and I both laughed in response and Adrian, shaking her head, responded, "Isn't that the truth!?"

"OK. That's all I have for now. Keep me posted about what you find out, and I'll do the same."

"Will do," I assured her.

"Good bye Agent Hebert. It was nice to meet you," Adrian said as we all ended the connection.

The blank screen stared at us as I turned to Adrian and said, "It's not like any of this is a surprise."

"No, it's not."

"I'll try to revisit the van and cab in a few days. I want to make sure I'm mentally prepared. I really, really don't want to revisit the murder of the cab driver."

"I don't blame you. Plus," interjected Adrian, "I want time to talk to Jen and see if there's anything she can come up with to help alleviate the headaches."

I silently nodded my head in agreement, shut down the computer and went to prepare dinner.

•   •   •

Adrian called Jen, without Josh. It wasn't that she was hiding anything. After all, she told Josh that she was going to talk to Jen. Well, maybe "not hiding anything" was an exaggeration. She was hiding the fact that she was becoming increasingly concerned about Josh's welfare. Although they had taken whatever precautions they could think of, the headaches were still coming after each episode. She was worried not only about the short-term effects of the space/time travel, but about any possible long-term effects as well.

When Adrian called Jen at home, after working hours, she was greeted with an enthusiastic "Adrian! I'm so glad you called. I've been giving Josh's situation a great deal of thought."

Surprised by the level of excitement she heard in Jen's voice, Adrian cautiously responded, "Really? So have I. As a matter of fact, that's why I'm calling."

"OK. Tell me what's going on."

In response, Adrian told her about some of the "watching" experiences Josh had had since Jen performed the scans. She did not go into details, nor did she tell her about the FBI. Jen had read some of the previous "watching" recountings, so it's not that she didn't want her to know what had happened. It was just that she didn't think the details were important to the reason behind her call. As to not mentioning the FBI, she knew from years of living with an attorney that Josh would say not to provide any information that wasn't necessary to the goal. It was a natural adjunct to his admonition to not answer any question that hadn't been asked, which she had heard so many times that it was imprinted in her gray matter. She also told Jen about the headaches and what they had done to fight off the effects, all of which Jen silently absorbed.

Having completed her narrative, Adrian awaited Jen's response.

"Hmm. Interesting," were the first words she spoke. After a moment, she asked, "How long do these headaches last?"

"It depends. Since he started taking the ibuprofen immediately upon coming out of it, I'd say about 2 hours or so. The after effects, a light headache, an aching behind the eyes, sometimes swirlies in his vision, can linger anywhere from one to three or four days."

"The accountings of his experiences that I read tended to be jarringly violent. Does the level of violence have any effect on the severity of the headache?"

Considering what Jen had just asked, Adrian did not instantly respond. "I've never considered it in those terms. I really don't know. Why?"

"No reason, really. It was just a thought." She stopped, lost in self-deliberation. "Hmm, if the level of violence affects the headaches, it could be more from an emotional reaction than a physical reaction. Or, the emotional reaction could be informing the physical. Interesting. I'll have to give it some more thought."

Adrian had the distinct feeling that Jen was getting lost in her own thought process and attempted to bring her back to the conversation. "So, Jen, is there anything you can do? I'm worried."

Hearing Adrian's voice, Jen was brought back to reality and said, "Oh, sorry. I think there might be. I said I'd been thinking about Josh's case a lot lately. Actually, I've been doing more than that. I still have that blood sample he so willingly gave," she said sarcastically. "I've been doing some analysis. Give me a few days to see what I can come up with."

The relief evident in her voice, Adrian said, "Oh, that's great. Let me know as soon as you can, please. And Jen, thank you."

"Of course. I'll talk to you soon."

• • •

In the few days that had passed since Agent Hebert had spoken with Josh and Adrian, she found herself absorbed in matters relating to other cases that had actual evidence to examine and clues to hunt down. Doing so helped to ease the frustration she felt in relation to the Garden Museum case, at least to a small degree. She had come to the realization, and more importantly, the acceptance of the fact, that the return of the Garden Museum art had become conflated with the clearing of her father's name and justice for Sheriff Joe and his victim. She felt herself becoming more personally involved in this case than she knew was appropriate. Nevertheless, for seemingly the first time in her life, she was willing to take the advice meted out in one of her favorite movies, *Risky Business*: "Sometimes you just have to say, what the fuck." She was willing to just say "What the fuck" when it came to accepting the bizarre nature of the leads coming her way. She was willing to say "What the fuck" when it came to following up those bizarrely obtained leads, if, in fact, they could be considered leads at all. She was willing to say "What the fuck" about considering them leads. She was willing to say "What the fuck" about the possible repercussions to her career if it became known that she was relying on what most in the agency would term "psychic bullshit." All because she was willing to say "What the fuck" if it all led back to her father's exoneration. Her motivation had become, "Let's find this art and get this wrapped up so I can convince Josh to help me with my father's case." She hadn't mentioned it to Josh, yet. She thought it would be best to wrap up the Garden Museum case, especially if they were successful in finding the art. She knew the whole process was hard on him and didn't want to come across as just another selfish asshole looking out for herself. But, she felt, if they could recover the art, and he could see how successful he could be, it could be a powerful persuader. Plus, having that five million dollars would probably put him in a pretty good mood. In the meantime, she'd have to work the other cases and take what was presented to her as it came in this one.

•   •   •

After Adrian had spoken to Jen, I noticed she seemed to have something on her mind. She was giving me furtive looks when she thought I wouldn't notice, but after so many years of living together, I didn't really need to see to know. I could feel it in the room's energy. Each time I asked what was bothering her, she said "nothing" in that way that definitely meant "something." If you've been in any kind of relationship, you know exactly what I'm talking about. I also knew enough, at this point in our lives, to let it go, at least for a while. Late into the afternoon of the third day after her conversation with Jen, out of the blue and à propos of nothing, I said, "You know, I'm fine."

She turned her head to give me that look meant to convey, "I don't know what you're talking about," and instead began to gently cry. "Are you?" she was able to say as I gathered her in my arms.

"I am," I said as I continued to hold her. "My headache is gone, even the after effects. I'm ready to go back in."

That caused her to pull away and look at me, hard. "I'm not sure that's such a good idea."

I started to respond when she cut me off.

"No, don't," she commanded. "I know you. You'll say that nothing is wrong just because that's how you want it to be. But you really have no idea.

Like it or not, you're having seizures." For emphasis, she repeated, "*Seizures!*" After letting that hang in the air for a moment, she continued, "That can't be good, short or long term. You may not notice anything now, but who knows what's really happening? You could have a stroke, or worse."

She was really worked up, so I wisely kept my mouth shut. After staring at each other for a count of ten, she gave me that look, with her eyebrows raised, head nod and hands open, that wordlessly said, "So? What do you have to say?"

I sat down, looked at her and said, "You're right."

She waited for me to continue, but I was at a loss for words at that moment.

"I'm right? That's it?"

As she came to sit next to me, which I took as a good sign, I said, "Yes, you're right. I have no idea what this is doing to me." After a pause, I asked, "Do you want me to stop?"

She thought and said, "I know you feel as if you can't. But I'd like you to hold off, at least until Jen has a chance to chime in."

"I have no problem waiting for her to come up with something. But, regardless of what's happening, at some point I have to see this through. I can't just let it go, unresolved, and," before she could say anything, which I saw she was about to do, "it's not just about the reward money. I started this. We started this. And now there's somebody else that's bought into what we're selling. I owe it to her to not drop the ball and make her suffer the career consequences. Not to say anything about the fact that I'm curious as hell to see where this goes."

"Even if it means a stroke or heart attack, or worse?" she said, not being able to bring herself to utter the word "death."

"Adrian, I could be hit by a car later today, but that doesn't stop me from going outside. I've got to do what feels right, regardless of the consequences."

Standing, she looked down at me with an unreadable expression on her face. "Let's hope it doesn't come to that," as she turned and walked away.

Watching her, I could only mutter to myself, "Yeah, let's hope."

All the while Agent Hebert was working on other files and waiting for Josh to come up with some information she might do something with, a niggling thought kept rattling around the recesses of her mind. Sleeping and awake. It was one of those thoughts that just evades one's grasp until, when focused on some other mundane task, it jettisons from the recesses to the "deal with me now or I'll drive you crazy!" portion of the mind. It was while she was in the break room at work washing her coffee cup that this transformation occurred, almost causing her to drop the cup. Instead, she regained her motor control and said, "The mole!", just a little too loudly.

Somebody behind her said, "Excuse me," seemingly perturbed.

Turning, she saw three women sitting at a table, one staring at her as if ready to pounce. As she looked at the staring woman, she noticed a mole present at the right corner of her mouth, as if she were the embodiment of Anne Francis. Embarrassed, Agent Hebert stammered as she attempted to regain her composure. "Oh, uh. Hi. I didn't realize anybody else was here. It was just something occurred to me in relation to a case regarding a mole in the agency in the 70s," she said as she backed out of the room, reached the door and scurried towards her office. Rubbing her eyes as she fled, she muttered, "Oh shit. That was horrible." Passing her boss's office on the way and seeing the door open, she abruptly veered into it and stopped just inside the doorjamb. Agent Bonet, sitting at his desk and buried in paperwork, heard someone enter and, seeing Agent Hebert, said "Yes, Star. What can I do for you?" attempting, unsuccessfully, to keep the exasperation out of his voice.

"Sorry, boss. I was just passing by and wanted to ask you a quick question."

Waiting, Agent Bonet said, "OK. Ask away."

"Did you ever hear anything about a mole in the FBI's Boston office in the 1970s?"

Pausing before answering, he said, "No. Why?"

"Oh, nothing really. Something that just came up in some research. Thanks. Sorry to bother you."

She quickly exited, wanting to avoid any further questioning, especially as she was unsure where this was going, or why. As she passed Ms. Wilson's desk and said hello, she remembered her long tenure at the agency and posed the same question, receiving the same answer. She thought, "Either there was nothing to this, it was kept local or it was covered up."

Back in her office, she scoured the mountain of boxes containing the files compiled by Agent Decker and his team, searching for any reference or mention of the mole. Nothing.

"Strange."

As she considered how best to proceed, she thought, "I wish I could talk to ether Decker or Moretti." Out loud she said, "Yes! Where the hell are they?"

Attacking her keyboard with renewed vigor, she instituted a search for both retired agents. The information contained in personnel files was not available to agents of her stature, but general information was. She quickly discovered that Agent Decker was deceased, having died in 2006 at the age of eighty-three.

"Unless Josh can suddenly speak with the dead, Decker is a dead-end," she mused, chuckling to herself.

Continuing her search, she typed in Moretti's information. It was revealed that he was retired and currently eighty-eight years old. There was a short rundown of his career, but no current contact information. In reviewing his career highlights, she noted that the number one accomplishment was the arrest and conviction of Don Ricky.

"At least he got his closure."

Contacting personnel, they instructed her to complete an information request form, which she did, marking it urgent. After all, he was old, and she wanted to talk to him before what could be an imminent death. She sent the form via email and followed up with a call in an effort to convey a sense of urgency, knowing that the effort was most likely wasted. To her pleasant surprise, the individual with whom she spoke was receptive to the fact that she required the information quickly and promised to get to it posthaste, actually using that word, which brought a smile to Agent Hebert's face. Twenty minutes later, she received an email with the current contact information for retired Special Agent Moretti.

"Wow!" She couldn't help but be amazed that something in the agency had gotten done so quickly.

Opening the attachment, she discovered that Moretti currently lived by himself in a small townhouse on the outskirts of Boston. Making a quick, if not rash, decision, she instructed Ms. Wilson to contact Moretti and find out what a convenient day and time for a visit would be. In her instructions, Agent Hebert specified that her first name was not to be used, only "Special Agent Hebert." She had a feeling that an old school former agent of his age would be happy to speak with an agent, just not of the female persuasion. Her intuition was spot on.

•   •   •

"Who are you?" was the greeting she received from a cantankerous Moretti as he opened the front door to his small townhome. Agent Hebert had climbed the three stairs leading to his door and was standing under a small portico intended to shield guests from the frequent bone chilling wind and rain that so often comprised Boston's weather. It sufficed to perform its intended task, but had no effect in shielding her from the cold gusts of mental energy that emanated from the person standing in front of her.

As sweetly as she could bear, she held out her credentials and said, "Hi. Special Agent Hebert. Thank you for agreeing to see me."

Not bothering to glance at the proffered identification and offering no sign that he intended to let her into his home, he gruffly said, "Why'd they send a secretary? Don't I even rate a visit from a real FBI agent? Is that how little the brass thinks of us old guys?"

Losing any attempt at sweetness and taking a calculated risk as to what would resonate with him, she replaced her credentials in her pocket and said, "Mr. Moretti, I assure you I'm a 'real FBI agent.' As for what you rate, I can also assure you that the 'brass,' as you call them, don't give a rat's ass about you. Now, are you at all interested as to why I'm here or are you going to make this a total waste of taxpayer money?" Crossing her arms, she silently stared at him, being certain not to even blink.

Holding her gaze, he finally chuckled to himself, muttered something unintelligible, and stepped aside, motioning for her to enter. As she passed him and entered the house, she let a smile of satisfaction grace her lips.

She took a few steps into the room and waited as he closed the door. Taking in her surroundings, it surprised her to find a bright, well-appointed room with a modern fireplace as its focal point. Prints of various art were hung around the room, taking in various styles and genres. He stood and watched her as she made her assessment.

"Surprised not to find a dark, dank dungeon of a space, are you?" he said as he moved past her into the room.

Looking at him, she didn't even make an attempt at lying. "A little bit," she said, as he took a seat and motioned for her to sit in a large wingback chair opposite him. The smell of cigarettes was overpowering, as she noticed the antique ashtray stand next to his chair, a plume of smoke gently rising to the ceiling, where it hovered before being dispersed by a fan. She noticed a portable oxygen tank in a corner of the room and he followed her gaze.

"I know, I know. Smoking and oxygen tanks are not a good combination. Don't even think about lecturing me."

Sitting, she said, "I have no intention of lecturing you. If you want to kill yourself, that's entirely your choice."

"Good. So, why are you here?" It sounded more like a challenge than a question, but she ignored his tone.

"I'm investigating the Garden Museum theft. Do you remember it?"

"Of course I remember it. I'm old, not senile."

"Good. Then perhaps you might actually be of some use." In response, he actually harrumphed. "What can you tell me about it?"

"There's not much to tell. Some morons broke in, stole a bunch of art and got away. End of story."

"What makes you think they were morons, and why didn't you and your team investigate?"

Moretti took a long drag from his still smoldering cigarette, blew the smoke toward the ceiling, watched it be blown by the fan, and asked, "What division of the Bureau did you say you were with?" Somehow, he made it seem like an insult.

"I didn't, but since you asked, the Art Crime Team."

"Ha. Figures."

"Figures? What is that supposed to mean?"

"It means a bunch of academics playing make believe detectives." Taking a long last drag from the cigarette before extinguishing the stub, he said, "We didn't investigate because we were involved in another investigation that involved the mob, murder, extortion, and other various serious crimes. We didn't have time to deal with the art." Sitting back in his chair as he hunted for a fresh cancer stick, he said, "Besides, from what we'd heard, the Museum was under the watchful eye of the Don and he was going to deal with it." Finding the object of his desire, he put it in his mouth and lit it with the waiting Zippo lighter, an apparent relic from the last World War.

"And you heard that from Caprietti?"

The surprise at hearing that question was apparent on Moretti's face.

"I see you've been reviewing some old files. Good for you." Stalling, he took another drag from the cigarette before answering. "Yeah, Caprietti mentioned it. We were using the heist as a way to get Capprietti back into the good graces of the Don."

"How'd that work out for you?" asked Agent Hebert, eager to hear what he'd say.

"If you've seen the files, you know he offed himself before he could really be of any use."

Leaning forward and staring directly into his eyes, she said, "But you don't really believe that he killed himself, do you?" Sitting back, she said, "At least Decker didn't believe it, did he?"

Again, the look of surprise flashed on his face before he could get it under control. "What makes you say that?"

Reaching into the leather carryall sitting at her feet, she removed a manila folder, opened it and handed Moretti a copy of the handwritten note she'd found in the file. "That's Decker's handwriting, isn't it?" The tone she used to ask the question clearly indicated that she "knew" it was.

Reaching for the note, Moretti studied it.

"Have you seen that before?" asked Agent Hebert.

Handing it back to her, he said, "No, I haven't, but that is Decker's handwriting."

Replacing the note into the file, she hid her elation at finally having some direct confirmation of at least one thing. To Moretti she simply said, "Um hm." Looking back at him she asked, "Did you have any reason to think that his death was connected to the Museum theft?"

More relaxed, he answered, "Nah. We figured that if he'd killed himself, it was because the Don had found out he was working with us and had threatened his family, or worse. If he'd been killed, it was for the same reason. Either way, he was of no use to us anymore and there was nothing to tie the Don or anybody else to his killing."

"Did you and Decker ever look into the fact that the street Caprietti lived on was closed and the streetlights were out until, miraculously, right after he died?"

"How'd you know that?" asked Moretti in a manner that clearly indicated she had his attention.

Not answering, she asked, "Have you ever heard of a guy that worked for the Don named 'Anthony?' He was a killer who apparently did a number of jobs for the Don."

Intrigued as to where this was going, Moretti said, "Yeah. Anthony Scolletti. Real sweetheart of a guy. He'd just as soon kill somebody as go for a plate of pasta. Why?"

Continuing to ignore his questions, she asked, "Did you ever look into him for the Caprietti killing?"

"No. Why would we? Even if Decker had his suspicions, there was nothing to indicate that Anthony, or anybody else, was involved."

"Did you have a file on Anthony?"

"We had a file, but only relating to his association with the Don. And nothing about killing Caprietti." Stopping, he looked at Agent Hebert and asked, "Where are you going with this?"

"I went through boxes of files that you, Decker, and your team had in relation to your investigation. There were files for Tiny, Ralphie and Jimmy. There was a file for Joey the Animal. But nothing for Anthony." Stopping to let that sink in, she continued, "Any idea what happened to the Anthony file?"

"What? There was definitely a file on Scolletti. Not much in it, but definitely a file."

"Think the Don's mole may have taken it to protect him?" She said it matter-of-factly. It landed like a slap across Moretti's face.

Sitting upright, he said, "What do you know of any mole?"

His response confirmed two things in her mind. First, that there was a mole and second, that it was supposed to have been a secret. Saying nothing, she reached back into her carryall and removed another file, from which she removed and handed to Moretti a piece of paper and said, "I'd like you to read this."

Taking it gently from her hand, as if it might bite, he read Josh's account of his and Decker's conversation in the car after Caprietti's death. She watched as the color drained from his face and he struggled to regain his composure, as he reached for his ever present smoking crutch. Clearly shaken, he dropped the paper onto the coffee table, looked at Agent Hebert and said, "What the hell is this? Who wrote that? It's not possible."

"Oh, apparently it is very possible," as she reached to collect the paper and replace it into her file. "Does that conversation ring a bell?"

Seemingly frightened, he said, "I remember it because of his quick look at the back seat and what he said about seeing somebody. That was really weird, because there's no way somebody could have been in the back seat of that car without us knowing. And, there's no way anybody, and I mean *anybody*, could have known about that." Taking another hit from his cigarette, he said, "What the hell is going on?"

Continuing to ignore his questions, she said, "So, who was the mole?"

Hesitating, he decided to answer. "We had a young kid on the team. Agent Orland. We discovered it was him. Instead of confronting him, we decided to keep it quiet and use him to feed false information to the Don. It worked. We were able to install a false sense of security in the Don."

"I see." Switching gears, she said, "What did you think of Jimmy Russo?"

Struggling to mentally keep up, he repeated, "Jimmy Russo?"

"Yes. Jimmy Russo. You had a file on him and even brought him in for questioning, hoping to squeeze him into becoming a snitch. What did you think of him?"

Thinking, he finally said, "Jimmy? Skinny kid. Smart-ass. Everybody thought he had something to do with the Museum theft. Him and those two friends of his, Tiny and Ralphie."

"That's the one. What did you think of him?"

"Not much. Nobody could figure how those three morons could have pulled something like that off, especially since the Museum was under the Don's protection. We just chalked it up to misdirection. We found out that the Don was interested in looking into him, so we brought him in to see what was what."

"Why was the Don interested in him? What did he think of Jimmy?"

"Well, until something happened, we didn't know what, the Don thought about Jimmy the same way as everybody else, as far as we knew. Just a low-level goon who was great at following orders, usually, but not much in the thinking department. Then we heard the Don was looking into him because he heard the kid was smarter than he led on. Why are you so interested in Jimmy?"

Before answering, she asked, "Can you remember if the Don's attitude about Jimmy changed right after Ralphie was killed?"

Pondering the question and smoking as he did so, he finally said, "You know, I think it might have been? Why?"

Deciding to finally answer a question he'd posed, she ignored the last and answered the previous. "I told you I'm investigating the Museum theft. As you've said, everybody was looking to Jimmy, Tiny and Ralphie. I'm trying to find out as much as I can." Having answered his question, she posed another. "Did you decide to look into Jimmy, too?"

"We started to, but not long after we squeezed him, he was dead. We figured the Don discovered Jimmy was somehow involved in the heist, squeezed him for information and offed him as another example to the lower ranks. With Jimmy, Tiny and Ralphie all dead, the Don had tied up his loose ends."

Considering, Agent Hebert reached back into her bag-of-tricks and came out with yet another manila folder. She handed it to Moretti and asked, "Is there anything that you found out about Jimmy that isn't in that folder?" He looked through the folder, which contained only the information placed into it by the FBI and nothing provided by Josh.

Having completed his review, he replaced the documents, closed the file and handed it back to Agent Hebert. "Nah. It seems like everything is in there. Like I said, we couldn't come up with much."

"Thanks. That's what I thought." As she replaced the file, a thought occurred to her. "You said you'd heard the Don was looking into him because he'd heard the kid was smarter than he'd let on. How'd you hear that?"

Actually thinking about the question and not just dismissing it with a quick "I don't know," which itself showed a slight change in attitude, he said, "It must have come from a wire-tap. Or maybe a snitch. We had one or two of them." Closing his eyes and apparently deep in thought, he pulled on a cigarette and silently smoked while Agent Hebert watched. Eventually, he came back and said, "You know, I do recall hearing something about the Don saying that Jimmy had some low-level relations in Detroit, or somewhere around there." Straightening himself in his chair, he refocused on his visitor and commented, "As I said, once Jimmy was dead, we gave it up."

Deciding that she'd already gotten any information that she was going to get, she made the determination that there was no reason to tell him about Josh or anything she'd discovered through him. After all, she had no idea with whom Moretti may still be in contact and she decided safe was definitely better than sorry. Gathering her things, she stood and thanked Moretti for seeing her, however reluctantly.

He walked her to the door and, before she passed through, said, "Hey, sorry about my initial reaction to your showing up."

She turned to face him and, gauging his sincerity, said, "I appreciate the sentiment, but no, you're not."

He laughed and said, "You're right."

Knowing she shouldn't, but unable to stop herself, she whispered "What the fuck" to herself and, before he could close the door, she stepped forward and blocked it with her foot. Leaning in, with her mouth next to his ear, she quietly said, "Jimmy didn't die in that car." Satisfied with the look on his face, she removed her foot and confidently strode away, knowing that Moretti was watching her with his mouth agape.

· · ·

In the afternoon of the day two days after Adrian and my conversation about continuing the "watchings," our doorbell rang. I was in my office, so Adrian answered the door to find a messenger with a package waiting on the stoop. She signed for the package, came into the house and called my name.

"Who was it?" I asked.

On the kitchen island was a small brown box, the torn plain brown wrapping paper lying next to it. Adrian was holding and looking into a small clear bottle in which was visible a milky viscous liquid. In the box were four more identical containers.

"This is from Jen."

I approached, removed one bottle from the box, and mimicked Adrian. We stopped our inspections and were looking questioningly at one another when she reached into the box and removed a folded piece of paper. It was a typed message from Jen, which Adrian read aloud.

"Hi guys. As you know, I've been analyzing the blood sample that Josh so willingly left behind. After our conversation, Adrian, I delved more deeply into it, with the goal of coming up with something that might help to alleviate the effects of the experiences. I could get into the scientific explanation for why I've done what I've done, but I know that you'd both just tell me to skip that part, so here I am, skipping. Suffice it to say that, among other things, this should, theoretically, help contain the electrical charges to a more reasonable strength and frequency. I've had no way of actually testing this, because, Josh, in this matter, you are, to my knowledge, unique. So, here's my admonition, which, as

a lawyer, I know you'll appreciate: Proceed at your own risk! I have every reason to believe that this should work, but, you know, I can't provide any guaranty.

If you decide to proceed, as I'm sure you will, drink 2 ounces of this delightfully tasty liquid not less than 30 minutes or more than 45 minutes before you take your time/space journey. The result should be that, when you come out of it, the headache, if any, should be much less severe and for much less duration. Be sure to keep these magic elixirs in the refrigerator after opening.

Good luck and let me know how it works.

Love,

Jen"

She put the letter down and we each once again picked up a bottle, looking into it as if we were each Pandora holding our own version of the famed box.

I looked at Adrian and said, "So, what do you think?"

"I think that, since you're going to do it one way or another, I'm glad we have this."

•   •   •

The next day, we prepared for another foray into the past. We got comfortable on the couch, had the laptop within reach and a glass of ice water waiting. Trusting in Jen's concoction, we decided to forgo the ibuprofen in an attempt to manifest the desired results. I poured two ounces of the liquid into one of those little plastic measuring cups that come with most cough medicines and similar remedies. I smelled it and was pleasantly surprised that it didn't really have much of an odor. Buoyed by this, I put the plastic container to my mouth, threw back my head, and swallowed the contents as if doing tequila shots.

Oh My Fucking God! It was the worst tasting thing that's ever been placed into my mouth. I had a hard time keeping it down, but, in the interest of science, I forced myself. Think of the worst tasting anything you've ever had to eat or drink. Like a combination of the alginate that dentists used to make dental impressions, mixed with stale ashes from an overused ashtray, with just a hint of rotten egg to top it off. When I say horrible, I don't think I can really convey the depths of my dislike. I didn't know if drinking water was a good idea or not, but I had to at least take a sip to get the worst of it out of my mouth, followed by a quick trip to the nearest sink to spit out whatever residue lined the interior of my mouth. Ugh!

That ordeal behind me, I set a timer for thirty minutes and got my laptop set up. Since this was an attempt at revisiting a prior "watching," something I'd never attempted, we both thought the best way to go about it would be to use the same visual cue I had used the first time. Once it was up and ready, I closed the laptop to ensure that I wouldn't be launched before the countdown had been completed.

As soon as the chime sounded indicating that the required time had elapsed, I took a deep breath to steel myself, concentrated on returning to the scene of my last experience, opened the computer and looked at the picture. As I let my breath out, I focused on my visual cue and...

The man is standing at the reception desk of the hotel, his two large suitcases waiting patiently off to the side of the desk, having been brought down by the bellman. He's dressed in freshly cleaned and pressed blue jeans, with a dark green Nehru jacket over a white Beatles T-shirt, and blue and white Adidas Campus sneakers on his feet. His brownish blond hair is stylishly long and he wears round horned rimmed glasses with yellow tinted lenses. Approaching the receptionist, he flashes a friendly smile and says, "Good morning, Liz. I'd like to check out."

I realized I had returned to the targeted "watching" at precisely the same time and place as it had originally begun. As soon as I became conscious of this fact I thought to myself, "I wonder if there's a way to start somewhere else," and I then realized that the scene I was watching was frozen in time, as if I had hit a "pause" button. I mentally swiveled my head and was rewarded by a 360° movement of the scene, much like that used by real estate agents in their online listings. Fascinated, I used my mind to manipulate my view, but try as I might, I was unable to move to a different vantage point. My frame of reference was fixed. As I considered what to do, I again thought to myself that I didn't want to relive the entire experience. I was here with specific goals. First, I thought, I needed to make an attempt at viewing the van's license plates. Having thought this thought, and apparently having decided this was a top priority, the scene became a blur. As if having pressed "»" on a mental remote control, it was fast forwarding at a speed which caused me to feel disoriented and slightly dizzy. As abruptly as it had begun, it came to a complete stop and just as abruptly began to play at what I can only think of as regular speed. I could swear I felt myself rock back and forth, as if in a car that had performed the maneuver. I found myself viewing from outside the storage container...

As Jimmy locks the container and searches the area. Satisfied that the coast was clear, he walks to the van, passing the rear doors...

At which point I hit the mental "pause" button, freezing the frame. The door of the container was visible, as I'm sure it was the first time I saw this. However, this time I thought to locate and note the container number, if I could. The container was a dirty white, with most of its identifying marks either covered by dirt or having been scraped off. What I could see meant nothing to me, but it might to Agent Hebert or somebody who was familiar with these kinds of things. 114, either a 5 or an S, 67. I hoped, as I concentrated and said them aloud in my mind, that these numbers would somehow be helpful. Turning my attention back to the van, I could see that the rear was clearly visible. I also noticed that, it being a panel van, there were no windows in the rear doors. Next, I noted that, as the rear was visible, the license plate was also visible. However, being in this particular state of consciousness did not serve to improve my eyesight. Focusing, I was still unable to move forward or change my vantage point, but I found that by imagining my fingers on a touch pad, I was able to zoom in and enlarge the section of the van housing the license plate. Concentrating in an effort to memorize the plate, I thought about identifying and saying the state and number aloud, white plate with blue embossed numbers, Massachusetts,

37836, 1970 tag, unaware of whether I was able to speak aloud. Repeating the state and number in my mind over and over, I felt I would remember, at which point my view zoomed out and returned to normal as...

Jimmy continues his stroll to the van, gets in, starts the engine, and drives away.

This was exactly the point at which the prior "watching" ended. Realizing that, I thought, "I'll follow the van and see where it goes." As I stood there, thinking about doing exactly that, the scene paused. No, not paused. Stopped. I could run it backwards, but each time I attempted to run it forward past his driving away, it just stopped, jarring me as if having run into a wall. Stymied, I stood staring at the stuck scene before me, trying to come up with another plan to move forward, but nothing came to me. Instead, I thought about my other goal in revisiting this "watching": to discover the identity of the cab driver. Focusing on the new goal, the scene rewound with the same dizzying speed, stopping as...

Jimmy returns to the cab, starts the engine and drives it into the now empty container. Exiting the car, he opens the passenger door and sees the still unmoving body of the severely injured, but still breathing, driver. Reaching into his pants pocket, he removes a four-inch stiletto style switch blade knife...

NO! The thought howled and reverberated through my mind with such force that I could swear I was hurled backwards, stopped by some unseen pair of hands. As soon as my mind screamed, the scene paused, Jimmy standing with his stiletto frozen in time. I was determined not to rewatch the murder and made the decision that I would rather not gather the information than put myself through that again. Considering my dilemma, I came to realize that there was another opportunity to gather the facts I required, specifically, when Jimmy/Mr. Martin entered the cab, or at least at some other point in the journey. Having zeroed in on a target, the scene immediately rewound to the point in time in front of the hotel...

As Jimmy gets into the waiting back seat of the Yellow Cab. Before the door closes, and within earshot of the still loitering doorman, he instructs the cab driver to take him to the airport, checking to make certain that the doorman, making every appearance not to be listening, clearly hears the direction. Smiling to himself, Mr. Martin closes the door and the cab pulls away from the curb.

I hit my mental pause button, becoming more at ease with the process of control. I engaged the 360° viewer, moving the interior of the cab up and down and side to side, unable to see the cabbie's identification card, which I knew had to have been posted on the passenger side on the front of the dashboard. Having failed in this attempt, I hit "play," mentally speaking as…

Mr. Martin says, "You know what? I've changed my mind. Instead of the airport, please take me to the Regent Hotel in Cambridge."

Gazing at his passenger in the rear-view mirror, the cabbie asks, "Are you sure? That's really out of the way."

I thought, since I could see the cabbie in the mirror, it might afford me a better opportunity to glance at his ID card. So, I again paused the scene and engaged the 360° mode. This time, as I maneuvered the view, I saw, clipped to something on the front of the glove box, a Yellow Cab Company identification card. Zooming in, I saw it: Sean O'Shea. Once again, I concentrated on the information, repeating it in my mind over and over, hoping that somehow I was able to verbalize my thoughts. I didn't think I'd be able to remember all the information I was attempting to gather, but was determined to try. Rather than let the scene continue, I kept it static while I thought about my next move. I realized we didn't really know where the storage container was located and that, although Agent Hebert was attempting to discover the location using technology, any tidbit of information I could gather might be helpful. I willed myself to the location, and knowing what to expect, braced myself for the speed and abrupt stop. Knowing didn't help. I still felt rocked and disoriented. As I gathered my wits...

Jimmy's eyes suddenly pop open and he begins to silently wretch. The cabbie, unable to ignore this display, looks into the mirror and, seeing his rider in distress, immediately pulls off the road and stops the car, turning around to ask through the clear bullet-proof plastic divider if there was anything he could do. Mr. Martin, looking outside and seeing what appears to be a deserted shipping container storage area, nods his head and points, saying through clenched teeth, "Go behind one of those. I don't want to throw up where somebody might see me."

I thought I might be able to see some street sign or other form of identification, so I paused the scene and rotated it. From my vantage point in the car, there was nothing helpful I could find, so I started the scene and...

Obediently, the driver turns and drives to the indicated spot behind a stacked row of rusty looking containers. Once the car has come to a complete stop, out of view of any potential witnesses, Mr. Martin throws the door open and runs further behind a container, where he bends over and dry heaves. Concerned, the cabbie opens his door and exits the vehicle, approaching his passenger.

I thought for certain that, now freed from the confines of the car, I would be able to see something. Again pausing and going 360°, I stretched my view as far as I could, zooming in and zooming out, using everything in my new arsenal. Tucked away behind the containers, there was nothing to be seen, just as Jimmy intended. Instead of terminating the "watching," something told me to let it run forward. Thinking about the controls on an actual remote, instead of using my mental remote to pause, fast forward or rewind, I thought, "What if I increase the volume?" Instantly, the sound increased, but all I heard was a constant whine. Thinking that I had some sort of mental tinnitus, I was about to give up when I realized the whine was the sound of fast moving tires. There was a highway somewhere nearby! Satisfied, I used my mind to reach out and hit the "Stop" button on my mental remote, sending me back to my couch and Adrian.

. . .

The return process was much smoother than in the past, my being able to control when I stopped making a tremendous difference. It was more like the slowing of a motorcycle by removing my hand from the throttle and less like the controlled crash of landing a fighter jet on a moving aircraft carrier in heaving seas. The fact that I did not witness a murder probably had something to do with it. You may be thinking, "Really dude, what's the big deal? You've probably seen hundreds of simulated deaths over the years in movies and television shows." That's what I would have thought, had I expected to witness violence, which I hadn't. But, having now been in that situation more times than I would have liked (one being an accurate number for that particular statistic), I can tell you with absolute certainty that it bears no resemblance to the moviegoing experience. When viewed in a movie or television show, the mind is fully aware of the simulated nature of the violent act. The screen acts as a kind of buffer between the act and one's psyche. When viewing the act of violence in a "watching" experience, there is no buffer of any kind. I am in the midst of the act. I can feel and experience the fear and adrenalin, smell the blood. Thankfully, I do not experience the pain. It's bad enough without the pain. The toll it takes on me, both physically and mentally, is hard to explain, yet it is most definitely a hard toll. So, my relief at not having to experience the murder of Sean O'Shea for a second time was palpable.

When I opened my eyes, Adrian was sitting beside me. When I smiled, instead of cursing, she smiled back and handed me a glass of water. I drank, not realizing how thirsty I was. It helped to invigorate me, just a little.

Before doing anything else, I needed to memorialize the information I had tried so hard to memorize, and told Adrian as much as I reached for the laptop. She reached out with a gentle hand and touched my extended arm, stopping my motion. When I looked at her with a puzzled expression etched into my face, she reached over and handed me a piece of paper on which she had transcribed the information I was about to attempt to recall.

"You were very vocal and animated this time. When I realized you were reciting a license plate number, I thought it might help to write what you were saying. Then, when you talked about other things, I continued."

I reviewed her writing and was so relieved I felt as if I would collapse. Instead, I took a deep breath, sat back and sunk into the couch. "Thank you. I wasn't sure I'd be able to remember everything I needed to, so I thought about speaking what I saw. I had no idea if you'd be able to hear me."

I drank some more water, closed my eyes, and recounted my experience. I opened my eyes when I told her about my level of control, mostly so I could see her expression, not because I was any less exhausted. And exhausted is exactly what I was. I hadn't realized just how tired I was until I got up to use the bathroom. It was all I could do not to fall back on the couch and ask Adrian to bring me an empty bottle. Instead, I stumbled to the commode, sat down to pee, and managed to get back to the couch without falling on my face.

Concerned, Adrian asked, "Are you OK? How's your head feeling?"

I hadn't even thought about my head since emerging from the past. Considering, I said, "Actually, it's not too bad. There's a slight throbbing, but nothing like the almost migraines from before. Maybe Jen really is the proverbial mad scientist."

Adrian breathed easier and said, "I'm so relieved."

"I am, however, really and truly fucking exhausted," I said, flopping backwards on the couch and letting my head loll and hang over the top of the cushion, just to make my point. Returning my head to a less awkward position, I looked at Adrian and said, "I feel as if I've just run a marathon," not really knowing what that would feel like. I was surmising.

"Well, you were really animated this time. Bouncing around, moving forward and backwards, and stopping suddenly. At one point I had to stop you from falling over."

"Did you put your hands on my back?"

Stunned, she replied, "Yes! Did you feel it?"

"I did. It was just as I thought I was going to have to watch the cabbie's death again and my mind screamed out, NO! The reverberation from the mind scream pushed me back with what felt like a physical force, but I had no idea it translated to my body. Amazing!"

"This whole thing is really unbelievable. And it keeps getting stranger." Pausing, she pondered, "I wonder how much of the new stuff, like your ability to control forwards and backwards in time, is related to Jen's concoction."

"Just thinking about it makes me want to retch," I exaggerated. "I was wondering about that myself. Or could it be because this was a revisit? Or a combination of the two? I have no idea."

Yawning long and loudly, I said, "I really need to get some rest." Struggling to my feet, Adrian arose, put her hand out and gave me a much needed assist. On my way to the bedroom, I stopped, turned and said, "At least we have some good information for Agent Hebert, although we're still no closer to the art. I'm getting really tired of having information we can't do anything with."

"I know," agreed Adrian. "It's frustrating, but I think we're getting closer."

Ever the optimist, I replied, "You know what they say about being close. It only counts with horseshoes and hand grenades."

IS THERE ANYTHING TO FIND?

It had been a little more than a week since Agent Hebert had spoken to Josh and Adrian, with no communication of any kind having been exchanged. She was busy with other cases, but the longer she went without hearing anything, the more anxious she became. She wanted to do something useful in the case, rather than just waiting for Josh to get back to her. To that end, she decided to check on the various searches she'd begun. As she did so, she was surprised to see that she'd missed some emails that had somehow gotten lost and then redelivered. Scanning those, she discovered one from Josh that had come just that morning and one from her location search for the shipping container ghost town, among other matters not related to the Garden Museum heist. Opening the email from Josh, she read.

> *"Good morning Star. I revisited my last 'watching' experience, as we had discussed. I'll tell you about the details some other time. Suffice it to say, it was interesting and, I think, successful.*
>
> *The van that Jimmy was driving had the following plates: white plate with blue embossed numbers, Massachusetts, 37836, 1970 tag. There were no back windows, it being a panel van, so I was unable to ascertain whether the art was inside. Sorry.*
>
> *The cabbie's name was Sean O'Shea. I could read his Yellow Cab ID card.*
>
> *Finally, I was unable to ascertain the location of the shipping containers. I was able to discover that it was close to a highway, but that's all.*

Please let us know what, if anything, you are able to discover. I'll keep at it as well. I'm getting very frustrated that I can't come up with any definitive information regarding the art and am sorry for wasting your time. Hopefully, we can find something solid soon.

Thanks,

Josh"

She could almost feel the frustration emanating from her computer monitor, it was so palpable. Knowing how such frustration can affect somebody, and not wanting to succumb to it herself, she dashed off a quick return email.

"Josh, thanks for the information. I'm sure that we'll be able to find something about Sean O'Shea, which will be a great comfort to his family. Don't let the frustration get to you. I know this isn't what you normally do on a day-to-day basis, but I can tell you that in any investigation there are long stretches of frustration. It only makes the successful outcome that much sweeter. We'll get there.

Talk soon.

Star"

She reread it before sending and hoped that it sounded sincere, as she knew how important it was to keep the spirit up and engaged. She was really attempting to believe it herself.

Now she turned her attention to the email regarding the location search. She read it quickly, then more slowly, ending with a fist pump and a "Yes!" before sending another email.

"Josh, how's this for a quick update? I just received the results of the location search for the shipping containers and, believe it or not, it still exists. And, as you said, it is located just off a major highway. My information states that it had been involved in ongoing major litigation which, until recently, had tied the hands of the City. The litigation has recently been concluded and work is

beginning on cleaning up the place. I'll check it out and let you know what I find out.

PS: How's that for coincidence?"

The first thing she did was submit a request to run the license plates that Josh had given her. Next, as promised, she delved into the details of the container location and discovered that it had been effectively, if not actually, abandoned nearly forty years before. The City of Boston, nearly fifty years ago, had an ongoing feud with ownership which, reputedly, was controlled by organized crime. With various administrations coming and going over the years, each with different priorities and varying commitments relative to organized crime, the ownership group was able to alternately get the item placed on the City's back burner of matters to deal with and flood the courts with enough paperwork to make it very time-consuming and expensive to proceed. Ultimately, the City and ownership settled for an approximately ten million dollar payment to ownership based on an eminent domain proceeding. As a result, the property was now under the control of the City of Boston, which was trying to clear it for future development.

Working the phones, she was able to determine that the City was in the process of removing the containers, but was unable to ascertain how far along they were. There were just too many divisions and governmental sections involved to get a straight answer. Rather than send the matter to the local field office and let them take the credit for anything that might be discovered, she decided to take the initiative and personally investigate. After all, it was her contact that led to the shipping container connection with her case. Besides, she was overdue for some serious recognition by her so-called superiors. So, the following day, she was off to Boston.

• • •

She arrived in Boston and picked up a rental car at the airport as arranged by Ms. Wilson. Instead of checking in at or with the local FBI field office, as she was required to do, she put the coordinates of the shipping container site into the GPS of her phone and drove straight there. Her reasons for skipping the necessary check-in were two-fold. First, she really wanted the credit for whatever it was she might find, and second, she was worried that she might find nothing and, as a result, be held up to ridicule by the "good old boys" of the FBI. No matter how much it seemed, to outsiders, that things at the agency may have changed, from a gender relations standpoint, the changes were almost meaningless. So, she hedged her bets.

As she approached the site, she couldn't help but envision what Josh had related in his written recollection. Stopping the car at the outskirts of the site, she saw, in her mind's eye, the cab drive up and pull over as the passenger gave directions to move out of sight. She moved the car toward the site and was surprised to find it alive with activity. There were trucks hauling containers, cranes holding containers in the air as they swung precariously before finally being lowered onto waiting flat-bed trucks, and men and women workers in hard hats and reflective vests scurrying about in what appeared to be haphazard fashion, although there must have been some method to the madness. She found what she thought was a safe place to park and got out of the car as she looked around for somebody in charge. Not seeing anybody that appeared to fulfill that requirement, she stopped a passing worker and asked where she could find the foreman.

The person she had stopped, a woman who appeared to be in her mid-to-late thirties, unabashedly looked Agent Hebert up and down, as if by her looks she could somehow determine whether or not to grace her with an answer. Having somehow concluded that Agent Hebert was worthy, she directed her to a construction trailer which sat around a corner and just out of sight. Thanking the worker, Agent Hebert purposefully strode to her new destination, trying not to get too filthy in the process.

She climbed the three steps to the trailer and, just as she was reaching forward to knock, hit a man in a yellow vest squarely in the chest as he violently pulled the door open and almost bowled her over. As she was about to apologize, the man, muttering unintelligibly under his breath, stormed past her down the stairs, obviously not happy with whatever encounter he'd just had. Turning back to the now open door, she took a deep breath and entered.

She stood at the doorway and took in her surroundings, which were nothing to behold. A desk, cluttered with paperwork, a computer and monitor that appeared to have come from a museum, file cabinets, and an old black telephone. Yelling into the phone was a large man that appeared to be in his late fifties, although the belly which hung over his belt could just make him look older. He was so intent on the phone call, his face and neck becoming flush as he shouted, that he took no notice of his visitor. Agent Hebert closed the door behind her, took two steps into the room, and waited. And waited. And waited. Finally, the receiver to the phone was slammed down as the man muttered, "Stupid mother fucking piece of shit," before noticing that he wasn't alone.

"Who are you?" he grunted in her general direction.

She ignored his tone of voice and general rudeness and presented her FBI credentials and politely introduced herself. "Special Agent Hebert, FBI. I wonder if I could have a moment of your time."

He glanced at the credentials, looked her up and down and said, "I don't really have a moment of time. In case you haven't noticed, we're busy."

"Oh, I have noticed. If you'll cooperate with me, I think I could be out of your hair in no time at all."

"And if I don't cooperate with you?"

As sweetly as she could, she answered, "Well, in that case, I'll make a phone call and this place will be swarming with FBI agents who'll shut this whole operation down until we get what we want." She stood and stared at him, not breaking eye contact or giving him any other alternative.

He took a deep breath and said, "Well, shit. What do you want?"

"First, I'd like your name," ignoring the name tag he openly wore.

Pointing to that very name tag, he said, "Falcone, in case you can't read."

Again ignoring him, she said, "Do you have a first name, or are you like Cher or Beyoncé?"

Puzzled, he said, "Yeah, I got a first name. Tommy."

Not attempting to keep the sarcasm out of her voice, she said, "Ah, now we're getting somewhere, Tommy."

Upon hearing her tone of voice and actually recognizing the sarcasm, he said, "You know, I don't like the tone you're taking, lady."

She took two quick steps forward and adopted an aggressive stance before she replied, "You know, I don't really give a shit, Tommy. You've been an ass ever since I walked into this shit hole of a trailer and unless you start cooperating, nicely, I'll shut this whole job site down. Are we clear?"

With a newfound respect, Tommy Falcone replied, "Yes, ma'am. Sorry. How can I help?"

Placated, she relaxed her stance, pulled out a piece of paper on which was written the description of the container provided by Josh, and handed it to the foreman. "I'm looking for this container. It was on the ground level so, hopefully, hasn't been moved yet. Any idea where I could find it?"

He studied the paper and shook his head. "There's really no way to know from this." He handed it back to Agent Hebert, who placed it in her pocket.

"In that case, Mr. Falcone," attempting to show more respect based on his new attitude, "I think you're going to have to take me on a tour."

Tommy led Agent Hebert out of the trailer and looked around, considering which direction would be best. Agent Hebert, recalling the description of events provided by Josh, pointed to her left and said, "Let's start that way."

Prompted by her direction, he led the way, winding in and out of paths that currently exist, exposing paths that once were and were no more. She tried to envision the path that Jimmy would have followed and, to her surprise, found herself, after about twenty minutes, standing in front of what was once a mostly white container. She removed the paper from her pocket and compared the numbers on the paper to what she could see in front of her. The foreman, standing next to her, craned his neck to see the paper, not having memorized what was written, so she handed it to him. He looked from the paper to the container once, twice, three times, before he said, "I think this is the one."

Agent Hebert took the paper back, replaced it in her pocket, and said, "So do I."

She walked to the container, put her hand on it and gently tapped on it with her fist, not really sure what she thought she'd be able to ascertain. She fingered the pad lock, rusty but still functional, and asked Tommy, "Do you routinely open the locked ones to make sure they're empty before you remove them?"

"Yeah, we do."

She motioned toward the lock and said, "Open it."

He didn't immediately move to comply, and asked, "Don't you need a warrant or something?"

"Mr. Falcone, you're going to have to open this anyway, when you eventually get to it, so why ask for a warrant? If you really want one, I'll have to put a halt to your operation, make the application, and come back here in a few days with a slew of agents running roughshod over your work site. You'll lose three or four days of work just to do what you're going to do anyway. Do you really want a warrant?"

Considering the alternative, he nodded his head in assent, reached for the walkie talkie hanging from his belt and ordered a worker to come to his location with a large set of bolt cutters.

· · ·

They waited in silence until Falcone finally asked the inevitable. "What are you hoping to find?"

As the worker with the bolt cutters approached, she replied, while she stared at the front of the container, "I'd rather not say, just yet."

Both she and the foreman moved out of the way as the worker cut the lock, removed it and handed it to his boss.

"Open it," he instructed.

Doing as he'd been told, the worker lifted the latch and swung the door wide, revealing a decades old yellow cab. The worker looked questioningly at his boss, who in turn looked questioningly at Agent Hebert, who ignored them both. Trancelike, she slowly approached the waiting cab, moved to the rear passenger door on the driver's side and peered in the window. Lying what would have been face down, had there been a face, were the tattered remains of clothing on a skeleton.

· · ·

Two hours later, the construction site was crawling with an FBI forensics team, forcing the work to be halted for everybody's safety. As the forensics team did what they do, taking pictures, dusting for fingerprints, removing the body, and generally leaving no stone unturned, Agent Hebert stood to the side and watched. Watching her as he oversaw the proceedings was the head of the Boston FBI field office, Special Agent Richard Stone, a forty-three-year-old, play by the book agent who reached his level of authority by not pushing boundaries or making waves. Agent Hebert watched as he approached her, having a pretty good feeling about what was coming next, which was nothing to feel good about.

"Agent Hebert, a word, please?"

"Yes, sir," said as if all were right with the world.

"I don't believe you checked in with my office when you arrived in my city and before you came here." It wasn't a question.

"No, sir, I did not."

He waited for further explanation, and when none was forthcoming, was forced to ask, "Why not?"

"Sir, as you are aware," not knowing whether or not he was aware, "I am part of the Art Crime Team. I was merely following a lead that relates to a fifty-year-old cold case. A rather questionable lead at that. Rather than waste the valuable time of your office, for what would most probably be nothing, I thought the best use of all of our time would be for me to check it out on my own first. In addition, I was aware that the shipping containers were in the process of being removed and wanted to be certain that I arrived here before the removal of the container in question." She was trying to downplay her lack of official contact in the hopes of not being formally reprimanded, which never looked good in one's official file. She also intimated that she was searching for art, which was not really within Agent Stone's jurisdiction, if you ignore the actual location of her search, which she did.

"That may be so, Agent Hebert, but protocol should still have been followed."

"I understand, but, if you'll consider, the investigation into the theft of art is the sole purview of the Art Crime Team and, with the threat of immediate removal or destruction, I believe that my decision falls under an agent's right, while in the field, to make judgmental calls in order to preserve life or evidence."

Agent Stone considered her statement and gave it due consideration. Before he could respond, she continued.

"And," she said, with an emphasis, "once I determined that there was no longer a threat to any person or evidence, I reported to your office without delay."

Unable to present a counter-argument that didn't amount to "Well, yeah, but, nah nah nah boo boo..." he said, "Very well. My report will indicate as much."

"Thank you, sir, as will mine. Will your report also mention that, while in the course of exercising my duties and following a lead, I uncovered a body in a fifty-year-old missing person's case?"

That last question made it seem to him she may know more than she was letting on, which got his attention. "What makes you think it's a missing person's case, Agent?"

Trying to recover from a possible slip, she responded, "Well, sir, as I'm sure was obvious to you," not knowing what, if anything, was obvious to him, "the cab was at least forty years old, if not more, and the condition of the body indicated that it's been here, undisturbed, for probably as long. It only seemed reasonable that the person in the cab would have been reported missing, back in the day."

His suspicions having been allayed, the hackles on the back of his neck relaxed as he said, "So, you noticed that, too," making it seem that he actually noticed those facts. "Good work, Agent Hebert."

Smiling inwardly, so as not to seem too smug, Agent Hebert said, "Thank you, sir. I appreciate it."

As a tow truck pulled the car out of the container, he said, "Well, we should head to the office and file our respective reports."

"Yes, sir." As they turned to leave and were walking to their cars, Agent Hebert asked, "Are you going to notify the next of kin, sir?"

"Once we figure out who it is, of course. I don't know how quickly things go at the Art Crime Team, but out here in the real world, that might take quite some time."

Successfully hiding her distaste at his intimation, she responded, "Yes, sir...although," as if she just had the thought, "aren't cabbies required to display a company ID, usually somewhere on the dash? That might be a good place to start."

He glared at her and nodded to himself as he begrudgingly muttered, "It just might be."

Being an intelligent woman in a man's world had given her manipulation skills of which even she was unaware.

· · ·

It was later in the evening than usual for my phone to ring, so when it did, it grabbed my undivided attention. Checking caller ID, I looked at Adrian, who was sitting close by, and answered.

"It seems the FBI is working overtime today," I said into the phone.

"It's not every day the FBI discovers the skeletal remains of a body in a cab stashed inside a shipping container after having disappeared fifty years ago," was the response.

Rendered speechless for a moment, I recovered enough to say, "You're kidding? The car and body were still there?"

"They were."

I put my phone on speaker and laid it on the couch as Agent Hebert informed us of the history behind the container site and described the events of the day, beginning with her arrival at the site and continuing with her interaction with the foreman and the discovery of the shipping container. She talked about the arrival of the FBI forensics team and her interactions with Special Agent Stone.

"That's absolutely incredible," I said, unable to keep the amazement from my voice. "And congratulations to you. This should be a nice feather in your professional cap."

"Thanks. It should be. And God knows, as a woman in the FBI, I can really use it."

"I can only imagine," was Adrian's truthful response.

"Aside from that, you realize what this means, don't you?"

I pondered the question, and before answering, looked at Adrian for guidance. She shrugged, as if to say, "No idea. You're on your own with this one."

"You mean, it's nice to have found the body, but we're no closer to finding the art than we were before?" I said, perhaps revealing more of my state of mind than I intended.

"No! It means, without any shred of doubt, that your experiences are one hundred percent genuine and can be counted on. It means that, eventually, we *will* recover the art, if it still exists to be recovered."

"You're absolutely right!" was Adrian's enthusiastic reply.

I was less convinced, still not sure where this whole thing was going.

"I hope you're right," was the best that I could muster.

"I am," responded Agent Hebert. "In my world, this is a big win. It should be in yours, too."

"Thanks. I'll try to look at it that way, too," I said, not very convincingly. With more enthusiasm, I said, "We're both thrilled for you, Star. We really are. I hope this works out well, career-wise. I can't really see how it couldn't."

"Thank you both. I have to head for the airport, but just wanted to make sure you heard the news from me. Let's talk soon."

• • •

Agent Hebert was walking with a light-hearted, happy step when she arrived at work the next day. She greeted Ms. Wilson, who couldn't help but notice her good mood as she bounded to the break room for her second coffee of the morning.

"It looks like you're feeling good this morning, Agent Hebert."

"I am, Ms. Wilson."

"I take it things worked out in Boston?"

"Yes, as a matter of fact, things did work out well in Boston."

"Glad to hear it."

"Thank you, Ms. Wilson," was Agent Hebert's reply as she continued on her way to her office, coffee cup in hand.

Arriving at her desk, she got comfortable, checked her calendar and got to work, quickly losing track of the time. She was making significant progress in another case and was eager to bring it to a successful conclusion. Suddenly, she felt as if her career could be headed in the right direction, despite all the obstacles placed in the path of a woman agent, whether knowingly or unknowingly, by those performing the paving.

Taking a break to check her email, she first saw a response to her request to track down the van's license plates. She opened it and learned that the plates had been registered to a 1967 Chevrolet Impala which had been reported stolen. "Well," she thought, "you win some and you lose some. Not too much of a surprise there." Still buoyed by her good mood, she continued through her Inbox, where she found that she had been copied on a correspondence from Agent Stone to her boss. Eager to see what he'd written, she opened the email to find a copy of Agent Stone's report of the previous day's events. Opening the attachment, she read.

"On this day, at approximately 3:10 p.m. I received a call from Agent Starling Hebert, who is attached to the Art Crime Unit of the FBI, headquartered in Washington, D.C. Agent Hebert reported finding the remains of an unknown individual in the interior of a Yellow Cab which had been stored in an apparently abandoned shipping container for approximately forty to fifty years. Agent Hebert was following a lead in a cold case art theft and traveled to Boston from Washington, D.C. in pursuit thereof. Upon her arrival in Boston, Agent Hebert failed to notify the Boston field office, and more particularly, myself, Agent-in-Charge Richard Stone, of her arrival in my jurisdiction. She further failed to identify the intended target of her investigation, putting in jeopardy a large scale deconstruction project being performed under the authority of the City of Boston, who has registered a complaint with this office based on the interruption to the performance of the work at the job site. Had agent Hebert followed proper protocol in the discharge of her duties, this office would have been able to notify the proper City of Boston authorities and avoid any animosity between the agency and local government.

I request that Agent Hebert's immediate superior, Special Agent Maurice Bonet, place a formal reprimand in the file of Agent Hebert."

Any remaining good feelings from the beginning of the day were immediately destroyed when she exploded at her desk, figuratively, if not literally.

"That no good, lying, rotten, self-serving, self-absorbed, self-righteous, Son of A Bitch!"

Still fuming, the color in her face matching her now foul mood, she printed the attachment, ripped it from the printer, and stormed to her boss's office.

•   •   •

Not bothering to knock on either the door or its frame, the door being open, Agent Hebert entered the office of Agent Bonet like a Panzer Division on a blitzkrieg mission. Nothing but destruction could possibly ensue, including the destruction of the meeting currently taking place between Agent Bonet and another agent of the Art Crime Unit. When she finally noticed that her boss was not alone, she put on her brakes and stood, breathing hard, unable to speak, and visibly seethed. Agent Bonet, having never seen her in this state and having noticed the sheet of paper clutched and wilting under the weight of her fist, excused the bewildered agent sitting across from his desk. As the agent left, he closed the door behind him, knowing innately that this was going to be that kind of session. Agent Hebert had regained some small level of control in the interim, walked to the desk, remained standing as she unfurled her fist and held the sheet of paper in front of her, offering it to Agent Bonet. Wordlessly, her boss took the paper, laid it flat on his desk, ran his hand over it to smooth out the series of creases, and read. Having completed his perusal, he opened his web browser and checked his email. Finding the correspondence from Agent Stone, he opened it and confirmed that the attachment was identical to the one handed to him by his distraught agent.

Calmly, he said, "Star, please have a seat. Let's talk about this."

The calming tone of his voice had the desired effect and she sat, although stiffly.

"Okay, tell me what happened."

After taking a couple of deep breaths to further calm herself, she recounted the story of the previous day and her visit to Boston. She told him about discovering the body and her subsequent call to the local bureau field office. She chronicled what happened after the forensics team arrived on site and explained in detail her conversations with Agent Stone, including her rationalizations for not immediately contacting his office.

"The son of a bitch actually told me it was, and I'm quoting here, 'Good work'." Pointing at the piece of paper still lying on the desk, she said, "And then he goes and does that! I find a dead body missing for at least fifty years and this is how he thanks me!" Under her breath, she finished, "Asshole."

After hearing her out, Agent Bonet told her, again in a calm tone of voice, "I can understand why you're so upset, Star." Sitting back in his chair, he continued, "However, from a technical standpoint, he's correct. And, from what I've heard, technical standpoints are his bread and butter." Holding his hand up to cut off the coming protestations, he persisted. "But, I also have to consider your rather creative and, I might add, mostly valid reasons for not reporting in on your arrival." A hint of a smile leaked to his lips.

"Thank you, sir," was her truly humble reply.

Shaking his head, he responded, "Because he sent this," motioning to the crumbled paper, "I'm fairly certain he also sent it to others in his chain of command. As the ultimate decision is mine, I'm going to note that you did not contact him immediately upon your arrival, but positively state that your failure to do so was guided by your overwhelming desire to preserve evidence in a case where destruction seemed imminent. I will further commend you for your swift and appropriate actions and note that you were responsible for the discovery of the remains in the container." Now relaxed and smiling, he asked, "Is that satisfactory?"

Overcome with emotion, she looked away and didn't immediately respond. When she turned back to face him, she said, "Yes, sir. That is very satisfactory. Thank you." After a moment, she said, "And, I'm sorry I barged in here the way I did."

"Yes. About that. Let's not have a repeat. Understood?"

"Yes, sir. Again, thank you." As she rose from the chair to leave, she was interrupted by her boss, and again took a seat.

"Star, what case were you working on that sent you to Boston?"

Since this was totally within his purview, she thought nothing of it as she answered, "The 1970 Garden Museum art theft. You had assigned it to me a while ago."

"Oh yes. I remember now. Making any progress?"

"I guess it depends on what you mean by progress. I was able to follow a lead to Boston, where the museum was located, and was lucky enough to discover the cab and body. But, so far, no art."

Curious, he asked, "What kind of lead did you get in such an old case? I would think that everybody involved was either dead or long gone."

The warning alarm bells in her head had now started to loudly clang, traveling from the sub-conscious to the conscious at the speed of thought. She realized she was now in the place where she needed to tread very carefully, lest all the good that had just been done became unraveled.

"Well, sir, it's a confidential source that I'm not yet comfortable revealing."

A partial truth was better than an outright lie, especially if the whole truth were ever to come to light.

"A confidential source in a fifty-year-old case, huh?" he asked, skeptically. "I take it this 'source' is concerned about possibly incriminating himself or herself?"

Again not wanting to outright lie, she replied, "He or she is concerned about...repercussions, shall we say?"

He determined that now was not the right time to push this matter, so decided to let it go, for now. "OK, Agent Hebert. But be very careful with this 'confidential source,' won't you? Let's not cross any more lines."

Relieved, but trying her hardest not to show it, Agent Hebert again stood to take her leave, and replied, "Of course, sir. And, again, thank you."

With raised eyebrows, his only response was a non-committal, "Um hm."

. . .

As Agent Hebert reflected on the roller coaster of events and emotions she had just endured, she came to the realization that, no matter how much she would have liked to believe that things in the Bureau were getting better for her gender, the fact of the matter was that the deck continued to be stacked against her. Whether it was the disrespect and pandering she faced in the field from outsiders or the by-the-book male insiders, she now knew for certain that she needed to be more careful. Her attempt to manipulate Agent Stone, while seemingly successful, turned out to be anything but. On the other hand, it heartened her to have a boss that understood and didn't seem to care about gender in his dealings. He was fair and reasonable, and, he had shown, had her back. So, perhaps all hope was not lost, although he was definitely in the minority. That he had come from academia, as she had, may also have something to do with his attitude. Still, she had to remember to always be on the alert for those that would harm her career just because she was a woman. It was a lesson she would not soon forget or ignore.

GREAT, BUT WHAT ABOUT THE ART?

Based on my recent conversation with Agent Hebert, Star, it was apparent that our relationship had somehow transformed from that of information provider or source to, dare I say it, a friend, of sorts. Perhaps a confidant would be more accurate. I suppose one can be a confidant without actually being a friend, although, in my mind, the two go more hand-in-hand. In any event, it was evident that the relationship was not as it started. The reason behind my conclusion was that she had called me to vent. There was really no other reason for the conversation. We didn't discuss the state of our case, what our next moves might be, strategy, or my "watchings." We didn't talk about the weather or current affairs. What we talked about, and when I say we, I mean she, as I was there mostly to listen and lend support, was the current state of gender relations in the FBI, based specifically on her most recent experiences. She had previously told Adrian and me about her interactions with Agent Richard Stone while at the construction site. So, when she told me about his subsequent report and its contents, my initial reaction was, "What a Dick. His parents must have known from an early age." This at least elicited a laugh from Star, which helped to improve her increasingly fraught mood as she relived the day. After having told me about this most recent male betrayal, she spoke in general terms about how hard it's been in her career dealing with the bureaucratic patriarchy. Humans really are their own kind of cruel. While other species engage in their own forms of what we would judge, if we were anthropomorphizing, as cruelty, for the most part they do it as a matter of survival. Humans seem to have taken it to the level of sport and engage in it for sheer enjoyment. Listening to the stories she told me, not only about herself, but of others both in and out of the FBI, had me ashamed to be part of the male gender of our species. What our conversation brought home to me in a very definitive way was that my actions in moving forward with our investigation needed to be such that I didn't put her in a situation where anybody at the Bureau could place her career in jeopardy.

· · ·

I relayed to Adrian my conversation with Star. She was appalled, but by no means surprised. She was already accustomed to my rantings about the human species on this planet, so I spared her another round of my observations and theories. Instead, I opened a discussion about how to best proceed with our search for the art. I was struggling with how to advance the pursuit, having lost track of Jimmy once he left the shipping container site. I remembered I hadn't heard from Star about the results of tracing the license plate, so I shot her a quick text asking about it. Immediately, I received a response.

"Sorry, I should have told you before. Those plates were registered to a 1967 Chevy Impala, which had been reported stolen. Not all that surprising."

My verbal response was, "Well shit!", as I handed Adrian the phone so she could read the message.

"Well shit, is right," was how Adrian responded.

"I was hoping to get a location from those plates. Somewhere he might have gone. He could have literally driven to anyplace in the U.S. Hell, he could have gone to Canada or Mexico and then on to South America."

"Let's try to place ourselves in his shoes for a minute," suggested my wife.

"OK. Go on."

"If you had stolen something, you'd need to find somewhere to either store it or sell it, right?" she asked rhetorically.

I answered anyway. "I would. And, assuming that was how I made a living, I'd probably know people in the same business."

"Right, so you'd seek them out."

"Again, I would. So, assuming that I worked mostly in the Boston area, my contacts would be local?" I presented it as a question because I wasn't convinced.

Adrian considered the question and didn't immediately respond. At last, she said, "That's a good question, and really the crux of our problem, or at least one of them."

We both lost ourselves in thought for a few moments before I realized we weren't looking at it from Jimmy's standpoint at all. My body brought itself to attention, which Adrian immediately noticed, as I said, "But Jimmy is different. He was working in Boston, but he seemed to have had a long game in mind and created different identities to carry out the plan. I think he'd get outta Dodge, especially with a load of goods that were as hot as the art."

"Good points. OK, so if he left town to unload the art, where did he go?"

"I don't know, but I can guarantee that he had a plan. He didn't just drive around haphazardly looking for a suitable spot to stash the stuff while making a deal." I couldn't sit still any longer and paced as I thought and talked. "I still think he'd go to someone he knew. Somebody else with a criminal past. But the psycho was so good at hiding his identity that we don't even know if Jimmy Russo is his real name or where he's from. If he's at all like other people, in any way, he went somewhere familiar."

"That makes sense," agreed Adrian. "So, how do we figure out where?"

Still pacing, I didn't respond because I had no answer. She watched as I moved back and forth repeatedly. My mind was at a complete loss.

"Is there anything you've seen in your 'watchings' where you could go back and search, like with the cabby's name?"

I thought about the question and replayed the recollections in my mind. I thought about the different places I'd seen Jimmy, and the only place remotely personal was the hotel room. Even that didn't seem personal to him, but seemed more to reflect Mr. Martin. I couldn't think of anyplace else to revisit.

"I can't think of anyplace that would have any information," I said, more than a hint of dejection in my voice.

I returned to my place on the couch and we sat in silence, each deep in our own thoughts. After an indeterminate amount of time, I broke the silence and said, "I'm going to reach out to Star and see if there's anything she's come across that might help. I've got nothing."

She nodded her agreement, so I grabbed my phone and wrote a text to Agent Hebert.

"We're at a complete loss for how to find Jimmy. With the plates having been stolen, we have absolutely no idea where to even begin to look. Our best theory is that he had a plan and went to someplace where he was familiar with the territory and people. Someplace not Boston, because the art was too hot to do anything with locally. Probably somebody in the criminal world. If we had any idea where he was from, it could be helpful. Any ideas?"

I handed Adrian the phone and she reviewed the text. Nodding her assent, she handed it back, and I hit "Send."

Minutes went by as slowly as I'd ever experienced. At some point, my text notification sounded and I grabbed the phone. It was a reply from Star, which I read aloud.

"There may be something. I have a vague recollection but need to check my notes. Standby."

"It's better than telling us she has no clue."

"Yes, it is. Still a glimmer of hope," said my ever hopeful wife.

We both sat staring at my phone as if it were an oracle about to dispense ancient wisdom. After what seemed an eternity, the notification sounded. I grabbed the device, opened the text, and read aloud again.

"I checked my notes from the conversation I had with the ever charming Moretti. He said he thought he remembered hearing something, probably from a wire-tap or snitch, that the Don had heard Jimmy had some low-level relations in Detroit, or somewhere around there. That's the only information I can find. Hope it helps."

"Detroit. It's a place to start, at least," I said.

"Yep. It's definitely better than 'I have no idea.'"

I shot a quick reply back to Star.

"Thanks. At least it's a direction. You don't happen to know if Jimmy, or James, Russo is his real name, do you?"

The response was immediate.

"Sorry, no."

"It was worth a shot," I noted. I reread the prior text and needed to clarify something. I asked Adrian, "By 'low level' do you think she means in the criminal world?"

"I would think so, but let's not make any assumptions. Ask her."

I posed the question via text and was rewarded with an affirmative response.

"OK, so that fits with our theory about having criminal connections someplace not in Boston. And family would probably be a safe bet for him," I mused.

"I agree. Now let's decide how we're going to put this information to use."

•   •   •

With the internet at our fingertips, we each began our own search. I searched for "James Russo Detroit," "Jimmy Russo Detroit," "Russo Criminal Family Detroit," and, out of sheer desperation, "Crime 1970 Detroit," which produced enough information to make a set of Encyclopedia Britannica. Adrian, with whatever her searches were based on, was having the same level of success as me. We verbally compared notes and concluded that James or Jimmy Russo was not his name.

"Why am I not surprised?" I asked.

No answer being required, none was forthcoming. Once again, we found ourselves at a silent impasse. Grasping at straws, we broke the silence by batting different ideas back and forth, playing a sort of verbal tennis. After a few sets and no decision, I took a different tact.

"Let's start with what we know."

"We know Jimmy Russo is not his real name. We know James Russo is not his real name. We know he's a psychopath. We know he's a criminal. We know he was in Boston. That's my list," was Adrian's response.

"All true." I began my pacing, which somehow seemed to open pathways in my mind. "I can't help but feel that we're missing something."

We again let the silence descend as I continued pacing and Adrian continued thinking while anchored to a single location. I stopped so suddenly that I almost gave myself whiplash.

Looking at Adrian and holding her direct gaze, I said, as if a major revelation, "We know what he looks like."

Her less than enthusiastic response was, "OK. So how does that help?"

"If he was from Detroit, or the Detroit area, he probably went to school in the area, at least until he was of the age to drop-out. Something tells me he graduated from high school."

"OK?"

"If he went to high school, even for a year, there's a chance that his picture, and real name, are in a yearbook, somewhere."

Adrian instantly perked up, seeing where I was headed.

"And," she said, "there are websites filled with yearbooks going back decades from all over the country, just waiting for someone to search through those pictures."

"Exactly," I said with genuine enthusiasm for the first time in what felt like forever. "I think they even have some kind of search function. If we can upload your drawing and use that as a basis of a search, maybe we can find a match in a yearbook."

Catching my enthusiasm, she said, "I think I can find some software that can de-age my sketch. If I can do that, it should be easier to find a match, since he's going to be a lot younger in the yearbook than he was when you saw him."

"That would be outstanding," I responded.

"It would be. The only drawback is that this is going to take some time."

"I can live with that. At least we have a plan."

Having a plan seemed to give me a renewed sense of purpose. Not just the fact that we had a plan, but a plan for which I had high hopes.

. . .

During the week or so after Agent Hebert had returned from Boston, she thought it would be smart to keep as low a profile as possible. Word had already spread through the office about her Panzer attack, spread, no doubt, by the agent whose meeting had been destroyed. As was the case in most offices, regardless of size, the rumor mill was hard at work, coming up with various scenarios that could have caused such an outburst. Stories varied from her having had a run-in with a major muckety-muck (not too far from the truth) to having interfered with and screwed-up a major ongoing investigation. Word was that she had been disciplined and reprimanded, with serious career implications. She felt that, since the boss knew what actually happened, and noted as much in her file, her best course of action would be to keep her mouth shut and concentrate on work, which is exactly what she did.

She checked on the various searches she had started and discovered that Sean O'Shea had been listed as a missing person, with no sign that his remains had been found. She knew that identification could be a long process, but had hoped that the identification card found in the cab would have helped expedite the matter. Apparently not.

Not being able to focus on other matters, and having no plan as to how to proceed on the Garden Museum case, she let her mind drift in the hope of gliding straight into an idea. Instead, she found herself thinking about her most recent conversation with Josh. She had vented about what happened with Agent Richard Stone, or as she had come to think of him, Agent Dick. She wondered whether she had crossed a line in discussing FBI matters, but, as she thought about it, she concluded it belonged squarely in the "What the fuck" category. It felt good to have somebody to talk to that would listen and be supportive. It had been such a long time. Since her father's death, really. She knew there was no way anything she said to Josh would make its way back to anybody at the Bureau and, she felt, it was nice to have somebody with no reason to sabotage her career. The opposite, actually. It was best for him if she maintained as much credibility as possible. It was the only symbiotic relationship that she was currently involved with. For that matter, it may be the only such relationship she could ever remember being involved with. Their mutual success really depended on one another. She discovered she had missed not having such a relationship, if one could miss something of which they had been unaware. In any event, she was grateful to have somebody rely on her as much as she was reliant on them. Having come to that conclusion, line or no line, she was glad to have talked to him about it. Now, it was back to letting the mind find a path through the Garden Museum case.

The most recent texts from Josh had been in relation to Jimmy, his whereabouts and real name. She agreed that the key to finding the art, which was the ultimate goal, lie in finding this mysterious vagabond. If the Don was correct, there was a decent chance that Jimmy had headed West to the Detroit area. She instituted various searches for James Russo and Jimmy Russo, all centered on Detroit and its environs. Even with FBI resources at her command, she could get no further than Josh and Adrian had with their similar searches.

Sitting back in her chair and pausing to gather her thoughts, she reviewed what information she had about Jimmy. She knew he'd been in Boston. She knew he worked for Don Ricky. She knew from Josh's observations that he was both crafty and intelligent, having successfully fooled both the Don and FBI agents. She knew, also from Josh's observations, that he was a psychopath. She knew he was in a blue panel van sporting stolen license plates. Closing her eyes, she recited the list to herself repeatedly, hoping for something to jump out and bite her in the consciousness. No luck. She searched for her file on Jimmy and reviewed it in the off chance that she had forgotten something. She hadn't. She removed the drawing that Adrian had prepared and stared at it in an attempt to divine some new information. Nothing. In the act of replacing the sketch, she stopped and looked at it once again. Something gnawed at her mind. The more she stared, the more the gnaw. Finally, it gnawed its way to the forefront of her thoughts.

"I know what he looks like," she said aloud.

She felt gladdened by the revelation, but remained unsure why. Still holding the sketch and looking at it, she raised her eyebrows as she said, "Detroit. If the Don was right, and there's no reason to believe otherwise, Jimmy was from Detroit."

Quickly, she rolled her chair closer to her keyboard, opened her intra-agency directory, and found a contact in the Detroit field office. She prepared an email, explaining as best she could who the attached picture was, the approximate year in which it had been prepared (a necessary white lie) and informing her colleague of the various aliases of which she was aware. She asked if they could run the picture against their local database in the hopes of finding a match and the real name of the individual. Satisfied, she sent the correspondence on its way, pleased with herself at being able to, maybe, move the quest forward.

• • •

After work, Agent Hebert made her way to the bus stop and, whether or not she wanted to, found herself huddled together with the others waiting to end their workdays. Once the bus arrived, it was too crowded to find a seat, so she grabbed a hanging strap and hung on for dear life as the bus driver recreated what must have been an unsuccessful Formula 1 racing career. None of the passengers seemed to notice. At the Rhode Island Avenue stop, she squeezed through the remaining throngs of passengers, having a much more intimate experience than she was in the mood for.

She lived in Brentwood, a very nice neighborhood a short bus ride from the office. On the walk to her 1990s style apartment building, where she rented a spacious two-bedroom apartment, she stopped for takeout Chinese food. As she entered the restaurant, she was pleasantly greeted by name and handed a waiting bag of food, having paid for the order on-line. Continuing her walk, she found herself in the midst of similarly aged people, all of whom looked slightly familiar as they made this same pilgrimage most days of the week. People seemed to be friendlier than they were Downtown, perhaps because they were more relaxed, their work day being completed. Passersby greeted her and, just before she could escape into the safety of her building's foyer, she heard the familiar voice of one Brenton Moore. Closing her eyes and whispering, "Damn, so close," to herself, she turned to find Brenton, a nice looking twenty-seven-year-old attorney, dressed impeccably in a gray pinstriped suit, approaching from the other side of the street.

Trying for friendly, but not inviting, she non-committedly said, "Hi Brenton."

"Hey, Star. I'm glad I ran into you."

"Are you? Why is that?"

Laughing, he replied, "Always the suspicious FBI agent, aren't you?"

"I can't seem to help myself."

"I was hoping you'd be able to join me on Thursday at a firm cocktail party. Maybe we could have dinner afterward?" He'd been asking her out so often that he couldn't help but couch this latest attempt as a question.

Surprising herself, she placed her dinner bag on the ground, reached into a pocket, and extracted a business card. Holding it out to Brenton, she had to laugh at his expression, a mixture of total disbelief and elation. "Call me and we'll see how our schedules work out."

He couldn't grasp the card quickly enough. Knowing enough not to say anything to screw this up, he smiled and said, "I will. Have a great night." As he backed away, he glanced at the card, looked up and said, "Talk to you soon," before turning and walking down the street, a noticeable bounce to his step.

As she watched him make his way down the street towards his building, she smiled and said, "What the fuck?" Picking up her dinner, she continued into her building, checked her mail (nothing but advertisements and bills) and took the short elevator ride to the fifth floor, where she disembarked and made her way to apartment 255, which, for security purposes, didn't list the floor number first. Waiting outside her door was a 12" x 12" box wrapped in brown paper, clearly addressed to her. Placing her dinner on top of the box, she first opened her door and then bent to pick up the box and its passenger, noticing the return address of her mother. Entering the apartment and closing the door behind her, she placed the box on her coffee table and continued into the kitchen to eat her dinner before it got cold, not giving the package a second thought.

.   .   .

Adrian had been painstakingly working with the new software she had purchased to de-age her drawing of Jimmy. I had thought it would be a matter of uploading the drawing and pressing a big red button labeled "De-Age Now!" Shows you just how little I actually knew about technology, in any of its various shapes and forms. As with seemingly everything else, it was not as easy as it should have been. Had this been the only thing on her agenda, she could probably have completed the task in a few days. As it was, with everything else going on in life, she was able to work on it intermittently and, after a week, was to where she felt the drawing was good enough to use for a yearbook search. Okay, maybe she was a bit of a perfectionist. In any event, in order to get to the point of a search, she had to join a website set up for just that purpose, at a cost that I would have thought would be less than half of what it actually was. If this kept up, we'd really need that reward.

She'd set the search parameters both as narrowly and as broadly as we could think of in order to assure the best possible results. Having uploaded the de-aged picture and setting search parameters, she was finally to the point of pressing the "Search" button. The least they could have done was make that button a bright Victory Red in order to instill a sense of impending success, but, alas, their marketing team was probably too young to have ever heard of such a thing. With literally thousands of pages to peruse, there was nothing for us but to wait. And wait. And wait some more.

We had estimated Jimmy's age to be between thirty and thirty-five in 1970, which would put his year of birth between 1930 and 1935. To be on the safe side, we expanded the search parameters to include people born between 1925 and 1940. That was literally thousands of people that would have reached high school age between 1939 and 1954. During those years, Detroit was a booming industrial city, with a metropolitan area population of nearly 2,000,000 people, making it the fifth most populous city in America. Knowing this, it was no surprise that it took nearly a week to get the search results. When they arrived, fifty-seven potential matches confronted us. Apparently, it's not as exact a science as we thought. All possibilities were approximately the same age, height, hair and eye color, and all had lived within one hundred miles of Detroit. We had our work cut out for us.

We disobeyed our usual rule of not printing anything unless there was no other choice and printed a copy of each potential match. We then divided the stack into two piles and, with Adrian's original sketch and de-aged drawing prominently displayed in our lines of sight, we used separate computers to perform internet searches on each. We hoped to find more recent photographs to compare to the original sketch, some detail about the life of each, such as what they did for a living and the possible different locations in which they had lived, whether they were still alive, and other similar information. Anything to help us narrow the search. As I looked at the stacks, I was both heartened that the person we knew as "Jimmy" was possibly within grasp and disheartened by the number of possibilities with which we were faced. I could see that Adrian was feeling the same mixed emotions.

Over the ensuing four days, we spent whatever time we could spare trying to cull the stack. At the end of that time, we had narrowed the most promising possibilities to a list of five. We were both relieved that the number was not any larger. Five felt manageable. We both felt that we'd done all we could to narrow our list of suspects, based on the information available to the public. It was time to bring to bear the full power of the federal government, the heavy hitters, the big guns, the big honcho. The FBI. With the resources they had available, we knew it was time to let Agent

Hebert know what we'd done, share our results, and let her do what the FBI does. Investigate.

. . .

"That was fucking brilliant, you guys!" read the text from Star. She used her personal phone rather than risk sending a non-professional email over her work server.

After sharing it with Adrian, I responded, *"We thought so, too!"*

"I love the modesty! I'll send this to the Detroit office and have them add this to the search I've already had them start. IKYP."

I showed the reply to Adrian and had to ask. "IKYP?"

After giving it some thought, she said, "I'll keep you posted."

"Ah," was all I could say.

. . .

Thursday arrived and Agent Hebert was surprised to find herself behind the closed door of her office after hours and changing into a black cocktail dress, after which she moved her essentials, including her weapon, into a small black clutch. After a last check of her make-up and hair, she left her usual handbag locked in her desk drawer, turned off the lights, and headed to the law firm of Bellini, O'Rourke & Schwartz.

She had agreed to meet Brenton after work, since they both officed Downtown within a five-minute walk of one another. After spurning his advances for months, she had decided to embrace her new philosophy to the fullest. It had been quite a while since her last date and she had come to the realization that she missed the companionship, at least when the relationship was right. And, as some English playwright had said, therein lies the rub. The older she got, the less her capacity for dating bullshit. She found that concentrating on her work kept most of the dating bullshit at bay, although the increase in work bullshit seemed to take up the slack. Since it was essentially a bullshit trade-off, she thought she might as well get some enjoyment for her efforts. Those were the thoughts passing through her mind as she entered the swanky offices at which Brenton was striving to become a partner.

She took the elevator to the thirtieth floor, which was just one of ten floors occupied by the legal powerhouse. Wondering whether she should text her date and arrange a place to meet, she handed her coat to the coat check person, got her ticket and turned to find Brenton waiting for her off to the side. He smiled and waved to her, and she returned both gestures as she moved to his position. Uncertain how to make the proper greeting, he opted for the European air kiss, which amused Star.

"Hi. You look wonderful," was his opening gambit.

"Thank you. You look quite dapper yourself, as always."

Pleased, he offered his arm and said, "Would you care for a drink?"

She nodded, entwined her arm into his waiting appendage and said, "Lead on."

· · ·

As the evening progressed, both Brenton and Star became more comfortable with one another, and she found herself enjoying his company. It surprised her because she had always thought of lawyers as rather staid and boring, but he was engaging and funny. When she realized he reminded her of Josh, she wasn't quite sure what to make of that fact. Perhaps, she thought, my conception of lawyers was a misconception. It occurred to her that most people probably thought the same thing about FBI agents, which brought a secret smile to her face. As they were mingling, she saw a familiar face mixed in with the crowd. She excused herself and approached a man in his early thirties dressed in a black suit, white shirt and black tie, otherwise facetiously known as the FBI Uniform. Watching her approach, a look of horror, mixed with dread and fear, spread over his features. Seeing no escape, he succumbed to the inevitable.

Star noticed his reaction, even as he attempted to hide it, and countered with a beaming smile.

Tentatively, he returned the smile.

"Hi, Doug. I didn't expect to see you here."

"Hi Star. I can say the same."

"Hey, I never got the chance to apologize for breaking into your meeting with the boss. I must have come across as a crazy person. I'm sorry."

"Well, you certainly had a moment of insanity. I hope everything worked out."

"It did, thanks. The boss is the best. I'd just like you to know that he did not formally reprimand me and, in fact, turned the report into something most favorable."

"That's great, Star. I'm glad for you."

A smile plastered to her face, she continued. "Thank you, Doug. So, I'd just like to say that I'd really appreciate if you would stop spreading rumors about my mental state and the state of my career. If not, it's a game that two can play. I'm not keen to play it, but if you don't leave me a choice," she shrugged, "what can I say?"

He stared at her with a look of confusion etched on his features. "Star, I don't know what you're talking about. I would never spread rumors." The slight involuntary twitch in his eye belied the truthfulness of his statement.

Moving closer to Doug, she lowered her voice as she said, "Doug, please don't insult my intelligence like that. I've heard you. It's hard enough at the Bureau for someone with a vagina, so don't make it any harder. You don't want me becoming the insane bitch that you perceive me to be, do you?" Stepping back, she saluted him with her drink and said, "Thanks, Doug. See you at work."

Returning to Brenton, who was deep in conversation with a colleague, she could feel Doug's gaze boring a hole through her back. Crossing the room, she noticed Doug was not the only person wearing the unofficial uniform. Letting her eyes roam, she noticed quite a few agents, some of which looked familiar, most of which were strangers. "Interesting." She hadn't realized how closely aligned with a law firm a federal agency could become, but she was learning.

As she reached her destination, Brenton pulled himself away from his conversation, smiled, and introduced her to his colleague, Jessica Davis. After exchanging introductory pleasantries, Star asked if there were many women at the firm and was surprised to learn that approximately twenty percent of the three hundred or so attorneys were woman.

"It's definitely better than it used to be, but there's still a long way to go," opined Jessica. "What about at the FBI?"

Glancing momentarily back at Doug, Star replied, "It seems as if the world of law is far ahead of the Bureau. It's definitely an uphill struggle. Hopefully, we'll get there."

Jessica gracefully disengaged from Brenton and Star, leaving the two alone for the first time since Star arrived at the party. Watching as an empty hors d'oeuvre tray passed by, a look of disappointment found its way to Star's expression. Noticing, Brenton laughed and asked, "Hungry?"

"Famished!"

"Me, too. I think I've fulfilled my obligations. Let's go eat."

• • •

They walked down the street to a modern, fashionable bistro where, after a brief wait, they were escorted to a table along a far wall with a view out to the street. The interior was dimly lit, but sufficient to read the menu and observe the surroundings. The noise level was such that, if they sat close together, they could hear one another over the din, creating a sense of intimacy that would otherwise have been lacking. Since it was near to where they both worked, they had both previously been patrons, adding to the feeling of general comfort each felt.

They were enjoying drinks while waiting for an appetizer when Star said, "I noticed quite a few FBI agents at the party." With a twinkle in her eye, she continued, "Am I an attempt to meet some kind of quota?"

Without missing a beat, Brenton smiled and said, "Yes. We're each required to go on at least one date a month with an FBI agent and to bring them to a firm function as proof." Pausing a beat to watch her, he continued, "You must be an extraordinary agent to have ferreted that scheme out so quickly."

Playing along, Star replied, "Oh, I am. It just shows that you choose well."

"I believe I did," he said as he raised his glass in a toast, to which she acceded by the obligatory clinking of glasses.

"Really, why were there so many agents there?"

"It's D.C. and we're a large law firm. We get a lot of business from the government. There's always some politician, politician's aide, lobbyist, fund raiser or FBI agent lurking about."

"So, your firm does work for the Bureau?"

"Firm folklore has it that the original founders of the firm were close with Hoover himself."

"Well, that doesn't really speak too well for them, does it?" she half joked.

"Ha. No, it doesn't. But it seems to have been good for business, don't you think?"

"Apparently so." Sipping from her nearly empty glass, she asked, "What kind of work does the firm do with the Bureau? Do you do any? I don't want either of us to run afoul of any conflict rules."

Quickly, he said, "Oh, no, I'm not involved in that. I work mostly in the real estate area. You know, developers taking small tracts of dirt and creating mega giant buildings. Nothing the FBI need get involved with."

"So, what work does the FBI need to get involved with?" She was determined not to let this go, just yet.

Pondering the question, he took a sip from his dwindling supply and answered, "You know, I'm not really certain. I'd heard that, back in the day, we helped unravel some corporate matters that the mob used to try to hide assets. Straw men, shell companies, off-shore accounts, that sort of thing. Why do you ask?"

"Just curious." Deciding it would be acceptable to share some of what she was doing, without breaching any confidences, she said, "I'm working on a cold case that also involved a Bureau investigation into organized crime and it made me wonder what a law firm could have done. Interesting."

Just then, the server appeared with refills of their drinks and a Thai calamari appetizer. They watched it land on the table and, with mouths nearly salivating, attacked the dish.

• • •

She had ignored the package from her mother long enough. The relationship with her mother was a complicated one. There was no doubt about there being mutual love, but the abandonment of her father those many years ago was still a raw, open wound that refused to heal and colored all dealings with her mother. The contents of the box could either be salt on that wound or a temporary band-aid. Her life had recently taken a pleasant turn, and it all seemed to coincide with her being contacted by Josh and Adrian. She had broken down and gone out with Brenton, which turned out to be an excellent decision. She had seemingly made strides at work, with the pleasant surprise of her boss's backing. She felt herself coming into her own. She found herself reluctant to delve into the boxes' content for fear of upsetting the new status quo. Rational or not, she was honest enough with herself to realize the truth. The box had moved from the coffee table to the floor on the side of her couch, where it sat unopened and, mostly, ignored for days. At home during the day on a weekend, she confronted her dilemma and, having decided, reached for the box and tore it open.

Inside, she found an old sweater she had left at her mother's, a box of homemade cookies and, at the bottom, a folded piece of paper sitting atop a black and white speckled note book. She removed the paper, unfolded it to find a handwritten note, and read.

"Star, you had asked whether your father had written anything about his visions and I told you that, if he did, he didn't share them with me. That was the truth. Until you asked, I hadn't thought to look, but since you did, I looked through some boxes that had been stored in the garage. I found this notebook. I don't know if this is what you're looking for and haven't read it. If he didn't want me to see it then, I'll respect his wishes now.

Star, please, please be careful. Sometimes when you dig for something, what you find is not what you'd hope for or expect. I don't want you getting hurt.

Love, Mom."

She held the notebook in one hand, running the other hand gently over the cover with clear reverence. She sat like that for nearly five minutes before she opened the cover. Inside, she saw the shaky script of her father. He'd used a blue ball-point pen that, if he paused on the page, left a little glob of ink. She touched one of these globs and was surprised to find the ink rub off on her finger. It also surprised her to have to wipe a tear from the paper, not having realized she was crying.

• • •

I don't know what's happening to me and I'm scared. Donna don't want to hear about any of this. I think she's scared about what people are gonna say. Hell, I'm scared too. I got nobody I can talk to to figure this out, so I'm going to write down some thoughts.

First of all, when I say I had visions, I mean what I say. I saw Sheriff Joe doing terrible things to a little girl. I couldn't stop him. It was like I was there, but I wasn't there. I know I wasn't dreaming, cause dreaming is different. I can't explain it any other way. Anyway, the Sheriff was at his property, the one he lives at. It's a large property, probably 30 or 40 acres. There's some outbuildings, like a barn and a shed. What I seen wasn't in no building, though. It was underground, I'm sure. I could feel the dampness and see the dirt floor lit up by the hangin' string of light bulbs. Gave everything a yellowish tone. The Sheriff was younger than he is now. So, I'm guessing that what I saw happened a while ago. I don't know when. I tried to stop it, I really did, but there was nothing I could do. When I woke up from this vision I was scared and crying. Thinking about it now makes me want to cry. I told people about it, but nobody would believe me. Can't say that I really blame them, though. I probably wouldn't believe it if it was somebody else's story.

I hope to God this don't happen again.

·   ·   ·

Star set the book aside and let herself cry. The wound in her soul was torn open afresh; deeper and wider than at any time since she was a child. She placed a palm on the notebook and sobbed, letting out long held emotions. She felt for her father in a way which had been previously impossible, never knowing what his experiences had been like. She cursed her mother for not being more understanding and helping the person whom she supposedly loved, for better or worse. And she revisited and renewed her rage at Sheriff Joe.

· · ·

It happened again. Damn it! I saw Sheriff Joe doing terrible things to a young girl, and I swear it was a different girl. Looked a little like the other one, but I think a little older. Maybe 9 or 10. I still tried to stop it, but couldn't do anything. Just like the last time, it was like I was there and not there. He was at the same place, I'm sure. Underground.

Nobody believes me!!! I don't know what to do! I need to do something. This has to stop. He needs to be stopped!!! I don't know how.

The headaches are getting worse every time this happens. Brain tumor? Could that be what's causing it?

· · ·

Star had to stop reading. The raw emotion of her father's suffering was too much. As committed as she had been to bringing Sheriff Joe to justice, she now knew that she'd never be able to rest until the truth came out.

· · ·

I'd never spoken to anyone in such a torn state of emotions as Star had been after reading part of her father's journal. She called me shortly after opening the package from her mother. She hadn't quite processed what she'd read, and I'm not sure she'll ever really be able to. I felt a sense of responsibility toward her since it was my introduction to "watchings" that had revealed what her father had really experienced. Sometimes I think certain things are best left undiscovered, but I knew, in the long run, knowing the truth about her father would be for the best. No coincidences. I found her because she was the only one in a professional position with the type of life experience that could help our quest. She had found me because, to our knowledge, I was the only one on the planet who could bring her the peace for which she so longed.

WELCOME TO DETROIT

In the office on Monday morning, Agent Hebert attacked the Garden Museum file with renewed fervor. Instead of emailing, she called the Detroit field office, asking for Agent Brian Mulveny, to whom she had sent both her initial request and the follow-up with the information from Josh and Adrian. Frustrated that he wasn't available, she left a voice mail message, stressing the urgency of a reply. She felt in her bones that the key to breaking the case was the real identity of Jimmy Russo. She found herself gazing at the sketch prepared by Adrian, still unable to ascertain any hidden truths.

"Damn!"

Nothing else to be done, in this matter, she turned her still divided attention to other cases. Checking email, returning telephone calls, speaking with an insurance adjuster. The typical day. Nothing from Mulveny.

Having been gone and back from lunch, she could not contain herself any longer and redialed Agent Mulveny. Voicemail. She checked the clock and realized that, with the differences in time zones, he was probably still at lunch.

"Damn!"

An hour later, she tried again. This time, he was in and answered his phone.

"Hello Agent Hebert. I was just about to call you back."

"Yeah, right," she thought. Aloud, she said, "Thank you. What have you been able to find?"

"I'll email the findings over, but with the original sketch and the additional research, which, by the way, was a great idea, good job, I think we were able to find your guy. Johnny Ricardo. Same initials as Jimmy Russo, which is a fairly common thing to do. He was born in 1935 and graduated from Horace Mann High School in 1953. From the records, it looks like he did pretty well in school. Smart kid. Anyway, he'd be 85 years old, if he's still alive. We have no record of his death. Not much about his life, either."

"What about family? Did he have any in the area?"

"Funny you should ask. His dear old dad, who, by the way, was named Jimmy, or more accurately, James, and his Uncle Pete, were low-level hoodlums. They tried for their entire lives to move up in the organization but really never became more than street hoods and enforcers. It seems that Johnny took off, leaving his cousins to inherit the family business, such as it was."

"Do you have his cousin's names, maybe some pictures? I don't care if the pictures are old, like from high school."

"I'll get you his family information, at least what we have. They all lived in the same general area, so there should be high school photos. Maybe even the odd mug shot or three. Give me an hour or so and it'll be in your Inbox."

Relieved beyond belief, she thanked Agent Mulveny profusely. "I can't tell you how much I appreciate this, Brian. Thank you so much. Bye."

She was determined to disconnect the call before he could ask why she wanted the information.

True to his word, the file was in her Inbox an hour later.

• • •

I heard the melodious tone of my email notification and opened my Inbox to find an email from Star.

"Check out the attached and let me know what you think. I think we struck gold!"

I opened the attachment, which was a rather large Zip File, and clicked on the first folder. It opened, and I saw what we hoped was the Holy Grail. "Johnny Ricardo."

"Oh my God. I think we actually found him!"

I quickly checked the other folders. High school transcripts. Family history. Family criminal history. Names. Pictures. Addresses.

I sent off a quick reply.

"I haven't digested the entire file, but, Holy Crap! I think the FBI just lived up to the 'I' part of its name. I'll get back to you after we've reviewed what we have and discussed the best way to go about landing in the right place and time."

"Outstanding!"

Her response was an emoji.

• • •

Adrian and I spent many hours over the next few days poring over the material. We learned about Johnny's father, Jimmy, and his uncle, Pete, mostly through copies of their rap sheets, which were extensive. Born into this type of family, we wondered what chance Johnny ever had to get out of the life, even being as smart as he was. Had he the proper support, he could probably have gone to college and fashioned a very successful career as a businessman, lawyer or, based on what we'd seen of his ability to transform into other characters, an actor. But that wasn't the case. Most of his male relatives had spent time in jail, including his father, uncle, and cousins, Billy and Pete, Jr.

James Ricardo, Johnny's father, died in 1969 at the age of 58. The cause of death was lung cancer. Certainly, the eight years in various prisons didn't help his health.

His Uncle Pete, James' brother and business partner in all things, from the looks of the records, followed later that same year from complications arising from emphysema and pneumonia. Again, the seven years he'd spent in various prisons probably didn't help his lifespan, either.

That left Billy and Pete Jr. to try to make ends meet. Curiously, the records omitted anything about the women that could have been in Johnny's life, namely his mother and aunt.

Pete Jr. was the closest to Johnny in age. They lived within a few blocks of one another and attended Horace Mann High School at the same time, although Pete was a freshman when Johnny was a junior. There were a few pictures of Pete, Jr. and Johnny, usually in sports uniforms of some sort. Baseball and football, mostly. Apparently, they were Tiger's fans. There was no indication of whether they stayed in touch with each other once Johnny left town and became Jimmy, among others. Sports aspirations aside, Pete Jr. followed in his father's footsteps. He worked the street for a local mobster, running numbers and enforcing. He appeared to have a legitimate job for a short time, since IRS records showed income from a local business named "Gloria's Glorious Containers." He died in a car crash in 1970. Pictures from the scene showed a mangled 1960 Ford Galaxie sedan under a Mack truck, crushed to the point that anybody inside would have been absolutely annihilated. Pete Jr. was inside at the time.

Less information was available about Billy. Two years younger than his brother, Pete Jr., it seemed that he stopped attending school in eighth grade. A string of arrests led to long-term incarceration for felony homicide. While on a burglary job, his partner shot and killed a homeowner. It didn't matter that Billy didn't pull the trigger; the homicide was on him as much as it was on the triggerman. He died in prison of an apparent suicide.

All of this information was interesting and gave us some insight into Johnny Ricardo/Jimmy Russo. What it didn't do was get us any closer to the art. We needed to find a way into the past that would lead us to Johnny. Since my other "watching" experiences had been kick-started by visual cues, we thought pictures would be the best entry method. To that end, we scoured the internet.

A family such as Johnny's did not, it seemed, plaster their images on the internet, especially from a time before the internet existed. Hard to imagine at this point, I know. As for after the internet was popular, it was unclear if there was any family still alive. The bottom line was that we were unsuccessful in finding anything that might serve as a visual launching point for my time/space adventure to Detroit.

Predicated on the information provided by the FBI search, it seemed to us that the person most likely to have been contacted by Johnny upon his return to Detroit was his cousin Pete. Based on the date of his death, Pete should still have been alive when Johnny completed his excursion. That is, barring any unscheduled stops, scheduled stops of which we were unaware, van trouble, or any of the other myriad possibilities that could have occurred during his journey. So, we concentrated on finding Pete. Or rather, on attempting to find Pete. Pete was an internet ghost. Part of a family of internet ghosts. No pictures online, other than an old grainy head shot that accompanied the story of his death. Just his head. No context as to time or location. It could very possibly have been a copy of one of his mug shots, since those seem to be his most frequent picture taking opportunities. We searched for information on "Gloria's Glorious Containers," only to find absolutely nothing. Our assumption was that it had closed decades ago, and no trace remained.

Of course, there were no pictures of Johnny. The FBI, which had checked local police records as part of their investigation, had no record of his return to Detroit. Assuming, for the sake of argument, and our sanity, that he actually went to Detroit, there was nothing to indicate how long he stayed. A family of internet ghosts.

Once again we employed the tactic of listing what we knew about the subject of our search, in this case, Pete, Jr. We knew he was close in age to Johnny. We knew he and Johnny grew up in close proximity to one another. We knew he and Johnny had played sports together. We knew he was a petty criminal. We knew he was dead. Adding it all up came to a sum of exactly...bupkis. Nada. Nothing. We concluded it was once again time to put the "I" in FBI to work. I prepared and sent an email to Agent Hebert.

"*Star, Adrian and I have spent hours reviewing the information you have provided. In our estimation, the most likely person to have been contacted by Johnny Ricardo upon his return to Detroit would have been his cousin, Pete Ricardo, Jr. We have searched the internet in vain for a picture of Pete Jr. that would serve as a visual cue for my excursion.*

Here is our list of what we know about Pete Jr.:

He was close in age to Johnny. He and Johnny grew up in close proximity to one another. He and Johnny had played sports together. He was a petty criminal. He's dead. We think he may have once worked at some place called Gloria's Glorious Containers, but can find no information on what is most likely a long defunct business of some sort.

We thought we'd give your crack team of investigators another shot at this before we move on to Plan B, whatever that might be. Let us know if you have a brainstorm.

Thanks.

J&A"

. . .

Agent Hebert was out of the office when the email from Josh and Adrian reached her inbox. In fact, she was having dinner with Brenton, an occurrence that was becoming more frequent, much to her pleasant surprise. Each of them had their phones on the table, so when the alert tone voiced itself, she glanced down in time to see who had sent the message. Attempting to ignore it, she continued to eat, but became noticeably distracted.

Brenton said, good-naturedly, "If you need to check that, go ahead. I can tell you're itching to."

She exhaled a sigh of relief and said, "Thank you," as she reached for the phone and opened her email app. Reading the message, a look of disappointment showed.

"Is it bad news?" asked Brenton, concerned.

Resuming her meal, she said around chews, "No, not really. It's just not the definitely positive news I was hoping for."

"Personally, or about a case?"

Smiling at him with genuine affection, she said, "Personally, things are great. It's about a case."

"Can you tell me about it or is it one of those double secret probation things?"

Laughing, she replied, "An *Animal House* fan, huh? In that case, I can tell you about it."

She gave him a general outline of the Garden Museum case, of course leaving out the whole space/time continuum thing. She told him, again in general terms, about the prime suspect, how he had fooled both the FBI and a mob boss into thinking he was just a low level street punk, when in fact he had out-thought everybody. She explained how they thought he had fled to Detroit with the art and gave him Johnny/Jimmy's family background.

"The kid never really had a chance, did he?" asked Brenton.

"It seems not. Under other circumstances, he could have been a legitimate whatever he wanted. But I have the feeling that he'd still have been a psychopath. Just a high-functioning psychopath."

"So, you're trying to tie this guy into some family in Detroit?"

"We are. We're going on the theory that he would have gone back someplace familiar, especially if in that place were familiar people with criminal contacts. Detroit fits the bill."

"We?" asked an inquisitive Brenton.

She looked at him with an inquisitive look and said, "Yes, we. Why?"

Brenton could see that her hackles were beginning to come up and laughed, holding both hands up in surrender. "Just wondered. You never mentioned anything about working as part of a team within the ACT, that's all." Laughing, he said, "Don't get all FBI on me."

Laughing in return, she said, "Sorry. I guess I'm a little suspicious by nature. Goes with the whole FBI thing, you know?"

"I get it," he said. "It's kind of the same with attorneys, even if we don't all go to court and cross-examine witnesses. Part of our DNA, I guess."

Hackles visibly withdrawn, she said, "To answer your question, I'm working with a confidential informant, of sorts."

"Of sorts?"

"Yes." She continued to eat what remained of her meal.

Brenton resumed eating his meal as he said, "Sounds mysterious."

"Oh, it is, truly."

They continued in silence for a few moments when Brenton said, "Hey, you said something about your suspect's relative. About his having worked somewhere."

"I did." Glancing back at the email message, she said, "Someplace called 'Gloria's Glorious Containers.' Apparently, it's long gone. Why?"

"Do you remember when you asked me about the firm's work for the FBI?" She nodded her assent, so he continued. "Well, it's my understanding that we have a certain level of expertise in unraveling corporate structure mysteries. Maybe I could help with that."

She paused, fork almost at her mouth, placed the fork onto her plate, and said, "Really?"

Pleased, he said, "Really. Get me whatever information you have and I'll have somebody check it out."

The food having finally found its mark, she smiled, trying not to lose what she was chewing, and said, "Brent, that would be great. Thank you."

As he excused himself to go to the men's room, she grabbed her phone and sent off a quick, cryptic reply to Josh.

"Working on it. Give me a couple of days."

The roller coaster of emotions in this job just never ended.

·   ·   ·

I received Agent Hebert's brief reply and gave her a couple of days. It wasn't as if I really had a choice. After those couple of days had passed, I resisted the urge to send a smart-ass email, thinking that, between Agent Dick, her mother, and her father's journal, she'd already had enough crap thrown her way. That's me showing my sensitive side.

Two days after the deadline of her original couple of days, we received a response.

"Josh & Adrian:

I had a friend at a large law firm in town check out Gloria's Glorious Containers. This is what he was able to discover:

It was a corporation formed in 1966 by a Detroit attorney, William Blair. Mr. Blair was listed as the registered agent, President and Secretary of the company. In 1968 a change of officer form was filed with the State of Michigan in which a Peter Ricardo, Sr. was listed as the new Secretary of the corporation. The corporation was involuntarily dissolved in 1972. It owned the property on which the business was located, with a mortgage held by a local bank. The mortgage was foreclosed in 1974. The property is located at 4819 E. Davison Street and is currently owned by The Sorenson Companies. The registered agent, President and Secretary of the Sorenson Companies is a Detroit attorney, William Blair, Jr.

Gloria's Glorious Containers was a self-storage facility. Gloria was William Blair, Sr's mother. The property seems to be basically vacant, except for a few remaining storage lockers, although there's no way to tell from the paperwork.

William Blair, Sr., was known to represent clients in the employ of the Zerrilli crime family. His son has taken over the law firm.

J&A, I copied and pasted the above from my friend at the firm. I was excited to see Peter Sr., listed on the paperwork. It's a definite link to the family. And, the fact that it was a storage facility fits as well.

I hope this is enough for you to prepare for your journey.

Star"

Adrian and I both read the information. We agreed that the fact of Pete Sr.'s involvement was an exciting discovery, even if we couldn't figure out what to do with it. It was good to know that there was a possible meaningful link. After all, the van had been stored in a shipping container. Could Jimmy/Johnny be following established patterns? Most people do, whether or not they realize the fact. Do psychopaths? I would think so, at least to some degree. If he was going to store the van, absent having a private garage under his control, a storage facility at which his cousin worked seemed like a logical choice.

As we discussed the possibilities, we concluded that, absent the kind of visual cue to which I had become accustomed, we were going to have to come up with a new, untested launch method. A daunting and more than a little terrifying prospect. We had Jen's magic elixir, but the purpose of it was simply to mediate my headache upon return. I didn't think that the potion had any effect on what happened in my revisit. My gut told me that the control was due to the fact it was my second time at that "watching," but neither of us could really say for certain. We tossed around different variations on launching methods, and finally settled on a type of meditation. We used Google Earth to get an actual picture of the location, hoping that, even though it might not be identical to how it appeared in 1970, it could still act as a frame of reference. Using the information at hand, after downing Jen's concoction, and trying not to vomit, I would concentrate on a location (Gloria's Glorious Containers), person (Johnny/Jimmy), and time frame (arrival at Gloria's). Without having an exact time, that last was a definite leap of faith. Then again, this entire process was a leap of faith, so what the hell? We scheduled my journey for the next night.

. . .

I find my consciousness outside the gates of Gloria's Glorious Containers, as identified by the garish pylon sign. It's light out, and based on the location of the sun above, it appears to be between 1:00 p.m. and 2:00 p.m. I try moving through the gates, mentally, and am unable to do so. I am able to focus my attention on different locations within my view. I just can't change the point of view, which matches what I could and couldn't do in the revisit. I attempt to fast forward to a different time, but, again, am unable to do so. I "stand" rooted to my current location, uncertain if I am anywhere near my target date.

As I have nothing else to do but wait, I notice that very little traffic is going on around me, either pedestrian or vehicular. Across the street is what appears to be a construction company, or more accurately, a storage area for a construction company's equipment.

Behind a locked gate is various equipment, heavy and otherwise. Dump trucks, diggers of various sizes, cranes, tanks for acetylene torches, and other items I don't recognize. On either side of the construction storage area are empty lots. I surmise that it is possible that the same shady company that owns Gloria's also owns the construction storage lot, construction seeming to be a lucrative business for organized crime. They probably even own the empty lots that border the construction storage location.

Other than that, nothing. No cars or trucks come or go. No people walk by. This is about as secluded a location as I thought one would be able to find within the confines of a large metropolitan area.

I wait like that for an indeterminate amount of time, time flowing at a different rate than I am accustomed to in my version of reality. From the movement of the sun, I estimate that at least two hours have passed. I begin to ready myself to call it a failure and attempt to return to my time and reality when I see a vehicle approach from two blocks away. A blue van. There are plenty of blue vans, so I don't want to get my hopes up, but as it continues its approach, it becomes clear this is the van for which I am waiting. Through the windshield, wearing dark sunglasses, I can see Johnny Ricardo/Jimmy Russo. Ever the law-abiding citizen, he puts his turn signal on as he approaches the driveway for Gloria's, slows to make the turn, and comes to a stop. He reaches out the window and punches a code into the primitive-looking keypad, causing the closed gate to roll to the side, creating a gap wide enough to drive through, which he does. Suddenly, I am pulled along, following closely behind the van as it drives to the main office, where Johnny pulls into a waiting parking space.

He doesn't immediately get out of the vehicle and I can't tell what he's doing. There is no visible movement which I can detect. Then, the driver's side door opens, my point of view suddenly shifts, and I watch as Johnny exits the vehicle and approaches the closed office door. I can feel the weariness and trepidation that emanates from him as he makes his approach. I had expected joy and relief, but that is most definitely not what I am experiencing. He reaches for the door handle, hesitates for a split second, as if having second thoughts about entering, and finally opens the door and walks through, pulling my mind along with him.

Fluorescent bulbs, one of which flickers intermittently, illuminate the office. I can smell the bad ballast. There's a row of three old red vinyl seats along one wall, dirty and torn, as if nobody cares if they ever see use. The counter is old, yellowing linoleum, speckled and dirty. On the wall behind the counter are posters announcing rental rates and the rules of the establishment. Nobody mans the desk, but as the door closes, a bell rings somewhere and a door, which is somehow hidden behind the counter, opens, revealing the slow motion dispersal of a man dressed in blue jeans and a red checked work shirt, large belly preceding muscular arms and a neck as thick as a Detroit phonebook of the day. As he glares at the man waiting on the other side of the counter, the deep scowl that seems to be permanently etched onto his face somehow becomes deeper and more menacing.

He slowly continues to the counter, stands directly in front of Johnny, and silently assesses his long-lost cousin. After an eternity he says, "Well, you piece of shit, you really have balls calling me and then actually showing up."

Johnny attempts a smile and says, "It's nice to see you, too, Jr. You're looking svelte." The sarcasm is dripping from Johnny, who seems impervious to Pete's attitude.

"Fuck you, Johnny. Why are you here?"

"Can't I drop in to visit my favorite cousin?" he innocently asks.

"No," Pete spits out. "You've been gone, what, 10, 15 years? Not a word. Didn't show up when your dad died. Didn't show up when my dad died. Left me in this shithole of a town to deal with both of 'em without a thought about what that would do to me. Then, out of the blue, there you are on the phone and, now, standing in front of me. So, I'll ask you one last time before I beat the shit out of you, why are you here?" He makes no attempt to hide the menace that lurks.

Without hesitation, Johnny says, "I need your help."

Unable to control himself, Pete Jr., laughs, that enormous belly bouncing as if it were a basketball being dribbled down court. "Now that really is rich." Motioning to his surroundings, he continues. "Mr. genius himself comes to my castle and actually needs my help. What happened, cousin," the venom in that last word being evident, "did one of your genius schemes backfire? Need some protection?"

Leaning on the counter with one elbow, Johnny says, "Actually, one of my genius schemes worked to perfection and I find myself in need of storage facilities." Looking around, he says, "it seems you're in the perfect business."

Not wanting to help his wayward cousin, but craving information about what could cause him to seek his help, Pete Jr. doesn't beat the shit out of Johnny before throwing him out, although I could feel his desire to do just that. Instead, he says, "No thanks to you, asshole. I keep an eye on the place for the boss, who finds it a handy way to stash certain goods that may have been obtained less than honestly. I'm not sure he'd want you as a client."

"But I'm the perfect client, Pete. I'll fit right in."

"Tell me," is all Pete says.

Considering what to say, Johnny just stares at Pete, not really wanting to let him know exactly what he has. I could feel the distrust between the cousins.

Dismissing Johnny with a wave of his hand, Pete says, "As honest and trustful as ever, I see." Turning to head into the backroom, he says, "Get the fuck out, Johnny."

Impulsively, Johnny says, "Wait!", stopping Pete in his tracks. Pete turns back to Johnny and just looks at him, letting the silence fill the space between them.

"Listen, I have some very valuable material and I just need a place to stash it while I line up a buyer. I'll cut you in. It's worth a fortune."

As Johnny waits, Pete returns to his spot behind the counter. "I need to know what you've got and see it before I agree to anything. I'm not gonna be played by you anymore. Understood?"

Agreeing, Johnny says, "Understood."

Johnny turns and walks to the door, followed by his wary cousin. As they approach the van, Johnny turns to Pete and says, "I need a unit large enough to drive this," motioning to the van, "into it."

"Won't be a problem," replies Pete. "Open it."

I know I'm not present in the corporeal sense, but I could feel the anticipation surging through my being. If I'd had a chest, the pounding of my heart would have been visible to the naked eye.

Reluctantly, Johnny agrees. With one of the back doors open, Pete leans in, blocking my view. I want to shove him out of the way and get in there, but I am helpless. Finally, he moves out of the way long enough for me to see frames and statuettes wrapped in protective blankets before Johnny slams the door shut.

The art! Holy crap, I've actually found the art!

"So, what is it?" asks a bewildered Pete.

"It's art," is the condescending reply.

"I know that, shithead. What's the deal? Why is it so valuable?"

Sighing, Johnny says, "Did you hear about the Garden Museum theft in Boston? Beginning of the year?"

Thinking, a look of recognition finds Pete's jowly face. "Yeah." Pointing to the van, he asks, "You?"

Johnny just nods his head.

Impressed, Pete says, "Maybe you *are* as smart as you always thought you were, after all."

"Maybe."

"So, what's my cut?"

As if having already considered this, Johnny immediately says, "I'll pay you 10 grand from the sale of the first piece."

I could hear Pete thinking, "Bastard thinks I'll settle for a mere 10 grand. Fuck him." To Johnny he says, "You cheap bastard.

If this is worth as much as you think, I want 20K from the first sale and from every sale after that, too."

Johnny thinks to himself, "All part of the game." To Pete he says, "20K from the first and 10K from the others."

"15" is the quick reply from Pete.

"Deal," says Johnny as he holds out his hand, which Pete eagerly shakes.

"Wait here while I find a container big enough for this thing and get a lock."

As Pete walks back inside, my focus remains with Johnny as I hear him think, "That wasn't as bad as it could have been." It's evident that he was expecting much worse, both as a reception and deal.

The door opens as Pete comes back, padlock in hand. He approaches the passenger door of the van, opens it and, not seeing Johnny moving to the driver's side, yells, "Let's go!"

Awakened from his reverie, Johnny gets into the van and looks at Pete, who says, "Back out. I'll direct you to the container."

Johnny does as directed, having a distinct feeling of déjà vu, harkening back to the storage container facility at which he disposed of the cabbie, with him playing the part of the cabbie. He thinks, "It's a good thing Pete never had the killer instinct that I do."

The target container is in the next-to-last row, out of view of the office or any street. Johnny looks around and notices that all the containers in this and the last row are of the same large size. Satisfied, he stops the van and lets Pete out. Pete opens the container door, revealing a large, empty space, easily able to accommodate the van. Pete motions for Johnny to drive in and steps to the side, out of the way.

Johnny drives the van into the container, turns the engine off, and leaves the keys in the ignition. He wants to make sure he knows exactly where they are when he needs them. He sees his cousin waiting for him at the open door, smiles and, as he walks toward him, says, "Thank you, Pete. I appreciate this. You won't regret it." It's almost as if he is sincere.

Pete steps out of the way, behind the front of the door, so that he can close and lock it, forcing Johnny to move away from the frame and wait for the door to clear his view of Pete. As it does, Johnny has just enough time to take in the barrel of the Colt automatic .45 caliber pistol and say "Shit" before his head explodes.

Pete stares at his handiwork and says, "I don't think I'll regret this at all, cousin."

• • •

I found myself sitting on the couch, Adrian waiting with a glass of cold water, which I gladly accepted and greedily drank. I handed her the glass as she handed me my computer, knowing by this point that I needed to record what I'd just witnessed. As I began to type, without looking up, I said, "I found the art. Jimmy/Johnny is dead." She said nothing as I completed my recollection. As had become our routine, I handed the computer to her after finishing my report. As she carefully read the chronicle of my journey, I laid my head back and closed my eyes. I could feel the exhaustion creeping into my being, body and soul.

I must have dosed off, because when I heard Adrian exclaim, "Hoy shit!" I jumped, startling Adrian, as well as myself. She reached out to touch my arm and apologized, having not realized I had fallen asleep.

"It's OK. I was just resting, not out for the night." Unsuccessfully having searched her eyes for a hint of what she was thinking, I asked, "So, what do you think?"

"That's quite the family, isn't it?"

"It really is. Makes you realize that, however fucked up your family is, it could be worse."

"True. Aside from that, you confirmed Johnny had the art. That's huge!"

"It is. You can't believe how excited I was when I was waiting for the reveal."

"Oh, I think I can. At one point, your breathing got very accelerated, your eyes widened, and your pupils became very dilated. I was thinking about trying to bring you back, but you quickly calmed down. I'll bet that was when you were waiting for the big reveal."

I agreed with her assessment and said as much.

"So," I said, "we know the art made it to Detroit. We even know where it went. My question is, why hasn't any of it ever turned up?"

We both just sat and thought. I decided I needed to think out loud and continued, "If Pete knew what he had, and he did, he knew it was valuable, especially since Johnny had told him so. He basically admitted that Gloria's was used by his boss, whomever that might be, to hide stolen goods, which clearly indicates that 'the boss' was involved in some sort of organized crime. Would Pete have gone to his boss to have the art fenced?"

After thinking about it, Adrian said, "That certainly would have been the easiest thing to do, wouldn't it?" Pausing, she continued, "But something tells me that Pete looked at this as his big opportunity. It seems that he had a huge chip on his shoulder about how his life had gone. And, it also seems that he blamed his cousin for a lot if it."

I agreed and beckoned for her to continue.

"So, if he thought this was his chance to score big, I'm not sure he would have gone to the boss. There's no doubt the boss would've taken a huge chunk of any money he realized from the sale. And, since the art was so hot, the sale would have to be at a huge discount, meaning that there wouldn't be much left of the pie for Pete." She thought for a moment and looked at me. "So, no. I don't think he would've gone to the boss. He'd want to keep as much of the money as he possibly could."

I swiveled my weary head so that I could look at her, smiled, and said, "That's great reasoning and I totally agree." Sitting myself more upright, I said, "So, he would continue to stash the loot until he could make a deal for himself." I wanted to pace, but didn't have the energy. "He'd probably be worried about the boss discovering, one, that he had the art, and two, that he was going to cut the boss out. I'd guess that having the boss know either of those two things would not end well for Pete."

"Probably not, based on how we've seen these things go so far," agreed Adrian.

"Would he move the van or leave it where it was?"

After a moment of silence, Adrian responded, "The easy thing to do would be to just leave it where it was. Why take the risk of moving it and being seen?"

As I paced in my mind, I replied, "It would be the easiest, but would it be the smartest?" I looked at Adrian, who motioned for me to continue. "Gloria's was a front for some mob guy. Pete had to go inside to locate an empty container, which meant he had records for which containers were being used. Then, he came out with a lock. No self-storage places give you a lock, although they will sell them to you. I think they provided the locks so they could control what came and went. Which means Pete would have had to report that the container with the van was being used. That would give rise to all sorts of questions from his boss." I looked at Adrian for confirmation.

"You're right. If Pete was going to keep this score for himself, he'd move the van."

We both knew what the next question was. I voiced it. "To where?"

Neither of us said anything, knowing that neither of us had an answer.

"Well shit," I said. "We're so close." I yawned so hard that I thought my jaw would dislocate. Adrian closed the laptop, stood, and offered her hand.

"Let's go to bed before I have to try to carry you to the bedroom."

·   ·   ·

I slept hard for almost twelve hours. Thankfully, Jen's elixir had done its job and my head did not hurt. I found Adrian in her studio/office working on a new painting. I loved to watch her work, so just stood silently at the door and did just that. I could tell she was "in the zone" and did not want to be the one that interrupted that most precious of occurrences. Having completed the portion of the work she had been concentrating on, she looked up and saw me.

"How long have you been standing there?"

"About an hour," I lied.

"Voyeur," she said as she smiled.

"When I can," I said, as I entered the room and gave her a quick kiss. "I'm famished. You?"

"No, I ate a while ago. I figured you'd be out for most of the day."

"OK. I'm going to make something and then go back to bed. Last night's excursion really kicked my ass." I turned to go to the kitchen, then stopped. "We should call Agent Hebert at some point today."

"I know. Let's do it after you get up from your nap."

I nodded my head and went in pursuit of sustenance.

• • •

It was late afternoon when we got it together enough to contact Star. I sent her an email with the account of my time trip to Detroit as an attachment and asked her to let me know when she might be available to talk. Fifteen minutes later, my phone rang.

I accepted the call, put it on speaker, and said, "I guess you're available now."

Instead of responding to my comment, she said, with evident excitement, "He had the art!"

Adrian and I both laughed as I said, "Yes, he did."

"Aren't you excited about that?!" she asked with enthusiasm. "After all this time and everything you've done?"

"You read how excited I was. It was huge. It *is* huge."

"So, what's up with the attitude?" Apparently, I wasn't showing the level of enthusiasm she'd expected. "Adrian, what about you?"

Adrian leaned towards the phone and said, "Hi Star. Yes, I'm excited. Maybe we've just had longer to live with the fact than you."

Appeased, Star replied, "OK, I can live with that answer." After a beat, she continued, "So, Johnny/Jimmy is dead. It seems he underestimated his cousin's killer instinct."

"So it does," I said.

"They're like birds or predators in the wild. One catches a fish or makes a kill and another swoops in to steal it," observes Adrian.

"That's a great analogy," agreed Star. "So, where did Pete stash his stolen feast?"

Neither of us answered, so I said, "That's the $5,000,000 question. We've been talking about that, as you can imagine."

"And?"

In response, we reran our skull session of the previous night, each playing our part. Star listened without interruption. When we had concluded, we waited for Star's response. After listening to silence, I said, "So?"

"I can't find a flaw in your reasoning. It all makes sense." After another pause, she said, "Now I understand the dampening of your excitement."

Sensing Star's deflation, Adrian jumped in and said, "At least we know for certain that Johnny had the art and where he took it. That's leaps and bounds ahead of where we were a couple of weeks ago."

"It almost makes it more frustrating. So close. So close. Damn!" We could almost hear Star forcing optimism on herself. "Okay," she said, "what's next? The two of you always seem to have a plan. Let's hear it."

Adrian and I both looked at each other and shrugged. I turned back to the phone and said, "Honestly, we haven't gotten that far yet. What are you thinking?"

I could hear Star sigh as she answered. "It seems as if you're going to have to go back and follow Pete. I'm sorry, but I can't think of another way. It's what got us this far."

Knowing she was right, I looked at Adrian, who mouthed, "She's right." Resignedly, I said to Agent Hebert, "You're right."

"Sorry Josh. I wish there was something I could do, but, when it comes to time travel, you're the only game in town," as she thought of her father and forced herself to keep it together.

"I know, and I appreciate it."

Adrian remembered the information about Gloria's and said, "Star, please thank your lawyer friend for that information about the storage place. We'd never have gotten this far without it."

Pleased, Star promised to do so.

After a few minutes of non-case related conversation, we were ready to end the call. "All right, Star. We'll let you know how the next phase goes."

"Thanks. Good luck."

We were back to the planning phase of my next journey into the unknown. It would be close to a week before we had the time and my mind and body had recovered enough for another attempt.

· · ·

The appointed time had come, and we took our usual places on the couch, the accoutrements of time travel at the ready. I reluctantly swallowed the potion provided by our favorite mad scientist and readied myself. Adrian had prepared a sketch of Pete Jr., so that I had something to focus on. Since the meditation method had proved successful the last time, we both thought there was no reason to make any change. As the timer made its presence known, I opened my eyes, concentrated on the sketch, thought about Gloria's Glorious Containers, and prepared to become aware in 1970 Detroit.

I concentrated on the sketch, thought about Pete Jr., envisioned launching through the space/time continuum, and waited. My consciousness remained in my home reality. I looked at where Adrian had been sitting, and found that she was still in the same spot, as was I.

I closed my eyes and began the process again. Meditate. Sketch. Gloria's Glorious Containers. Launch. 1970 Detroit. Space/time continuum. Still, I remained in my present, on my couch, next to my wife.

I looked at Adrian, who watched silently, afraid to say anything for fear of causing something to go wrong. I assuaged any such worry by saying, "It's not working."

"Are you feeling all right?" she asked.

I took stock of myself and answered, "I feel fine. It's just not working."

We had not been previously been confronted with a launch failure and were completely at a loss. Do we try again immediately? Do we wait? How long will the potion remain effective if we wait? Why the hell wasn't it working?

Trying not to panic, I closed my eyes for another attempt. Concentrate on the target. Visualize Pete Jr. Think, 1970, Gloria's Glorious Containers. Breathe steadily.

Nothing.

I looked at Adrian and repeated the obvious. "It's not working."

Before she could say anything, I held up my index finger in the universal "wait one minute" gesture, closed my eyes and concentrated on revisiting my last successful journey. Instantly...

I find my consciousness outside the gates of Gloria's Glorious Containers, as identified by the garish pylon sign. It's light out, and based on the location of the sun above, it appears to be between 1:00 p.m. and 2:00 p.m.

I experimented with my mental remote control and found it in perfect working order. I concentrated on the target of my most recent attempt and tried to jump to Pete at some point after he had killed his cousin. I could only move to the end of my last "watching" experience. I stood outside the container and stared at Johnny's prone body, blood spilling from where his head once resided. No matter what effort I exerted, I could move no further or to any other time not previously visited. I willed myself back to my present and opened my eyes to find Adrian waiting where and when I had left her.

"What happened?"

I explained what I had tried and the results. We were both completely baffled. We talked about the possible reasons and settled on the fact that Pete had not been involved with the actual theft from the Garden Museum, which is how this whole thing began. As long as I was trying to "watch" one of the participants, I had success. This was the first time I'd tried with somebody else. We concluded that my ability to "watch" was tied to the documentary, or at least the people involved in what the documentary was about. Maybe it was my connection to the source material, and the cause of my "seizures." We really had no idea. All we knew was that we were at an impasse with no obvious solution.

.   .   .

I couldn't wash the failure from my mind and had a difficult time sleeping that night. I tossed and turned as much physically as I did mentally. I played scenarios through my internal video player, considered potential solutions, and came to a conclusion.

It was obvious that we were both trying to avoid any mention of the failure to launch. At breakfast, I broke the spell.

"I think I have to go to Detroit. Physically go, like a for real trip."

Adrian looked at me and simply said, "Why?"

"Honestly, I don't really know. I couldn't sleep last night and went over a million possibilities. Going to Detroit just seems like the right thing to do. I can feel it."

Over our years together, we had often talked about following our gut feelings. If something felt like the right thing to do or not do, it most often worked out if we followed those feelings. When we went against that inner guidance, it was usually to our detriment. I could see her thought process playing out as I chewed my bagel, so I remained silent. Also, over our years together, I learned when to keep my mouth shut, mostly. At last, she came to a conclusion.

"All right. If your inner-self is telling you that's what needs to happen, do it." I could feel a "but" coming, so waited two beats. "But," she continued, "I want to point out that the property still seems to be owned by a company with mob ties. They don't play well with others."

"I'll be careful," I promised. She looked at me skeptically. "Really," I implored. "I'll be in and out before anybody knows I'm even there. I'll be a little Jewish ninja."

Shaking her head, she got up from her seat and said, "You better be."

.   .   .

My flight landed at Detroit's Metropolitan Airport early in the evening on a Friday. I had a carry-on suitcase and my laptop, so didn't need to wait for luggage. Instead, I made my way to Hertz and picked up a non-descript black four-door Chevy Impala. I drove to my hotel, a moderately priced Holiday Inn Express, checked into my room, and relaxed.

Darkness would soon descend and I had no place I needed to be or wanted to go. Detroit today is not the bustling metropolis it was in the 1970s. I ate dinner at the Outback Steakhouse across the street and was back in my room by 7:30.

• • •

I had the free breakfast offered by the hotel, showered, and found myself in the rental car by 9:30 a.m. I had already input the address of the former Gloria's Glorious Containers into the GPS app on my phone, so, after pressing the "Start" button, was off and running.

The hotel was about forty-five minutes from my destination, so I arrived around 10:00. The information provided by Star's lawyer friend stated that the former location of Gloria's was vacant. It must have been old information because a facility named "Metro Self-Storage" now occupied the site. Instead of going directly into the facility I elected to drive around the neighborhood. The construction storage facility was still located across from the storage location, which, for some unexplained reason, pleased me. Cranes, dump trucks and other heavy equipment were still visible through the chain-link fence. The adjacent lots were still vacant, but maintained in a much nicer manner. I drove by the Metro Self-Storage facility just to get an idea what it looked like. It appeared that not much had changed since I'd last seen it two weeks or fifty years ago. I drove around the block, just to see what I could see. As I noted on my first visit, there was a complete dearth of pedestrian or vehicular traffic, which I thought odd for a Saturday. I would have thought that Saturday would be a prime day for visiting a storage locker. Perhaps unloading stolen goods during the day was not a great idea.

After finishing my tour of the neighborhood, I returned to the entrance of Metro Self-Storage. I stopped in the driveway and then pulled up to the keypad, a modern-looking piece of technology that performed the same function as the keypad of fifty years ago. Hard as I tried, I could find no call button or any other way of contacting the office so that I could arrange entry. I thought it odd, unless it was still used as storage for stolen goods, rather than an actual business open to the public.

I pulled my car over to the side and used my phone to look up a telephone number for the location in front of me. Finding a 1-800 number listed, I dialed and listened to a recorded message. Press 1 for this, press 2 for that, and so on. It became apparent that this was a general number for a business with multiple locations, not the number of the office I was attempting to contact. As I disconnected the call, I gazed at the entrance, as if I could will the gate to retract. To my utter surprise, the gate did just that! I put the car in gear and drove toward the entry, where I had to wait for a black Chevy Suburban to clear the opening before I could scurry through. The windows of the Suburban were all heavily tinted, so I couldn't see who was driving or whether there were any passengers. As I passed it, the brake lights illuminated, causing it to hesitate, as if it wanted to back-up and find out what I was doing there. Instead, the red lights faded and it drove away, freeing me to make my way into the facility.

I had noticed security cameras on the fence, unlike fifty years ago. As I drove through the rows of containers to the office, I noticed security cameras at multiple locations, which made sense in today's environment. I wanted to get out and walk around, but thought it best to check-in with the office first, it being fairly certain that somebody knew I was there.

I found the office and parked in the same available space in which Johnny had parked upon his arrival. Getting out of the car, I noticed that not much had really changed on the exterior. It would be interesting to see the interior after all these years.

I opened the door and stepped in. It was like traveling through time, but with a physical body. Three blue vinyl seats had replaced the three old red vinyl seats, but not recently. They didn't appear torn, but I would want an antiseptic treatment after sitting in them. I approached the counter, which was the same dirty yellow linoleum. The bell must have been replaced by a silent alarm of some sort, because although nobody was at the counter, the door behind the counter soon opened and emitted a woman of somewhere between forty and sixty years of age, not over five feet two inches tall, and weighing in the vicinity of one hundred eighty pounds. A cigarette hung from her unadorned lips, smoke curling upwards towards her squinting eyes. I had to reassess my thinking on the silent alarm, as she seemed totally surprised by my existence.

She stopped dead in her tracks, peered at me through the smoke and, by way of greeting, rasped, "How the hell did you get in here?"

I pointed to the door.

She approached the counter, placing the file she was holding on top. "I mean, smart-ass, how did you get through the gate?"

"The gate opened and I drove through," I said, speaking the truth. "Isn't that how it usually works?"

She stepped back to assess my appearance and, probably, whether I was a cop.

"Actually, no, it doesn't. You need a code to get in and you can't get a code without having a storage unit."

"How do you get a storage unit if you can't get in to check them out and get one rented?" I thought this was a perfectly reasonable question. It seemed that I was in the minority.

She took a deep hit on the cigarette and placed it between two fingers, holding it at bay while she responded. "It's a conundrum, isn't it?" she said, with a touch of amusement.

I agreed.

Getting more comfortable with my presence, and perhaps realizing that I was not law enforcement, she said, "This ain't a public facility. You have to be, let's say, permitted to rent a unit here."

I let a look of confusion take its place before I asked, "Really? And from whom does one obtain such permission?"

"From whom? Well, la di da," she said, mockingly. Putting on the air of British aristocracy, she continued, "One does not obtain such permission. One has to be granted such permission by ownership, who only grants such permission to those in his favor."

"And how does one get in the favor of ownership?" I asked, playing along.

"One does not." Finished with the game, she said, in her regular voice, "now get out."

Taken aback, I let it show before I replied, "Fine. Have a nice day."

I left the office and stopped outside to look around. I noticed security cameras placed strategically around the perimeter, as well as on top of some of the storage units. The goal seemed to be to maintain a view of the different aisles, as well as the entrance gate and office. I turned around to see miss personality still watching me. I waved, and she gave me the one-finger salute. I was actually rather amused and laughed as I got into my rental.

I didn't go directly to the entry/exit. Instead, I made a driving tour of the facility, being sure to drive by the location at which the blue van had been stored and Johnny shot. A storage container still filled the spot, although there was no way to tell if it was the same one. I looked at the ground, half expecting to see a blood stain that refused to be removed. Thankfully, I saw no such thing.

As I continued my tour, I noticed a portion of the property remained undeveloped, no storage units having been erected. Just large patches of bare ground. I wondered if I were looking at the final resting place of one Johnny Ricardo.

•   •   •

I found an old time diner near to Metro Self-Storage and stopped for lunch. Most of the vehicles in the parking lot were pickup trucks, dirty and used for work, not the shopping mall pickups of most large cities. I parked, went inside and decided to sit at the counter rather than a booth. You meet some interesting people at diner counters and restaurant bars, and I was partial to both. I found an empty seat at the end of the counter and picked up a waiting menu. There was an empty seat to my right and, as I placed my order, a tall, hard looking man in his thirties filled it. He was wearing dusty jeans and work boots. Under his long sleeves, tattoos were visible. He nodded to the waitress, who brought him a cup of black coffee, without having been asked. A regular. He made eye contact, and I nodded in the universal man-greeting. He took a sip of his coffee, placed the cup gently on the counter in front of him, and swiveled his seat in my direction.

"Find what you were looking for at Metro?" he asked.

I was surprised but, utilizing a quick method of deduction, determined that he was in the black Chevy Suburban that allowed me entry into the facility. "Actually, no. I was hoping to get information about rental, but apparently, I'm not in, how did that charming lady put it, oh yeah, 'favor with ownership'. Odd way to run a business, but it's not the only storage facility in town."

Having heard what I had to say, he nodded, as if satisfied with my explanation, took another sip from his cup, stood, and walked out. I followed him out with my eyes and was not surprised to find him open the driver's door to a black Chevy Suburban.

When the waitress brought my patty melt, I asked her who that man was. "Nobody you want to know," was her reply, as she quickly moved to another customer.

"Interesting," I thought, as I ate my lunch, which was delicious, by the way.

. . .

On my way back to the hotel I took a meandering drive. I kept a close watch in my rearview mirror, just to make sure that my new friend, or one of his friends, wasn't tagging along. I varied my speed, took last-minute turns, and generally followed the lessons learned from years of reading spy novels and watching movies. When I arrived at my hotel, I was fairly certain that nobody had followed me. Paranoid? Maybe. As I had told Adrian many years ago, I'm probably not paranoid enough.

Once in my room, I called Adrian and recapped my day. I left nothing out. We both came to the conclusion that the storage facility was still mob owned and used for the same purpose that Pete had mentioned to his cousin.

"So, now what?" she asked.

"That's a good question. I'll have to think about it."

"When is your flight home?"

"Monday morning."

"Try not to do anything to arouse the suspicions of your new lunch buddy."

"Never even crossed my mind."

She let her disbelief be heard before saying, "Right, my little Jewish ninja."

I laughed and said, "Don't worry. I'll call you tomorrow."

"Bye. Love you."

"Love you, too."

•   •   •

I went to bed very early that night, having set my alarm for 3:00 a.m. I had decided that I needed to explore Metro Storage and the best time to try would be under cover of darkness early in the morning. I awoke at the prescribed time, dressed, and quietly left the hotel. Nobody was visible in the vicinity as I walked to my car. I opened the driver's door and quickly closed it, extinguishing the dome light. I sat perfectly still, watching my surroundings. Nothing stirred. I started the car, first being certain that the headlights would not automatically turn on. I drove for two blocks with my lights off, keeping one eye on the rearview mirror and one on the road ahead, being careful not to use my brakes. Seeing nothing behind me, I turned on the headlights and proceeded directly to Metro Storage.

I parked a block from the entrance, turned the engine off, and got out of the car. Standing perfectly still, I watched for movement, but detected none. My attire consisted of black jeans, black shirt and black windbreaker, as close to a ninja uniform as I could assemble. I had seen a place along the perimeter fence hidden by bushes with no visible cameras, and hastened to that location. The fence was not very high and I was able to make my way over, even if it wasn't pretty. Once inside, I made my way to the container in which Pete had stashed the van. I kept an eye out for camera locations, trying to stay as close to walls and underneath the radius of the lenses as possible. When I reached the target container, I stood before it and noticed that it was not locked. I would have been shocked had Pete's lock remained, but not surprised if another lock had replaced it. Unlocked, I could easily determine that the container was empty. I had only opened the door an inch or so, fearful of making too much noise. Seeing it empty, I decided not to close it, leaving it slightly ajar, again afraid of the creaking noise made by unoiled hinges.

Standing there, I tried to place myself in Pete's mindset. He had just stashed a van full of stolen art and killed his cousin. I surmised that the first order of business for him would be to dispose of the body. I remembered my drive out of the property and the large section of vacant land. My legs carried me in that direction, my mind being unaware of the decision. I stood in the shadow of a container on the edge of the vacant dirt. I became convinced that this was the location of Johnny's burial. It was close to where he died and nobody from outside would know.

The body having been disposed, Pete wouldn't be in a hurry to move the van. I guessed that he'd have a few days before he really needed to worry about it. If that were the case, he would have had time to find a prime location. Something not far and out of view, but accessible. I walked around the property, looking for such a location. As I walked, I concentrated on finding the likely location of the van, and lost sight of the fact that I was trespassing on dangerous territory. I was suddenly reminded of that fact when I thought I heard a noise behind me, maybe in another aisle. Moving to the end of a row, I stopped and peered around a corner. I saw movement at one of the containers, but no vehicle. I figured it must have been some kind of animal. As I turned to continue on my way and head for my exit point, I heard something behind me and turned. Before I could complete my turn, I felt something hit the back of my head, something hard.

The pain was like nothing I'd ever experienced. It was as if my head simultaneously imploded and exploded. All I saw in front of my eyes was a bright flash of light. Whether or not it was actually there, I had no idea. Overcome by the pain and the sound of my skull cracking, I tried to turn and run when another blow to the back of my head landed, I saw those proverbial stars, and then complete and utter blackness.

. . .

I lay on either a cold metal floor or concrete. It was difficult to tell which. My head hurt like never before. The pain I once experienced coming out of a "watching" would have been a welcome respite. I cautiously opened one eye, afraid that opening both at the same time would result in a final explosion of my head. When nothing else happened, I slowly opened the other.

I had no conception of time. A ray of light shone through a partial opening in a wall, causing a sharp pain to start in my eye socket and shoot to my brain. I smelled cigarette smoke, coming from where I could not determine. My last recollections were in the dark, so I could have been laying like that for an hour or ten. I tried focusing, but everything remained fuzzy, at best. I felt nauseous, glad that my stomach was empty so I could avoid laying in my own vomit. I moved my head, slowly. It still hurt. I brought my hand to the back of my head and it felt sticky. Checking, I looked at my hand and found it covered in semi-coagulated blood. The sight caused me to dry heave. I tried to sit up, but soon discovered that just moving my head was enough of an effort at this point in my captivity. Slowly moving my head, I could see two figures standing in the shadows, silently smoking and observing. Concentrating, I tried to make out faces.

"Johnny? Pete?" I croaked out the questions, barely audible.

One man stepped forward, leaving the other against the wall with a smoldering cigarette.

"You say something, asshole?" It was a deep voice, belying what I perceived as a youthful face. The face was too high above me to allow me to adjust my focus and get a good view.

I thought, "Could I somehow be in 1970, body and all?" To my guard I repeated, "Johnny? Pete?"

For my efforts, I received a kick in the ribs, right before he said, "Shut the fuck up. You don't know neither of us."

He resumed his position against the wall as I writhed in pain, unable to avoid the fetal position, eyes closed. I could feel tears running down my cheek, otherwise unaware that I was crying. I remained like that for somewhere between ten minutes and two weeks. I tried to form a coherent thought, but the electrical storm coursing through my brain made it impossible. It was as if I could see and feel the neurons firing. No pattern, just complete chaos.

Trying not to panic, I recited, "Calm. This will be OK" over and over. It came out as incoherent mumbling, but in my head it sounded perfectly pronounced.

At some point, through my closed eyelids, I could tell that the quality of light in whatever room I occupied changed. It was brighter. The brightness was accompanied by a creaking sound, which I came to realize was the door to a metal container. I was still at the storage facility. I heard footsteps approach and stop at my location. With eyes closed, I remained motionless. A steel-toed boot prodded me, causing me to flinch. I opened an eye and saw a work boot and the bottom of a pair of jeans.

A voice said, "Sit him up against the wall." It sounded to me as if he were using a bullhorn in a confined space, causing my brain to rattle in my head. I winced as two pairs of hands grabbed me and dragged my limp form about eight feet to the side of the container. Someone grabbed me under the arms, sat me up, and propped me against the ribbed metal wall. I passed out and remained unconscious until somebody splashed water on my face. I cautiously opened my eyes and found a hand holding a bottle of water in front of my face.

"Drink."

It took a monumental effort, but I was able to reach for the bottle, close my fingers around the plastic and bring it to my mouth. I drank, long and slow. Finished, my hand dropped to the floor, the plastic bottle rolling away and spilling its precious contents.

The voice said, "How many times did you hit him?"

"Just twice, Frank."

"With what, a steel girder? Look at him."

"We used the blackjack."

Disgusted, the voice said, "Figures. What else did you do to him?"

"Nothing," said a voice.

A different voice said, "You did kick him in the ribs."

I could hear a slap before a voice said, "Oh yeah. I kicked him in the ribs."

As I watched, the man with the water bent down so he could look me in the eye. When I saw his face I said, "Lunch guy. Still in 2020." I creaked a short laugh and said, "I thought I went back to 1970." I sounded drunk.

He reached behind me and felt the back of my head. His hand came away covered in sticky blood. With his other hand, he lifted one of my eyelids and then the other. Standing, he walked to his two underlings. "You hit him too hard and too many times. He's got a grade 3 concussion."

"What's that mean, Frank?" asked one of the voices.

"It means that he's not going to be able to answer any questions for a good long time. It means that we're not going to be able to find out why he's here. It means we will not be able to find out who he works for." Pausing, as if considering what to do, he said, "Did you find any ID?"

One underling shuffled his feet as he reached into his back pocket. "Yeah, Frank. Here's his wallet."

Frank took the wallet and inspected the contents.

"He's a lawyer," Frank told his subordinates. "At least he's not a cop or FBI."

I could hear Frank pace as he made a decision about my fate as the neurons in my head continued their fireworks display.

"We're going to have to get rid of him. He saw me yesterday and, even if he's incoherent now, he's seen my face. I can't take the chance."

"You going to kill him, Frank?" The excitement in the voice was apparent, as if the speaker wanted to watch.

I could hear Frank turn his entire body to face the man who made that last statement. "Don't get so excited, Adam. It's not something to take lightly." I heard Frank turn towards me and say over his shoulder, "Get out, both of you."

They scurried out the open door as Frank strolled in my direction. Once next to me, he reached behind his back and withdrew what looked to me to be a deck cannon from the Queen Anne's Revenge. I couldn't even pretend to make an attempt at crawling away, my brain having been scrambled beyond the point of motor control, so I sat placidly watching as my death approached.

Frank bent in front of me and quietly said, "I'm sorry, Joshua, but this is how it has to be."

I could barely comprehend his words, although I believe a part of me fully understood, as the fireworks in my head reached the finale stage.

Frank stood, slowly. He took a few steps away from me, when I thought I heard something outside. I assumed it was all in my head, but Frank must have heard it, too, because I saw him turn his head, the cannon automatically rising and following his gaze. I heard incoherent shouting coming from just outside the container's door, followed by cannon fire. The report of the weapons coincided with the fireworks finale in my head, the world went bright white, followed immediately by silky smooth blackness.

· · ·

I became conscious again at some point, but again refused to open my eyelids. I expected to be on a hard surface, but instead discovered something soft against my back, which gave me enough confidence to open my eyes, slowly.

The quality of the light which greeted me was a comforting, dim, soft white. I felt something touching me and slowly turned my head. Adrian was seated to my right, cradling my hand, a tentative smile forming. "Hey," I said, as a tear escaped and rolled down my cheek.

"Hey," was her quiet reply, a twin to my own rolling gently down her cheek. She had been advised that sounds that may not seem loud to her may sound amplified to a concussed person.

I used my left hand and touched my head. It was wrapped in fabric, and partially covered with some kind of probes, reminding me of Jen's helmet. I tried straightening up, wanting to sit more upright, when my ribs screamed their objection. I stopped squirming.

"You have a couple of broken ribs."

"Umm," was all I could manage as a nurse entered the room.

She checked my chart, probed my eyes with a small flashlight, which I could barely tolerate under the best of circumstances, and said, "Welcome back, Mr. Lowenstein."

Unable to control myself, I said, "Mr. Lowenstein? Is my father here?"

A look of concern crossed the nurse's face before Adrian smacked me on the arm and admonished me. "Stop screwing around." To the nurse, she said, "Sorry. He can't help himself."

The nurse gave a knowing smile, which I quickly returned. "Well, if that's his normal demeanor, it's a good sign. I'll check in later."

Adrian turned back to me and said good-naturedly, "Really?"

I shrugged as best I could.

"So," she said, "please tell me that your Jewish ninja career has ended."

"No doubt about it," I said with as much sincerity as she'd ever heard from me.

I finally brought myself to ask, "What happened?"

As she opened her mouth to answer, someone entered the room. I smiled as I saw Adrian rise to greet Star with a warm hug. She came around to the left side of my bed and stood, assessing my condition.

"Agent Hebert," I said. "Thank you for coming."

"Mr. Lowenstein," she replied. "Thank you for surviving." She bent down and gave me a kiss on the cheek.

"Pull up a chair," I implored. "Adrian was just about to fill me in. I assume you'll have something to add." I was fighting exhaustion, but really needed to know.

Star brought a chair over and nodded to Adrian.

"After we spoke on Saturday, and you told me about the storage place, I knew you were going to try something ninja-like. As soon as we hung up, my inner voice was screaming a warning at me."

To Star, she said, "We agreed years ago not to disregard our inner voices. Hard-won lessons."

Star nodded, so Adrian continued.

"I immediately called Star and told her what happened when you tried to 'watch' Pete after he killed Johnny. I told her about our conversation and your feeling that you needed to go to Detroit. I told her everything I could, including your itinerary and rental car company. I begged her to get in touch with you."

Adrian looked at Star, who took over the narrative.

"I contacted the local Detroit office and filled them in on as much as I could without revealing," she looked around, "you know."

I nodded as best I could.

"They told me about the owners of Metro Self-Storage, which they'd been aware of. Hearing what they had to say, I decided I needed to get to Detroit ASAP."

Pausing in her recitation, she stared hard at me and said, "You know, these are not people to take lightly. My FBI contact scared the shit out of me, which is why I got on a plane. What the hell were you thinking?"

Apparently, it wasn't a rhetorical question, as she awaited my reply. All I could think to say was, "It seemed like a good idea at the time."

She shook her head and continued. "I tried calling you on Saturday morning, but got no answer."

I interrupted, asking, "Oh yeah. Where is my phone?"

"In an evidence bag at FBI offices. One of those two idiots who clocked you had it in his pocket and hadn't even turned it off, which is how we were able to find you."

"You tracked my phone?"

"We did. Actually, we had Adrian do it, just to avoid any legal questions. Once we determined you were at the storage facility, we sent someone with a drone. He parked a few blocks away and flew over the site. With some special secret technology doo-hickey thing attached to the drone, he was able to determine that you were in a storage container and pinpoint which one. We had a local agent watching the entry and when he saw Frank drive in, knew there was going to be a problem, so he called us in. We found you and here you are."

I absorbed this information and lay quietly. I lifted my head, looked at Star, and asked, "Frank?"

"Dead."

I watched her face, but was unable to make a determination. "You?"

She simply nodded.

"I'm so sorry. Are you OK?"

"Surprisingly, I am. It happened so fast, and there was no question that not only was your life in danger, but so were the lives of every agent out there."

I reached out and squeezed her hand.

"Thank you." I turned to Adrian and added, "Both of you."

I laid my head on the pillow and closed my eyes, taking a deep breath and contemplating everything we'd been through. The neurons were still rapidly firing, but less painfully so. I must have winced, because Adrian asked, "What's wrong?"

I opened my eyes and told them about the electrical activity I'd been experiencing since having been struck with the blackjack.

Adrian reached for her phone and said, "I'm going to call Jen. I called her before coming to Detroit and she's been consulting with the doctors."

"She didn't tell them about...you know, did she?"

"No, but she said at some point she might have to."

I turned deadly serious and said, "Under no circumstances will I allow her to tell anybody outside of this room. Understand?"

Adrian could see that I was not screwing around, and said, "OK," as the call with Jen connected.

I looked at Star and said, "I still don't know where the art is."

Her look softened as she said, "I know. Let's not think about it for now. You've been through enough."

"All for nothing," I dejectedly replied.

Exhausted, I lay my head on the pillow and closed my eyes as Adrian spoke with Jen. I listened to the drone of their voices and thought I was drifting off, when the electrical activity in my brain reached a fever pitch, I watched as fireworks exploded and...

Pete Jr. is driving a medium-sized, self-propelled crane, which he drives across the road, to Gloria's Glorious Containers. He stops to punch in a code; the gate opens, and he drives through.

In my hospital room, two nurses came rushing in, alerted by the machines attached to my headdress. As they started to make adjustments, Adrian, still on the phone with Jen, shouted, "Stop!" Surprised, they obeyed immediately, before catching themselves and advising that they had to address the situation. Adrian, knowing what a "watching" experience looked like from this side of the space/time continuum, quickly told Jen what was happening and handed the phone to one of the nurses. After confirming to whom they were speaking, they reluctantly agreed not to administer any drugs and allow this "seizure" to run its course, although they insisted on remaining in the room.

Just as the sun goes down, he drives through the facility to a newly delivered storage container, which he hooks up to the crane. He slowly drives the crane, the container swinging in the air, to the large parcel of land, which now contains a dirt ramp leading into a large hole, a digger from the construction site sitting quietly next to an enormous pile of dirt. On one side of the hole, hugging the dirt wall, lay what remained of Johnny Rodrigo. Not bothering to even glance at the dead body of his cousin, he maneuvers the crane and its cargo into position, so that, when he lowers the container into the hole, the door will be facing the ramp and be able to swing fully open. Satisfied with his efforts, he moves the crane to the side, shuts it off and climbs out of the cab. Walking as hurriedly as he can manage, he makes his way to the container that holds the blue van and his financial redemption. He drives the van out of the container, not bothering to stop and close the container's door. Driving to the site of the newly dug hole, I sensed the satisfaction oozing from him. He's left the door to the van's new home waiting open and carefully drives the van into the chasm, calmly anticipating its arrival. Turning the engine off, he leaves the keys in place, just as his cousin had done, before he exits the container and closes the door. He doesn't bother with a lock. Scrambling up the ramp, he returns to the digger and proceeds to return the waiting dirt to its original home, spreading across the site what will no longer fit in the hole.

The hole filled and the container now invisible, Pete returns the equipment, comes back to the office of Gloria's Glorious Containers and locks up for the night. He walks to his waiting 1960 Ford Galaxie and thinks, "I see a new car in my future." Pleased with his night's work, he starts the car and drives out of the storage facility, looking forward to a beer when he arrives home.

As he drives down a dark, mostly secluded road on his way home, he approaches an intersection. Craving a cigarette, he reaches over to the passenger seat, onto which he had tossed a fresh pack. He takes his eyes from the road for a fraction of a second as he leans over and pushes the lighter in. Grasping the pack, he looks up at the last minute just as he enters the middle of the intersection, in time to see the grill and menacing bulldog hood ornament of a large Mack Truck barreling down on him, headlights off. It broadsides the Galaxie and turns it over multiple times before it comes to rest with the truck on its flattened remains. Pete Jr. dies instantly.

I slowly opened my eyes as the machines hooked up to my head calmed themselves and returned to a state of relative normality. The nurses rushed to check my vitals and were amazed at the fact I hadn't died. Jen was still on the phone, so the nurses reported on my condition and left the room, looking suspiciously back at me over their shoulders.

I yawned mightily and asked for a glass of water, which Star handed to me, complete with a bendy straw. Adrian disconnected the call and turned her attention to me.

"Are you all right? What the hell happened?"

I turned my head as best I could and said, "I'm fine. Tired, and I can feel a headache coming back, but fine. What happened was, I somehow launched into a 'watching.' No warning or anything, but there I was."

"Where?" asked Star.

I faced her and said, "Gloria's Glorious Containers. 1970. Pete Jr."

I paused for dramatic effect, turned to face Adrian and then back to Star, before I took a satisfying deep breath and said, "I found the art."

EPILOGUE

I remained in the hospital for two more days before convincing them to release me, with a lot of help from Jen. Since my concussion symptoms had not totally subsided, we rented a car and took our time driving back to Arizona. Adrian had to do all the driving, so we took it nice and slow, stopping frequently and making it a little vacation.

. . .

Star was able to excavate at Metro Self-Storage without a warrant, as it was the scene of an ongoing investigation, which itself had exploded as a result of my capture. Word somehow leaked to the press that a major discovery was about to be made, so there was a plethora of cameras available when the dirt was removed, the container uncovered, and the blue van hoisted to the surface for the first time in fifty years. As Agent Starling Hebert approached the back doors of the panel van, a wave of excited anticipation rolled over the gathered crowd, which included a representative of the insurance company. Although Agent Bonet had made the trip, he let Agent Hebert take the well-deserved spotlight.

Star walked calmly to the van, although her heart was pounding. Gathering herself, she reached forward and threw open both doors. Unmoving, she stared at what presented itself.

Canvasses wrapped in movers' blankets. Statues also wrapped for protection. Because they had been buried and kept from the sun, the art was as pristine as it was the day they had been taken from the Garden Museum.

She reached in, pulled out a random canvass and slowly and carefully unwrapped it, using her body to block the view from behind her. She found herself holding a Botticelli painting which had been all but forgotten. Beaming, she moved aside and held it for all to see. Applause erupted as reporters turned to waiting cameras and print reporters rushed to meet deadlines. Agent Bonet slowly approached and showed his credentials to the guards in order to pass the barrier which had been erected to protect the discovery. His face could barely contain his smile. He offered his heartfelt congratulations.

It looked as if Star's days being treated as a second-class citizen of the FBI were over.

.   .   .

Six months after the ordeal in Detroit, my head had recovered enough to allow us to travel, although I did get headaches more often than I used to. Adrian and I took a much needed vacation to our favorite hotel on our favorite Hawaiian island, Kauai. Three glorious weeks of doing only what we choose to do, which was not much.

Star successfully kept our identity confidential, and the reward check was safely deposited into our account.

All seemed well.

We kept in touch with Star and were glad to hear of her relationship with Brenton. He seemed like a nice guy and treated her well. She seemed happy and satisfied with her career. I knew she was reluctant to talk to me about her father and Sheriff Joe, worried about my mental and physical state, having seen what a time traveling trip did to me, especially one taken without Jen's elixir and while experiencing a grade 3 concussion. Not pretty. Nevertheless, Adrian and I discussed the situation and concluded that it was worth the attempt to help put her mind at ease and bring some peace. I texted her while at the pool and asked that she send her father's journal to our house. She called, and I assured her it was something we both really wanted to do and were committed to seeing it through.

When we arrived home, the package from Star was waiting for us. I left it unopened for a few days while we researched Sheriff Joe. We reviewed his career, found numerous pictures of him from local newspapers, and tried to find any complaints that may have been filed against him. We found no such complaints. The guy was either squeaky clean or powerful. We went with the powerful option.

After the Sheriff Joe phase of research, I opened Star's package and read her father's accounts of his "visions." I could feel his anguish. Had it not been for the support of Adrian, our relationship with Jen and current technology, I very well may have shared the same fate as Charles Hebert. I felt I could understand him better than anybody.

After reading the journal, Adrian and I also researched Sheriff Joe's property, since Mr. Hebert had been convinced that was where the atrocities had taken place. As he'd stated, it consisted of approximately forty acres and, surprisingly, was currently on the market. As a result, we were able, not only to see the property using Google Earth, but also to virtually tour it using the realtor's listing. I thought the familiarity would be helpful, and I was correct.

We prepared for the excursion in the same manner as we had for the Garden Museum case. We had the elixir, photos of the property, and photos of Sheriff Joe from back in the day. In addition, we had an old newspaper photo of Missy Williams, the first victim that Star's father had claimed to see. Using the journal of Charles Hebert as a guide, we made our first attempt at a "watching" not related to the Garden Museum theft.

. . .

The attempt, and the three that followed, was successful beyond our expectations. I will not put down on these pages what I saw during those excursions, to spare all of you the horror. Having had to live through each monstrous act, in a manner of speaking, I chose not to do so again. You'd thank me if you knew.

I had to experience three different acts of utter depravity before, in the fourth trip, I could determine the location of evidence which would be sufficient to put Sheriff Joe behind bars until death took him from this world. What I discovered on that fourth journey was that he used a particular portion of his property to bury the bodies. It was a large plot of land utilized as a flower garden. Frequent digging in a flower garden, especially by a renowned gardener, would not, and did not, arouse suspicions.

After my fourth time visiting the Kentucky of the 1980s and early 1990s, Adrian and I gathered enough information to present to Star. We arranged a time for a Zoom meeting after her normal working hours and while she was at her apartment. We felt it would be best if she were in a relaxed atmosphere and not around coworkers if she got emotional, which we fully expected to happen.

All of us were anxious, so we delved right into it. I asked if she wanted to read my recollections, while making the recommendation that she decline. Thankfully, she accepted my opinion and didn't put herself through the misery. It was enough that she knew her father had experienced the horror I described in general terms. I was able to identify the victims because Sheriff Joe had addressed each by their names while using various terms of endearment. Star noted the names so that she could search the missing persons data base for confirmation. Finally, I was able to relay the location of the bodies, which I thought would be sufficient evidence to put Joe behind bars.

"So, what do you think?" I asked.

Trying to keep her emotions in check, she said, "I think this bastard needs to die. That's what I think."

"I don't disagree. But what do you think from a 'what can you do,' standpoint?"

"Obviously," she started, "we need to get into that flower bed." Thinking about how to go about it, she continued, "our problem, unlike in Detroit, is that we have no probable cause to dig it up."

Adrian, listening, said, "Fuck probable cause! Go in and dig it up. Then let the bastard try to talk his way out of it. The court of public opinion will crucify him."

"I wish it were that easy," replied Star. "If I weren't an FBI agent, and of a different mindset, I'd do just that, but I can't. We need either to be invited onto the property or have a warrant, and we've got nothing for a warrant. I'd love to see Joe's face when the daughter of the man he had institutionalized asks for permission to come in and dig up his prized flower garden."

We stared at each other over the vast expanse of Zoom, until I remembered.

"Wait a minute."

They both said "What?" at the same time.

"The property is on the market."

Waiting, Star said, "OK. What about it?"

I looked at Adrian and said, "What if we either bought it or rented it?" Turning back to Star, I said, "I've never practiced in the criminal law area, but it seems to me that, if we had the legal right to occupy the property, we'd also have the legal right to invite the FBI in, especially if we happened to stumble upon something suspicious while working in the garden."

I could see Star brighten. "That could work. Would you be willing to do that?"

I turned to Adrian and said, "If we could rent, instead of buying, we'd probably be able to terminate the lease, or, if it's a short-term lease, it probably wouldn't cost all that much. They're only asking $160,000 for the whole thing. What do you think?"

Facing Star, Adrian said, "What the fuck, right?"

I could see Star tear up as she said, "Oh my God, you guys. That's amazing. Thank you."

"What the fuck. It's the insurance company's money, right?" I said.

Star laughed.

"OK," I said. "We'll contact the real estate agent and get back to you."

We ended the call and looked at each other.

"This is pretty crazy, isn't it?" I asked.

In response, Adrian kissed me and said, "What the fuck."

• • •

Over the next three weeks, I was able to hire a local real estate agent and negotiate a lease with purchase option. The terms of the lease were favorable since I sweetened the purchase price, knowing we'd never exercise the option to purchase.

We let Star know once the lease was signed, and we traveled to Kentucky. The first order of business was to have our friend Star and her boyfriend visit so they could help with some gardening work. We arrived on a Friday. By Saturday morning, Star and Brenton had arrived, and by Saturday afternoon, our local hardware and rental company had delivered a small skid steer to the property.

I manned the skid steer and headed for the first of the locations where I thought a body had been buried.

Before plowing ahead, I made sure everybody was ready for what we might find, including Brenton. Star had briefed him and he seemed game.

I worked the controls, drove to the first location, and put the bucket down. I went gently, afraid to disturb the bones which I was certain awaited. Star was standing right at the first cut and directed me. Following her directions, I dug gently, and moved dirt. After five small buckets of dirt had been removed, she yelled, "Stop!"

I stopped, turned off the motor and ran to join the others, all of whom had gathered around the hole. We stared into the earth as, clearly visible, a human femur reached towards the sky.

We all reverently backed away from the hole as Star got her phone and called the nearest FBI office.

•   •   •

Over the next two weeks, FBI forensic teams covered every square inch of those 40 acres. I had told Star where the hidden underground room was located, so she and another agent could happen upon it. There could be no question that Sheriff Joe was the monster Charles Hebert thought him to be, twenty bodies having been uncovered.

•   •   •

Local and national news couldn't get enough of the story. The daughter of a man who had been persecuted and institutionalized by Sheriff Joe uncovered evidence of the very thing reported by her dead father. They ate it up.

Star was given the satisfaction of placing Joe under arrest and reading him his rights. She appeared on numerous broadcasts and took every opportunity to talk about what happened to her father. As a result, the Governor of Kentucky issued a proclamation clearing the name of Charles Hebert and awarded him a posthumous special Kentucky Medal of Valor.

Unfortunately, it wasn't all good news for Star. During a private interview with Sheriff Joe, he realized she was the daughter of his original accuser and took that final opportunity to inflict emotional pain, verifying just the type of person he truly was. He told Star that her mother had accepted money from him in order to acquiesce to having her father committed and to help pay expenses for the move. Star had no doubt that he was telling the truth and compartmentalized the information, for the time being. She'd deal with her mother after the tumult died down. For now, she'd revel in the success of having cleared her father's name and being a rising star at the FBI.

· · ·

As for Adrian and me, as soon as the FBI left the property, we called the real estate agent and terminated the lease. We told him to tell our landlord that if he didn't like it, he could sue us. We went back to Arizona as fast as the jet stream could carry us.

"Watching" can be a powerful tool, even as it exacts a heavy toll. We discussed it and have come to the conclusion that we'll keep the ability between those of us who already know and revisit it only when the greater good is at stake. Until then, it's time to enjoy life.

So, be on the lookout for happy coincidences and remember, there's a time to say, "What the fuck?" You never know, it might just work out.

ᛏᛏ

ACKNOWLEDGMENTS

No novel gets written in a vacuum, and this one is no exception. Without the constant support and encouragement of others, the words on the previous pages would most likely still be stuck in my head, screaming for release. For all of our sakes, I am grateful we were spared that fate.

I would especially like to acknowledge and thank my wife, Alexis, for her constant reading and reviewing of my written pages, as well as for putting up with me as I enter what she refers to as my "possessed" state; my brother from another mother, Lee, a terrific writer himself, for his continued guidance, support and encouragement; my other brother from another mother, Ira, for his continued review of, and enthusiasm for, my writing; and the numerous others that were kind enough to read and provide feedback as, what I have now learned are, "beta readers."

And thank you all for indulging me in this story. I hope we cross paths again.

ABOUT THE AUTHOR

Photo by Elaine Belvin

Jeffrey Jay Levin was born and raised in Chicago, Illinois. He currently resides in Sedona, Arizona with his wife of so many years you wouldn't believe it if I told you. He makes his living as a commercial real estate attorney, but like so many in his chosen profession, has always been a frustrated writer. In his spare time, when not being totally consumed by his writing, he is rebuilding a 1976 Corvette Sting Ray and chasing his grandchildren around.

NOTE FROM THE AUTHOR

Word-of-mouth is crucial for any author to succeed. If you enjoyed *Watching*, please leave a review online—anywhere you are able. Even if it's just a sentence or two. It would make all the difference and would be very much appreciated.

Thanks!
Jeffrey Jay Levin

We hope you enjoyed reading this title from:

BLACK ROSE
writing™

www.blackrosewriting.com

Subscribe to our mailing list – *The Rosevine* – and receive **FREE** books, daily deals, and stay current with news about upcoming releases and our hottest authors.
Scan the QR code below to sign up.

Already a subscriber? Please accept a sincere thank you for being a fan of Black Rose Writing authors.

View other Black Rose Writing titles at
www.blackrosewriting.com/books and use promo code
PRINT to receive a **20% discount** when purchasing.

Made in the USA
Las Vegas, NV
25 July 2024